Ms. Mueller has combined fantasy with reality in a profoundly beautiful way. This story of a young girl's trials and tribulations gives everyone who reads it hope in human nature. The author's imagination brings out the beauty and wonder of all creation, and beyond. Enjoy!

Mary J. Foley, Illinois

Take a marvelous flight into an unknown world with Cynthia Mueller, an unusually gifted author, and set your imagination free!

Donald Abel, Illinois

Beyond the Garden Arbor

Beyond the
Garden Arbor

written by Cynthia Jean Mueller

Beyond the Garden Arbor
Copyright © 2007 by Cynthia Mueller. All rights reserved.

The opinions expressed by the author are not necessarily those of Imperium Publishing, Inc.

Published by Imperium Publishing, Inc.
1097 N. 400th Rd | Baldwin City, Kansas 66006 USA
www.imperiumpublishing.com

Cover design by Lindsey Behrems
Illustrations by Cynthia Jean Mueller
Interior Design by Sarah Leis

Published in the United States of America

ISBN: 978-1-64318-028-1
1. YAL Fiction
2. Fantasy

For my dear husband, Richard, for never trying to dissuade me from anything I ever wanted to do, and also my three beautiful children, and grandchildren, all of whom I love so very much. May your lives hold nothing but love and beauty.

And last, but certainly not the least, thank you God for the talent that you have given me. I realize that it is only on loan from you.

Contents

Beyond the Garden Arbor
a poem by Cynthia Jean Mueller

There's a secret place within my yard
that no one else has ever found.
Beyond the garden arbor
beauty and nature abound.
Past the crooked willow
near the water, by the waterfall
there's a secret I wish to share with all.
Beyond the rainbow full of light
exists a wondrous, ethereal sight.
Surrounded by flowers
in splendorous beauty
and awesome wonder
newly sprung from winter's cold slumber.
For when there is a rainbow
and butterflies float in splendid ardor
you shall see
what only me
and they have seen so far.
A magical treasure
and perfect world
where true love and complete peace are.
Take my hand,
be my forever friend,
and together we will see
just how marvelous life can be,
if only you will follow me...
to perfect peace and serenity.

Perhaps our lives all contain a hint of magic...

Abandoned in a Gazebo

Many years ago, near a sleepy, quaint little town bordering the Blue Ridge Mountains, a baby girl was born.

The town was quite enchanting, sitting at the base of a stunning mountain. It had only three short streets containing rows of lovely Victorian homes. Many were embellished with gingerbread, with wraparound porches holding wicker chairs and tables or porch swings.

Flowers bloomed in brilliance over the edges of flowerpots and planter boxes in the welcoming shade of the porches. Flower and vegetable gardens were abundant in the yards. Lovely, huge old trees lined the streets, with white picket fences bordering well tended yards and walkways.

In the coolness of the morning, a teenage girl from the mountains nearby sat in the barely dawning light of the new day in the raised, gingerbread-covered white gazebo in the park on the edge of town. She had given birth just a few short hours before. At the present, she sat crying for her lost childhood, and the fate of her tiny, sweet, unwanted baby girl, who lay sleeping in a small basket nearby.

Clasped around the newborn's neck was a small, delicate, tri-color gold, antique oval locket. The form of a beautiful butterfly graced the face of it. The inside contained no photograph. However, engraved on the back, there was simply a name: Katharine.

Minutes passed, and the quietly sobbing young woman realized that the daylight was increasing. Torn between what she wanted to do, and what she knew she had to, she finally leaned over, kissed the sleeping child's forehead, and breathed in the sweet new baby essence for what would be the very last time. Then, she whispered softly to the child, "I'm so sorry that I can't be your mommy. Someone will find you, take you home, and love you forever."

Then, crying softly, the teenager stood up, straightened her dress, sniffed and wiped her eyes, and walked off, disappearing into the nearby trees.

As the young woman vanished into the forest, she was followed closely by a large, beautiful Luna moth, itself retreating into the thick growth with the approaching sunlight of the brand new day.

As the sun began to rise, the newborn slept. It was going to be a beautiful, but hot August day. The sunrise was gorgeous, touched with warm, stunning shades of gold, purple and red. As the sun continued to rise, the early morning mist over the mountains disappeared, and the colors faded away. Then, they were replaced by a cloudless, breathtakingly clear-blue sky. The birds began to sing, and still the baby slept.

Near the park, bordering the woods, were a resplendent, crystal-clear waterfall and a mountain stream that bubbled and tumbled with frigid mountain water, even at this late time of the summer.

At times, the spray from the waterfall combined with the sunlight to create an awesome rainbow effect directly above the water.

Columbine and other wildflowers bloomed in profusion in the entire area. Large, drooping willow trees graced the edges of the stream, providing welcoming shade, and birds and other wildlife were in abundance.

Doves began their gentle cooing. Redwing blackbirds started their distinctive chirping. The bluebirds began flying about. Dragonflies and other insects commenced their daily movements. Frogs set about catching insects and croaking, and the fish in the stream scurried quickly to and fro in the chilly water. Butterflies initiated their daily flight, the bees began to buzz. It was a glorious new day, there was work to do, and there was not a moment to waste.

The heat of the day began to escalate. Old Mr. Nelson, who operated the general store a couple blocks down the street threw the front door of the store open, and began to move around inside in preparation for the new business day.

A neighbor lady went outside and initiated work in her garden before the heat became too intense. Small children began to rise, and with them, their parents. The hustle and bustle of the day was beginning.

The Great Depression had ended only a couple of years before. The country was at war. Most people had very little in these days, but were proud of what they did own, and took very good care of it. Being an unwed mother in this time held tremendous shame, and since money was so hard to come by, it was impossible for an unmarried woman to raise a child in these circumstances.

Young Pastor Farley opened up the windows and the heavy front doors of his white-steepled church. Standing at the top of the large stone stairway leading up to them, he sighed and wiped the sweat that was already beginning to form off of his brow. *Dear Lord, it's going to be a hot one today*, he thought absently to himself.

Back in the park, in the shade of the gazebo, the tiny baby whimpered and stirred, then quieted back down and returned to her peaceful slumber.

A maidenfly, or miniature dragonfly, flitted by, her colors of pale green and blue, and clear iridescent wings barely noticeable. Suddenly, the maidenfly slowed, and turned, and headed back toward the gazebo. *What was that tiny little bundle in there?* she wondered.

Delicately, she landed on the diminutive being's nose, the iridescent wings still in constant motion. The infant child stirred, raised her tiny, unpracticed fist, and attempted to rub her little pug nose. The maidenfly quickly lifted up on her agile wings to avoid the miniature fist, and now hovered over the child's face. *Oh my, this is a tiny human being!* she thought. *What should I do now?*

Perhaps, the maidenfly mused as she hovered moments longer above the baby, *something has happened, and the mother will return soon. I will stay nearby, and watch and wait.*

Back near the town square, the hustle and bustle of daily life had begun. People were walking along the streets here and there. The mercantile had opened for the day. Small children were playing in their front yards, some riding their tricycles or pulling each other along in their wagons, and laughing. Older children rode bicycles up and down the short streets.

Funny old Mrs. Applequist was out in front of her gracious home too, wearing a huge straw hat and floral-covered apron. She weeded her zinnias on her knees amongst the butterflies that had begun gliding to and from each one.

Her tortoise-marked cat, Zoe, was sitting nearby in the shade of the lilac bush, waiting patiently for one of the butterflies to forget that she was there so that she could snare the poor thing and amuse herself by torturing it to death.

Zoe was not a pleasant feline. She routinely followed Mrs. Applequist around the yard, but did not like to be petted. She also had a mean streak within her that caused other neighborhood cats, and even most of the dogs in the small town, to avoid her like the plague.

Her idea of contentment was sitting in the shade most of the day, drinking out of the birdbath in the corner of the yard, and occasionally stalking, catching and killing a poor, unsuspecting bird or other small creature. Eating from her food dish twice a day when her human fed her was also one of her requirements. She needed nothing else, and ruled her little territory ruthlessly.

Zoe did not appreciate it when another neighborhood pet would, out of curiosity; try to befriend her or Mrs. Applequist. Mrs. Applequist was *her* human, and other people's pets were usually treated to a ruthless swipe of her claws across their poor, tender noses if they were stupid enough to happen by. In fact, next door, Mr. And Mrs. O'Neill's poor dog, Homer, had experienced this nasty treatment more than once.

This particular morning, from the cover of the lilac bush, Zoe was suddenly intrigued by the sight of a poor, hapless bluebird splashing about in the birdbath. *Aha, my next victim,* she schemed evilly to herself.

Stealthily, she moved ever closer, attempting to maneuver into perfect position in order to pounce. Steadily, she inched her way toward the cheerful bird, too busy singing happily, and enjoying the refreshing, cool water in the mounting heat, to notice her approaching.

Meanwhile, back at the gazebo, the tiny cherub had begun to stir. It was now approximately eight-thirty in the morning. The temperature was getting hotter by the minute, it seemed. The exhaustion of just having come into this world had begun to wear off, and was being replaced with a gnawing sense of hunger. At first, the baby just grunted occasionally, then she started to whimper, and gradually she began building up into full-fledged crying. Since she was still so new, her crying wasn't terribly vociferous yet.

The maidenfly, which had been hovering nearby and watching this activity for at least a half an hour by now, began to become increasingly anxious. *Where is this poor thing's mother at, anyway? Perhaps,* she decided to herself, *it would be a good thing if I go find some of my friends. Maybe they can help me decide what to do!*

In less than a minute, the maidenfly was back at the mountain stream. Quickly, she spotted some swallowtail butterflies near some orange butterflyweed. She zipped on over to them, speaking in her wispy voice, "Please, help me, there is a tiny human in the park gazebo and I don't know what to do! She is crying! What should we do?"

The butterflies looked up in astonishment from their nectar breakfast, then quickly floated up into the breeze, and followed the maidenfly back to the gazebo.

When all of the winged creatures arrived there, the infant had again temporarily settled down, and one of the swallowtails alighted on her round little tummy, gazing up at her precious little face.

"Where is this poor child's mother?" the swallowtail asked the maidenfly.

"I don't know, I have been here on and off now for quite some time." the maidenfly replied. "There has been no sign that anyone even knows this child is here! What should we do?"

The other swallowtails floated above this precious scene wondering the same thing themselves, and asking each other the same questions. Suddenly, the swallowtail that was sitting on the baby noticed the oval locket.

"Look!" the butterfly exclaimed, "She is one of us! There is a butterfly on the necklace that she is wearing around her neck!"

Finally, then, looking to the maidenfly, the butterfly said, "You can fly so much more quickly than us! Please, return to the stream; fly into the rainbow and find the king and queen swallowtails. Perhaps we need a bit of magical intervention. They will know what to do!" Off zipped the maidenfly!

Into the ethereal, spectral light the maidenfly shot, surrounded instantly by the heavenly forms of all the delicately winged insects that had ever occupied the earth.

Reigning over this ethereal splendor, were the king and queen of the swallowtails. They were glorious, transcendent beings in their own ulterior world that were also able to materialize into ours. It was their appointment to watch over and care for all of the winged creatures in their charge, and to help keep them safe.

The maidenfly took a few moments to relay the other butterflies' message to these glorious beings, while they listened and took all of this in benevolently.

Several minutes later at the ornate gazebo, the king and queen swallowtails arrived. They were mesmerized and enchanted by the beautiful, sleeping, precious infant girl that lay in the basket, just now beginning to stir again. They observed the delicate butterfly locket resting on the baby's tiny chest. After conversing with each other for several minutes, they finally decided that the most prudent thing for all of them to do would be to try to draw attention to the gazebo from the townspeople.

They alighted together on the small baby's chest, and the king whispered to her, "Tiny sweet thing, we will help you. Even though you are too young to realize it now, we will help you find safety, not only now, but all of your life. You will always enjoy the sight of a butterfly, and it will make you happy. Life does not hold an easy path for you, but whenever you need us, we will be there, and we will never let you down! We will watch over you through the butterfly's eyes of your lovely locket. This is our promise, and our blessing for you. All you will ever have to do is touch your locket, think of butterflies, and we will be there!" With that, the king and queen swallowtails drifted upward, and began to float above the dear, sweet baby again.

Finally, after the king and queen swallowtail spoke briefly to each other, they again approached the maidenfly. "Go into the town," the king instructed her. "See if you can find some of the other butterflies. Together we will create some sort of magical commotion that will lead the townspeople this way." The maidenfly happily complied, and zipped on in toward town.

Back in Mrs. Applequist's yard, Zoe had nearly homed in on her prey! Creeping closer, with evil intent in her glowing, green eyes, she nearly had the poor, male bluebird within her reach!

By then, the maidenfly had reached Mrs. Applequist's zinnias, and had observed the wily cat and what she was up to. "Quick!" she whispered to the butterflies that were lazily floating over them and alighting on the colorful flowers. "The other butterflies need some help sent out to the park! And Mr. Bluebird needs some help, *now!* Send him back to his home by the stream! Alert him to what is about to happen to him by the deadly paws of that awful cat!"

Chirping and splashing happily in the birdbath, and cheerfully trilling his song at the top of his tiny little lungs, Mr. Bluebird was just about to meet his untimely end. Without warning, a butterfly surrounded by iridescent, rainbow-colored lights materialized right in front of his miniature beaked face. Awakened from his reverie, he then glimpsed the movement beneath him of Zoe the cat. Before he had time to fully take in what was about to happen, his bird intuition kicked in, and he leapt into the air and began to fly off!

The fierce feline began her pursuit, so eager was she to grasp the bird that she knocked over the birdbath with a loud thump, splash, and then a screech as it almost landed on her. She startled Mrs. Applequist with all the commotion, and woke poor old Homer from his shady snooze on the porch next door.

As the astonished pooch stood on all fours, he stretched and shook off his nap with haste, ears, jowls and tongue flapping, and saliva spraying everywhere. He felt a sudden surge of excitement move through his canine veins, and into his heart, and decided to join in whatever chase Zoe was already fully engaged in.

Through Homer's yard the cat hightailed after the bird, nearly knocking over the unsuspecting Mr. O'Neill as he came out the front door to walk down to his job as head of the sawmill. Homer the canine was barely able to bound around him, and was now in full, barking pursuit. Toward the mountain stream's safety the bluebird flew, well ahead of Zoe, and now Homer too, but still in a panic.

By now, quite a few people in the neighborhood were looking to see what all the commotion was about. Some were coming out of their houses to watch from their graciously shaded porches. Pastor Farley had stepped out of the large double doors of the church, and another neighborhood dog had also joined in the chase. The group of animals all ran directly in front of an old Model-T slowly puttering down the street, causing it to come to a screeching, unplanned halt.

The frightened bluebird flew haphazardly and with all its might, frightened to death in his pounding bird heart despite his vantage point of the air. Tearing between the two imperial and magnificent butterflies floating protectively over the infant, he knocked them totally off balance in the wake of his dizzying breeze, and spun them round and round.

He was followed closely on the ground by two dogs now chasing his nemesis, the cat. The dogs were barking up a storm, and the cat was shrieking and hissing her displeasure at the pair, both in hot pursuit of her. When all three animals were directly in front of the gazebo, Zoe attempted to slash poor Homer across his nose yet another painful time. Homer, however, backed up and continued barking and growling at her.

Mr. Bluebird zipped toward the safety of the stream and disappeared, out of breath but glad to be home at last!

Back at Zoe's house, poor upset Mrs. Applequist struggled up off the ground as quickly as she could at her age, and hobbled over to the O'Neill's front door to let Mrs. O'Neill know what had happened to Homer. She asked the woman if their teenage son would be willing to run down to the park to retrieve the animal, and perhaps coax her cat home while he was at it. After a few moments, the boy burst out of the house, heading straight for the park, and soon he was joined by a few other neighborhood children as well.

By now, most of the normally peaceful neighborhood was in quite an uproar. After all, this was more commotion in a few short minutes than most of them had seen the entire summer.

Elderly folks milled about in front of their homes, some holding cups of coffee, and having quite the time discussing the disturbance that the dogs and cat were causing. Being curious, and also rather bored up until that point, Pastor Farley began to walk toward the park, and more neighborhood children ran in that direction also.

Now Homer, being the big, loveable dufus of a dog that he normally was, was beginning to become tired. When he saw his boy coming to retrieve him, he quickly lost interest in the feisty little cat and other dog, and simply started running toward the boy. All he wanted to do now was head home and resume his nap in the coolness of the shady porch.

The teen began trying to coax Zoe to settle down, but the cat was still intent on dragging her little razor-sharp claws across the other dog's nose, so the boy began to back off.

Soon, however, the other dog began to tire of all the nonsense too. After all, he wasn't even quite sure why he had joined the chase to begin with, and it *was* very hot today. Maybe he would just go take a dip over in the mountain stream.

Off he loped in the direction of the water, leaving the ornery cat still spitting and hissing at anyone who ventured near. As the canine approached the waterfall, a beautiful, brilliant rainbow suddenly appeared in the bright sunlight, bursting forth with radiant beauty.

Aware that something had disturbed her, inside the gazebo, the tiny baby was again beginning to build up into a hungry tantrum.

Suddenly, the little girl let out a piercing cry that brought all the commotion around her to a complete, shocked standstill.

Astonished, all the neighborhood children and adults looked up toward the gazebo, and saw several dozen swallowtail butterflies floating near the ceiling. Tiny little rainbow lights sparkled here and there between all the butterflies.

The rainbow that shone directly from the vicinity of the waterfall seemed to extend right into the gazebo. Everyone began pointing, and oohing and aahing at the magical scene before them. Again, they heard the cry of a small baby, building with mounting gusto.

Zoe, disgusted at the predicament of having lost her prey to those two stupid dogs who had both run off, began to skulk back toward her domain and human with contempt. She scowled, hissing and growling occasionally and baring a claw or two even now at anyone attempting to coax her home.

At this point, Pastor Farley and a few of the adults had reached the gazebo area, and were now, to their astonishment, also hearing the cry of a small baby. The townspeople stood gazing at the glorious, sparkling spectacle, with utter astonishment, but none of them moved.

Pastor Farley decided that it was his place to take the initiative. After he climbed the steps leading up to the gazebo, he couldn't believe his eyes! In the center, on the floor, protected by the shade of the ornate gazebo's roof, was a tiny, precious baby girl, screaming her diminutive, purple, upset little head off! Several dozen butterflies and spectral lights all floated directly above her as if they were trying to call attention to and protect the screaming little thing.

"My God," he exclaimed, "it's a miracle! If that cat hadn't gotten into it with those two dogs and come running down here, it could have been hours before this poor child was discovered! She might have died in this heat! We must find out where this baby's parents are!"

By now, several of the other adults and their children had made their way into the gazebo. Most stood, gazing in astonishment along with the pastor, but then, one of the younger mothers stepped forward, and picked up the wispy-blond-haired infant. She announced to no one in particular that this child was hungry and in need of a bottle, and that she was going to take care of this matter right now!

Everyone else in the gazebo stood for a moment or two longer in stupefied silence, and then the pastor came to his senses, agreed with the young woman, and sent her on her way. He then announced to the other adults that a town meeting must be held later in the day to determine if anyone knew whose baby this was, and what to do about all of this.

For now, all of the excitement was over, and reluctantly, most folks headed back to their homes, still gossiping quite loudly and excitedly about all the melodrama that had just taken place. They wondered who this newly discovered baby was, and where she had come from!

Some children remained behind to play in the park for a while. They would push each other to and fro on the swings or round and round on the merry-go-round, sit in the shade of the large oak trees, or just play pitch and catch at the baseball diamond.

Satisfied that their mission had been accomplished, the rainbow lights faded away. The congregated butterflies and maidenfly headed back toward the stream, joyous that their small, temporary charge had now found her way into safety. Back to the butterflyweed they went!

Once Pastor Farley had made his way back into town, he stopped first at the general store, and then at the bank, to let the other town leaders know what had happened. He suggested to them that a meeting would need to be held.

The other men agreed that this matter should be discussed that afternoon at the town hall, and that they would get the word out to the other villagers.

Banker Janssen, who was also the mayor and town judge, held the meeting at two in the afternoon. There were several dozen adults present. With a loud bang of his gavel, the rather pompous mayor called the meeting to order. He then asked, "Does anyone know who this poor child belongs to?"

Mrs. Hennesy, the young mother that had earlier volunteered to give the baby a bottle, brought the infant to the front of the room. The sweet thing slept peacefully in her arms, completely unaware of all of the commotion going on around her, or that she was the center of attention. Hushed whispers could be heard, as people quietly exclaimed amongst themselves over her beauty.

The young woman finally spoke, saying, "I have discussed this with all the other mothers in the neighborhood. No one knows who this sweet little girl could possibly belong to. What are we to do?"

Mayor Janssen then addressed the crowd, asking, "Is there anyone who could care for the child, temporarily if nothing else, until we are able to determine who her parents are, or find a home for her?"

After several moments of loud discussion and gossip, the mayor banged his gavel on his desk, and shouted, "Order, please! Now, again, is there anyone who would be willing to take this baby under their wing until we have this matter resolved?"

With hesitation, Mrs. Hennesy stepped forward, and then said, "I will, but only for the least amount of time that is necessary. I already have several mouths to feed, and another baby at home to care for. It is just not reasonable that I should have to care for this one too with my hands already so full."

There were several more minutes of argument and discussion, and then the mayor again interceded, pompously pounding his gavel one last time and shouting, "Ladies and gentlemen, please! This matter is resolved, at least for now! Let us all go back to what we were doing, and if necessary, we will meet again to discuss anything further regarding this situation."

Mayor Janssen, satisfied that he had resolved this issue, for at least the time being, anyway, set his gavel down, and puffed his chest up quite proudly at his accomplishment.

After some grumbling and mumbling, the villagers began

to disperse. Everyone headed back to work or home, and Mrs. Hennesy returned to her home with the child. The tiny town was calm again, at least for now.

Several days passed. Sunday morning brought all the townspeople to church. At the end of the service, Pastor Farley asked Mr. Hennesy how things were going with the infant.

"My wife is at home caring for the child as we speak." the young father said. "She really has her hands quite full, as our young son, Paul, is only ten months old and just beginning to try to walk."

Pastor Farley nodded; then assured the man that he would try to arrange another town meeting that afternoon.

In the afternoon, most of the folks from town again gathered. Gavel banging to bring order to the meeting, Mayor Janssen then asked Pastor Farley to please speak to the crowd.

Pastor Farley stood up, cleared his throat, and addressed the throng, asking again, "Does anyone here know who the sweet baby girl, who is being called Katharine because of the locket she was wearing when she was discovered, might belong to? Has anyone heard anything, or known of anyone in the area who might have recently been with child?"

Low murmurs and discussion dominated the room, with everyone ultimately agreeing that no one had any idea who the baby's parents might be.

Pastor Farley went over to the mayor and conversed with him quietly for several minutes. The pastor looked quite saddened after this private discussion. He and the mayor both finally nodded their heads in unified agreement, shook hands, and then the mayor banged his gavel one last time.

He announced to the waiting crowd, "Pastor Farley and I have discussed this at length, not just now, but for the last several days. We feel that it is in the best interest of this little girl that we find a permanent home for her. Mr. and Mrs. Hennesy have been kind enough to take this child into their home and care for her, but this was supposed to be only temporary. We need someone to step forward now, and offer their home to this girl on a permanent basis, or we need to investigate the possibility of placing her with an orphanage in the city some distance from here. So, folks, what is it to be?"

More murmurs and loud discussion again took place, but no one stepped forward.

One mother in the crowd finally called out above the din, which quieted almost immediately, "None of us have much here, and another mouth to feed is really too much to ask of any of us. All of you know how it has been! There is barely enough food on the table at most of our homes these days."

She looked at other young mothers with emphasis, while low rumbles of agreement could be heard throughout the room. She waved one hand toward the group of young women, in compassion. "Elsie over here is expecting another wee one anytime now, and Margaret and Daisy and the rest of us already have our hands full." The other mothers nodded their heads in agreement.

Again, there was much muttering and rumbling, until finally Mayor Janssen interceded. "Well, then folks, Pastor Farley and I feel it would be best for the child if she were placed with the orphanage in the city. Surely there will be someone there that would be willing to raise this dear girl."

Pastor Farley nodded in agreement. After several more minutes of discussion amongst the crowd, Pastor Farley once more stepped forward to address the gathering. "Well then, I guess this matter is resolved. If any of you should change your minds, would you please let me know by the end of next week? Unless I hear from someone willing to raise this child, I will send word into the city and arrange for her to be transported to the orphanage."

After a few more murmurs and nods, the crowd began to break up and head back to their homes.

Alone with the mayor several minutes later, Pastor Farley

again pleaded with the man, saying, "Certainly there must be someone here that would want the child! She is a very well-behaved baby. If only I had a wife, I would take the baby into my own home. However, I know nothing about raising a child, and I already have so many duties associated with my church. It would not be a good life for the girl. She needs two parents to nurture her, and help her grow. Please, see if you can convince someone to take her in."

The mayor nodded, and shook hands again with the Pastor, "We will see what we can do, but in the meantime, maybe you can pray for all of us here; and for the little one too."

"Yes, I will do that," Pastor Farley affirmed. He then left with sadness in his heart, and went back to the church to pray.

Days passed, and the tiny town resumed its routine. No one offered to take the child in permanently, and the Hennesy family became increasingly stressed. Pastor Farley contacted a woman with "Our Saints Catholic Orphanage" in the city. He took up a paltry offering the next Sunday in the church to help the family out with expenses. He also held a small baptismal service for the child after the regular service.

Twelve days after Zoe the cat and the two dogs had chased the bluebird into the park, the maidenfly and butterflies had helped the infant, and the infant had been discovered in the gazebo, the woman from the orphanage in the city arrived. No one had come forward to claim the child as their own, and no one had offered to raise her.

When the woman knocked on the door of the rectory, Pastor Farley felt a huge lump in his throat. He had prayed sincerely for the health, well-being, and safety of this child, and felt an odd attachment to her and the Hennesys. Yet, he understood the reason behind their feelings in the matter, and could not fault them for it.

Mrs. Bailey, the woman from the orphanage, seemed very pleasant, and he walked her down the street to the Hennesy's home with dread in his heart for what was about to happen. If only someone here had wanted the poor child. Certainly, someone in the city would find it in their heart to adopt the beautiful little girl.

When the Hennesys opened the door, they too seemed awkward, and saddened, and lingered a bit before finally handing over the sweet baby to Mrs. Bailey. In the twelve days that she had existed, she had been well-cared for, and had filled out and grown somewhat already. Her pale blond hair had thickened slightly, and her eyes now appeared as though they would be blue in color. It was remarkable how well behaved the tiny baby was, and how aware of her surroundings she already seemed to be.

Mrs. Bailey was shown the locket the baby was wearing.

"Katharine," remarked Mrs. Bailey. "What a beautiful name, for such a beautiful little girl!"

Katharine cooed softly and did not complain or fuss when Mrs. Bailey took her into her arms, and remarked again at what a beautiful baby she was. She only fussed very slightly when they began to take her away.

Mrs. Hennesy went running after them as they approached the end of the sidewalk in front of their home, to give the sweet girl one last kiss. With regret, she handed Mrs. Bailey two spare bottles for her return trip to the orphanage.

Back at the rectory, Pastor Farley wished the woman well with her return journey on the train, and touched the baby's soft, chubby cheek for the last time. He said another silent prayer for her as Mrs. Bailey approached her car. A couple of butterflies playfully fluttered past him and the woman as she was getting back into the car that would return her to the train station. He watched and waved for several minutes as the car slowly drove away.

Later that day, by the waterfall, in the rainbow light, the butterflies and maidenflies congregated.

"The child is gone now, hopefully to safety," proclaimed the king of the swallowtails. "Wherever she goes, there will be more of our kind to watch over her and help her if she needs us. Now, perhaps, she will find a home of her own. That and a love-filled, joyous life are all that we could wish for her!"

"Yes, indeed." agreed the maidenfly with joy. And, following that, after a few moments of silence and reflection, all was bright and happy again and life went on as usual by the waterfall.

In another town, quite some distance away, Mrs. Bailey from "Our Saints Catholic Orphanage" boarded the train with Katharine, and a chapter in the baby's young life was over.

Adopted at Three

Some hours later, the train arrived in the city. Mrs. Bailey hailed a taxi to take Katharine to "Our Saints," and marveled at how good the precious girl had been for the entire trip. "Well, little one," she whispered softly to the sleeping baby when they arrived, "here we are! This will be your home for now."

She then walked the girl to the orphanage through the shade of the beautiful old oak trees that covered the lawn of "Our Saints Catholic Church". A couple of nuns walked by in their habits, conversing quietly with one another, and acknowledging Mrs. Bailey only with subdued smiles and a friendly nod.

Mrs. Bailey had attended Our Saints for years, and was the assistant to the director of the orphanage, a kind nun, named Mother Magdalene. While waiting outside Mother Magdalene's office, the little girl began to fuss somewhat as she awoke from the nap she had taken in the taxi on the ride home.

Soon Mother Magdalene greeted Mrs. Bailey, and then

motioned them into her office. "So, this is the little girl that Pastor Farley wrote to me about!" She gazed happily at the adorable little face. "What a perfect, sweet little baby! Katharine, is it? Such a precious girl! Well then, we will just get you settled in here as quickly as possible! Why don't you take her in back where the other children are, and they can get her cleaned up and fed and all settled in," she suggested.

Mrs. Bailey nodded and said, "Yes, Reverend Mother, I will see to it that everything is taken care of."

Mrs. Bailey proceeded to the large, bright room of the orphanage, which contained a multitude of beds, and some baby cribs along one of the walls.

Numerous children milled about inside, some quietly playing cards on their beds, some reading. The cacophony of many more playing outside in the playground resounded indoors, where their laughter could be heard. Mrs. Bailey loved being here, and hearing the sound of all the children. There was something about the sound of many children all talking at once, and laughing, that kept her feeling youthful, even though she was in her late fifties.

A young nun approached her, took the infant with a smile and marveled at how precious she was, and went on her way to go clean her up. Mrs. Bailey beamed with satisfaction. Her work was done for now. She was sure the small girl would grow to love it here for whatever length of time she stayed!

Once the young nun had gotten the infant all cleaned up and sweet-smelling, with a brand-new diaper and kimono, she admired the locket. She fed the little girl until she dozed, and then placed her in a crib that had recently been fitted with clean sheets and a blanket. Since Katharine was a little girl, the nun had hung a mobile of colorful butterflies over her crib that drifted lazily overhead. Boy's cribs had airplanes hung over them.

Satisfied that the sweet girl was comfortable and ready for a nap, the nun gently touched her adorable face as her eyelids began to flutter closed. Then, she smiled, and went off to attend to some of the other children's needs. *Katharine will be content here; and the Lord smiles down on her,* she thought happily to herself.

Weeks passed, and then months. The tiny infant grew into a chubby baby, then a busy toddler. Other children befriended her and helped care for her and the other babies.

Sundays were days to observe religion at the orphanage, but every Saturday, folks would pass through and look at all of the children. Sometimes they would choose one that they felt would make their family complete.

Katharine was too young to know or understand why these strangers would make their way through the orphanage. Sometimes, they would pause to look at her, and remark at the blueness of her eyes, or the blondness and waviness of her ever-lengthening hair. Now and then a young couple would spend an inordinate amount of time with her, only to leave eventually and move on to another child's bed and leave her sitting in her crib alone again.

In these times, many couples were looking for boys that would eventually grow big enough to be helpful on farms or with other work, so usually the boys did not stay there long.

The younger ones were at a particularly high premium. Therefore, often the poor girls were passed over in favor of a boy. Consequently, there were many more girls in the orphanage than there were boys.

However, it still was a joyous place to be, and Katharine had never really known anything else anyway. The nuns and children were always kind to her, and in the rare moments that another child got a bit mean with her, the nuns always made sure that a stop was put to it quickly.

Months passed by in a blur, and not long after Katharine had turned three, one Saturday morning another young couple came by her crib. They looked very well-to-do, dressed expensively and neatly.

The man seemed immediately entranced with Katharine, who was all dressed up very prettily in a frilly blue frock that matched her eyes. However, the woman didn't seem quite so sure.

With a wide smile that filled his turquoise-blue eyes, the nice man picked her up, and held her, and talked to her. She babbled a few baby words back at him, and then he threw back his head and laughed. "What an adorable little girl!" he exclaimed to his wife, who still kept her distance.

"Oh, come here!" he cheerfully coaxed the woman, then handed the little girl over to her whether she wanted to hold her or not.

After a minute or two, the woman seemed to relax a little, and then began to smile slightly, even bouncing the girl against her hip a bit. Katharine was suddenly entranced with the pricey sparkling baubles hanging from the woman's earlobes. She reached up with a chubby fist and grabbed one in order to examine it.

"Oh!" exclaimed the woman with pain. She quickly lifted her hand to remove the chubby fingers from her earring. In exasperation, she handed Katharine back to her husband. "Please, you hold her!" she directed him.

"Besides, I thought we were here to look at boys, although there doesn't seem to be much of a selection right now," she continued with slight dismay in her voice.

"We should speak with the nuns," the woman added, "and see if there are any outside in the playground that we haven't seen yet. After all, you wanted a boy that could help you with the store when he gets a little older."

The man nodded, placed the three-year-old girl back into her crib, and then acquiesced to his wife. They proceeded to walk around, and soon could be seen talking to one of the nuns. Finally, they disappeared outside for a little while.

Katharine quietly played in her crib once again, and one of the older girls came over and entertained her with a colorful stuffed animal.

Then suddenly, the couple was back at her crib once more with one of the nuns. The woman was holding the hand of one of the older boys, named Michael. He had always been kind to Katharine, and was seven years old. He had dark brown hair and brown eyes.

The kind-looking man had a broad smile, and happiness danced in his eyes. He picked Katharine back up out of her crib, chatting to her and playing with her for several moments more. He admired her beautiful locket.

Then he proclaimed to his wife, and the nun, "I want this adorable little girl also!"

The nun looked overjoyed, beaming happily, along with the man, while the woman stood quietly and unsmilingly unsure nearby.

"All right sir." the nun said professionally. "Let's go into the Reverend Mother's office then and take care of all the paperwork."

Katharine's prospective parents were told during the adoption signing that not much was known about her origins, only that she had been abandoned in a small town bordering the Blue Ridge Mountains. Michael's parents, although known, had both been killed in an accident just the year before, and no surviving family members had been found to care for him.

A couple of hours later, after the orphanage lunch had been served, and the few articles the children possessed packed into boxes, the newly formed family climbed into their expensive automobile.

The proud Edward first drove toward his place of business to show off their new children to all of his employees before heading home.

Katharine and Michael's new parents' names were Edward and Constance Abernathy. Edward was the owner of an expensive department store on the exclusive side of the city, aptly named "Abernathy's."

Edward Abernathy was tall and very good looking, with sandy-colored hair, and kind, turquoise-colored eyes. He was a good, kind employer, and all of his employees loved him.

However, not many of them cared for his wife. Rather, she was something merely to be tolerated and avoided whenever possible.

Constance Abernathy was beautiful, in a severe, haughty sort of way, with dark hair and emerald green eyes. She had exquisite taste, and a keen sense for fashion. Her husband had given her charge of the women's clothing department, which she kept very neat, orderly and stylish, and ruled with an iron fist. More than one hapless woman employee had crossed her in her day, she felt. Constance had never wasted any time sending them on their way out into the street, jobless and left to fend for themselves.

On this particular day, several employees glanced at each other with looks of disdain for the woman; and pity for the poor children and their new father. However, they were polite, and welcomed them into their new family and at the store just the same.

The children continued to hang back cautiously, shy and slightly dismayed at all of the newness in their lives. They just watched with huge eyes and listened to everything that was going on around them for the longest time.

One of the women employees finally asked if she could hold the adorable little girl. Then, all the other women and a few of the men gathered around. They exclaimed over the child's beauty, and her beautiful locket, her sweet, calm personality, and how absolutely adorable she was.

All the while, Constance stood quietly by while Edward beamed. Also, not wanting to leave the boy out, the store workers gathered around Michael and asked him what his name was, what he liked to do, and so on.

Soon, the children began overcoming some of their shyness, and started to smile a little at all of the nice people around them.

After quite awhile, Katharine began to rub her eyes, and Edward wasted no time in noticing this. He realized that it was probably time to introduce both the children to their new home, and so he bade his wonderful workers farewell for the afternoon.

Off the happy father went with his brand new family to their large, exquisitely appointed Victorian home on the outskirts of the city. Constance sat stiffly in her seat across from Edward, having difficulty adjusting to the fact that there were now two young children in the back seat of their car. She did not have the slightest idea of what to do with either one of them.

She and Edward had been married for nine years, and apparently were not able to conceive. It hadn't really made much of a difference to her. She had grown used to being around only adults, and wasn't particularly interested in children. Rather, she regarded most of them as brats.

Edward, on the other hand, had always yearned for children and had bothered her frequently for years about having them, so she had finally given in just to please him. At least this way, she had reasoned to herself to some extent, her exquisite figure would never be spoiled, after all. Nonetheless, all she really wanted was to keep her husband to herself!

Edward didn't notice her quietness during their ride one bit though, so enthralled was he with his new family that he had forgotten all about his silent and brooding wife for the moment.

Eventually, the new family arrived at what was to be the children's permanent home. A huge, breathtaking Victorian mansion came into view. It was what was commonly called a "painted lady", of very large scale. Its grounds contained many mature trees, gorgeous fountains, ponds, and gardens, and it was situated on an enormous piece of property.

A wrought iron fence wrapped around the entire estate, with gates that would need to be opened before the car could enter. Their wait was not long, however, for soon, a servant waiting in a small coach house nearby expediently opened the gates for the family, and Edward drove the car slowly up the winding drive to the mansion.

The children were awestruck. Even though they were children, they knew that this was someplace special. Their new daddy helped his wife, and then them, too, out of the car. Taking their hands, he guided all of them up to the large, sparkling, leaded glass double doors at the front of the mansion. Another waiting servant opened the doors before they even had time to knock.

The inside of the house was breathtaking, with a huge, ornately winding staircase coming down from the upstairs and ending near the front doors. Edward's new family entered, and the children surveyed the huge space with awe.

A humongous, glistening crystal chandelier reflected thousands of points of light directly overhead. Gargantuan rooms richly appointed with marble flooring and more chandeliers went on and on before them. Several servants walked by and paused momentarily to greet them.

Edward introduced them all to his new children. The help politely greeted them with smiles, and then proceeded on their way to take care of whatever special job that they had been assigned to do by the Abernathys.

Mr. Abernathy then finally spoke to the servant by the door, saying "Charles, the children are exhausted from the newness of everything. Would you please see what can be done about preparing Michael's and Katharine's new rooms for them, and also speak with Rosie about dinner arrangements as quickly as possible so that they can get settled in?"

Charles the butler nodded professionally, and walked briskly away.

Not much later, everyone was eating happily in the large kitchen while the cook looked on cheerfully. Rosie was a rotund, cheerful-looking woman that loved to talk, and the children loved her instantly.

"So, Mista Abanathy," the woman observed happily, "yestaday it was just you and the missus, and now, look at you taday! You have a complete family! What absolutely beautiful chillun!"

Mr. Abernathy agreed happily, while Constance just sat there, picking delicately at her food and only eating a few bites. Being such a woman of style, after all, required keeping a slim, trim figure in order to display all of the expensive styles she wore so proudly. *I would have preferred eating in the elegant dining room,* she mused.

Constance never ate much, but secretly, she did like to drink wine, and lots of it. The servants knew all about her little secret, but never mentioned it to anyone, not even her husband. He had always held his beautiful wife up on a pedestal, and never would have believed them anyway if they had told him.

When she had finished picking at her food, she quietly excused herself and got up, leaving the rest of the noisy bunch in the kitchen while she went into the parlor and poured herself a large glass of wine. *Perhaps this will help numb me to the annoying, cheerful noises coming from the kitchen,* she mused disdainfully. *I prefer peace and quiet, not all this noise, and certainly not snotty noses and every other nasty thing that comes with having children. Edward and I will have to look into hiring a nanny as soon as possible!*

After dinner, Edward took the children out onto the large, tastefully decorated veranda in back. Large pots, overflowing with flowers graced the area, along with beautiful bushes, a delicate arbor, and several fountains. Welcoming chairs and benches were scattered about, in groupings, to encourage conversation.

Beyond the veranda stretched a vast expanse of green lawn, as far as the eye could see. It too, was as stunning as the front lawn was, with beautiful landscaping, and many gorgeous gardens scattered here and there upon its far-reaching grounds.

The children began running around and playing close up by the house, but there wasn't really much for them to do, and Edward quickly saw that. He decided to himself that tomorrow he would look into the construction of a small playground for them.

Katharine was again beginning to rub her eyes. Her tummy was full now, and she had missed her afternoon nap.

So, Edward gathered the children back together, and took them up to their newly prepared rooms. Since there had never been children in the mansion before, there weren't many toys or other children's things, something that Edward also made a mental note to take care of as soon as possible.

The servants helped the children both get cleaned up and tucked into their beds, and sleepy little Katharine was out almost instantly. Edward chuckled softly to himself, and kissed her lightly on her forehead, and then went to check in on Michael. He was already becoming drowsy too. The day had been quite stressful for both of the children, with all the changes that had taken place, and they were exhausted. Soon, he was asleep also.

Edward went blissfully back downstairs and out on to the veranda, in the fading light of the day, where his wife had been for quite some time already. She sat in a small, ornate loveseat, fanning herself, and enjoying a glass of wine.

"Well, Connie, what do you think of all of this?" he asked her happily, feeling quite proud of himself, and plopping down jovially in a matching chair across from her.

"I'm pleased if you are, dear." she replied blandly. "Are the children in bed now?"

"Yes, Mamie helped me get everything all in order for them, and they both went to sleep almost instantly." he returned, smiling at the recollection. "I'm sure they must both be exhausted after all of the excitement of the day."

"Yes, dear." Constance said then, looking rather distressed and slightly annoyed after the long day herself. After pausing a moment, she then announced to her husband, "I want to look into finding a nanny for them in the morning. With my duties at the store I won't be here during the day, and the children will naturally need much looking after."

Edward felt rather distraught at hearing this. He was hoping that his dear wife would be overjoyed at finally having some children to be a mother to. He himself would certainly be busy at the store quite often, and not be able to be here, and Connie's position was not absolutely necessary.

He had given his wife her department years before only to ease her boredom at being home all of the time. But things had changed now. There were plenty of other capable women in that department that could oversee things just fine.

With some consternation, he finally asked her, "Darling, are you sure? I was rather hoping that you would want to look after the children yourself. We have waited so very long for this! Naturally, the servants would be able to do the diaper changing and such for you, if you didn't want to be bothered with that, but I *had* hoped you would want to be around to watch them grow and all! I was thinking that in the morning I should contact someone about constructing a small play area for them out back here a little ways. I also would like to have someone see to it that their rooms are filled with children's toys and books and such, so that they don't become bored."

"Well, all of that would be fine with me, dear." Constance returned with a slight edge to her voice. "However, I do still insist that I be allowed to continue operating the Women's Department at the store. I do *so* enjoy it, and you must know that I would be bored to death staying at home here all day long, like I was when we were first married before you started up the store." she argued.

"Please dear, why don't you just mull it over for a little while? I'm sure you'll want to change your mind after just sleeping on it a bit. The children should keep you plenty busy, and you most likely would no longer even have time to become bored!" Edward finally suggested, still hoping to change her mind. He was still thrilled at his new "daddyhood" and could not comprehend or understand his wife's reluctance.

Dismissively, Constance suddenly rose, glass of wine still in hand. Its contents nearly splashed over the rim of the dainty glass. She retorted with underlying rudeness in her voice, "Sleeping sounds like an excellent idea to me, dear, but don't expect me to change my attitude about this! I am going to bed now, to read and relax for awhile to help ease my nerves, and then to sleep, as you have suggested!" And off the veranda she strode, and into the house purposefully, leaving Edward feeling very frustrated, alone, and slightly hurt.

Later, Edward came up the stairs and entered their expansive, perfectly decorated bedroom. All the lights were off, and his wife was already sleeping, or so he thought. As silently as possible, he slipped into bed beside her. He laid there for a long time, unable to relax because of their earlier argument. Ultimately, however, the exhaustion of the day finally claimed him, and he fell into a fitful, but deep slumber.

In the middle of the night, Constance, who was still wide awake, rose and quietly went over to the small bar in the bay window alcove on the far side of the room. She silently poured herself another glass of wine in the moonlight. She was still very frustrated at her new predicament, and knew that she was going to have trouble warming up to these children. *Why, they aren't even my own! Perhaps if I had given birth to them, I would feel different. . . no, I have never really even liked children at all,* she concluded after some thought. *This had all been Edward's idea!*

Silently and deliberately, she wandered out the bedroom door and down the large, wide hall toward the children's rooms. Their doors were both slightly ajar so that the sleeping servant down at the end of the hall could hear them if they cried out in the night.

Constance paused outside Michael's door first, hesitantly reaching to push it open so that she could enter, but then changed her mind. Padding carefully just a little further down the hallway, she noiselessly pushed open the door of Katharine's room, and went in.

Moonlight streamed through the windows on this side of the mansion. The silhouette of a large Luna moth cast its shadow briefly against the largest window, its luminescent wings fluttering against the glass, and then, it disappeared.

Constance paid it no heed, and stood observing the small, angelic child sleeping soundly, and peacefully. The beauty and innocence of the sleeping girl didn't move her heart at all. Instead, Constance snorted derisively. Advancing closer, she peered at the sleeping child. Something flashed in the moonlight as Katharine stirred slightly in her slumber. Constance peered, a little closer. *What is this cheap little locket around the girl's neck? Butterflies!*

She reached out to touch it. Then, thinking better of it, she pulled her hand back quickly. She did not want to wake the little girl. She had always hated the sound of a crying child, and also did not want anyone to know she was in there.

Constance backed up now slightly, in dismay. Her lower lip protruded in a bit of a pout. All she could think about was all of the aggravation and upset that these children were going to cause in her selfish life. She stood rooted there several moments more, contemplating the events of the previous day.

At last, she went back to her and Edward's shared room, and quietly sat in a chair in a corner by the window for quite some time still, occasionally refilling the glass of wine and emptying

it. Finally, she climbed back into bed, and eventually drifted off
into a fitful sleep herself.

Beloved, Yet Abused

Weeks passed in the Abernathy household. The children appeared to be adjusting quite well to their new situation. However, Katharine didn't do much talking yet, and was a rather shy, reserved child.

Edward saw to it that the chain on Katharine's unique locket was replaced with a longer one. The delicate chain that she had been wearing had shortened considerably around her neck as she had grown. Edward loved to tease her. He had noticed her enchantment with butterflies by now, and sometimes referred to her as his "butterfly baby."

Michael was quite the boy, and enjoyed playing with cars and trucks and running around full of energy. He also loved to talk constantly.

Edward himself had taken quite a lot of time away from Abernathy's to spend with Michael and Katharine and help them settle in. He oversaw the building of the play area outside, and the re-decorating of their rooms, making sure that they were filled up with plenty of new toys and books.

Constance, true to her word, hired a nanny for them within days, an older and thankfully kindly woman named Aggie. Both Katharine and Michael warmed up to her quickly.

Edward liked Aggie too, and mellowed slightly about his wife's attitude toward the children and their having a nanny. He only wanted to placate his wife, but even now, her attitude toward *him* had not warmed back up completely. Maybe time would remedy that, he hoped sincerely.

She still does not spend much time with the children, though, he had noticed with dismay. In fact, after Aggie had been hired just a few days after they had brought the children home, Constance had returned to her post at the store and begun working even longer hours than before. She also began harassing her poor workers with greater venom than ever.

Edward was rather lonely of late also, their marital life had dwindled to almost nothing these past weeks, and he felt vague regret, and missed the closeness that they had once shared.

A couple of weeks after they had brought the children home, Edward's parent's came for a visit. They were very kindly older folks; that had always loved all of their grandchildren, and were so happy to meet their new ones now. They exclaimed to Edward over how beautiful both of the children were, and played with them and talked to them and Edward for hours during their first visit.

It wasn't long before they were visiting the new family on a weekly basis. The children also soon met Edward's older brother and his wife, George and Madelyn. They were not nearly as wealthy as Edward was, but just as kind. They were named the children's godparents.

Katharine and Michael enjoyed their new play-yard very much, and began to spend much of their time and energies playing outside in the sunshine.

Katharine was also especially intrigued with a nearby flower garden that contained a small bird bath, gazing ball and ornate arbor. Butterflies frequently visited it. Often, she would leave her brother's side and run over to the tiny garden. She would stand and watch in awe as the intriguing insects fluttered and floated almost effortlessly around the brightly colored flowers, landing on them occasionally and drinking their nectar.

In his time off from the store, Edward had found joy in the little girl's enchantment with the delicate creatures, and had delighted in watching her talk to them. He commissioned a local artist to come in and hand paint some of them on the walls of Katharine's newly repainted room.

Feeling that everything was in order now with his new family, Edward returned to work, running Abernathy's with his usual, kind professionalism. His employees were grateful to have him back.

One Saturday afternoon, in the days approaching the fall, Edward was still at the store, and Constance had finally taken a rare day off. Katharine was playing on the swing set while Michael was digging nearby in the sandbox.

Constance sat, lazily cooling herself in the breeze up on the veranda, while enjoying her third glass of wine for the afternoon. She picked at a small plate of food and ignored the children totally, however, while Aggie sat on the edge of the veranda watching over them.

After some time, Katharine tired of swinging. She again ran out toward the little garden, hoping to see some more butterflies there.

Aggie had watched her run over there often. She observed Katharine dash happily that way now, and didn't mind her going over there.

Katharine was always very good and came right back when she got bored. She was always so enchanted by the butterflies that Aggie thought her simply adorable.

After a little while, it occurred to Constance that the child was no longer swinging, and she asked Aggie where she was.

"Oh, just over there by the little garden, that is all, Mrs. Abernathy. Would you mind if I went inside for a couple of minutes?" she suggested. "I would like to see if Rosie has their afternoon snack ready yet."

"No, not at all, Aggie. I'll watch the children for a few minutes." Constance replied. She *had* been feeling slightly bored. *Perhaps a change of scenery, and just getting up and moving around would make me feel better,* she thought. She stood with her drink in hand, and, slightly tipsily, moved closer to the edge of the veranda.

Michael was still in the sandbox, pushing a large metal dump truck around and making motor noises. Constance could barely see Katharine, however, who was on the other side of the little garden. So, she steadied herself with the hand railing and made her way carefully down the steps and across the lawn toward the garden to see what the little girl was up to.

As she neared the garden, Constance could hear the little girl talking softly. *Why, those are more words put together at once than I have ever heard the girl say before!* she thought absently to herself. Constance was beginning to think there was something wrong with the girl. Perhaps she was afflicted somehow. She hardly ever spoke, especially when her new "mother" was around.

As Constance rounded the garden, she could see two beautiful butterflies fluttering over some flowers. The small girl was transfixed with them, standing quite close to the creatures and looking positively enchanting while she carried on her one-sided conversation.

An intense surge of dislike and jealousy toward the girl blossomed within her at that moment. The girl looked so sweet and innocent. She appeared to be captivated by the creatures, and looked so very happy.

After observing the whole scene for a few moments longer, Constance said to her rather sharply, "Come along, Katharine, Aggie has gone to get your afternoon snacks! Let's go join your brother and go back up to the porch to eat now!"

Katharine, who had always been a little afraid of the woman, and had not seen her approaching, now shied away slightly. Really, those were practically the only words that Constance had ever spoken to her, and she sensed that her new "mother" did not like her much!

Katharine stopped speaking, and did not reach out to Constance's unoccupied and offered hand. Instead, with huge blue, worried looking eyes, she only backed up more.

Constance, in her slightly drunken stupor, was rapidly becoming angry with the little brat. "Come along, now!" she commanded Katharine.

When Katharine still refused to take her hand, Constance lost all of her control and abruptly smacked Katharine on the side of her pretty little head as hard as she could. Then, she grabbed a hold of the child's tiny little hand and yanked Katharine toward her.

Stunned, Katharine looked at her wide-eyed and open-mouthed for a moment, and then, the poor child began to wail loudly. She grabbed at her head with her other hand in a futile effort to tear the pain away, with tears streaming from her eyes.

It was at that moment that Constance then again noticed the delicate locket around Katharine's neck, observing yet one more object of the little girl's enthrallment. Out of her angry spite, she reached to yank the tiny locket from her.

As she took hold of the delicate gold locket, hanging from its wispy gold chain, it instantly became fiery hot in her fingers. Quite suddenly, before Constance could entirely let go of it, Katharine instinctively reached for it and grabbed at it.

Iridescent miniature lights materialized between them, and then Constance experienced an unseen, but vigorous force quickly and strongly pushing her back away from Katharine.

In surprise and total shock, Constance lost her balance, landing soundly on her rump, and spilling the remainder of her wine all over her brand-new, obscenely expensive dress.

"Ohhh!" she cried out in a startled voice, so bewildered by what had just taken place that it took her a few seconds to recover from her shock. She even thought she saw tiny rainbow-colored stars, or bright little lights drifting and floating in front of her eyes for a few more seconds. *Must be the wine*, she thought! She shook her head vaguely, wondering just what this impudent little brat had done to her!

By now, Katharine had escaped the angry grasp of Constance, and was running away from the woman on her chubby little legs back toward her play area and to the safety of Michael and Aggie, as well. Aggie, who had just set the small tray loaded with their afternoon snacks on a table up on the veranda, noticed the screaming child with astonishment.

Katharine was still screaming as loudly as she possibly could at the pain in the side of her small head that Constance had just inflicted. The poor girl was sobbing almost uncontrollably by now, and Aggie ran down the steps and across the lush green grass as quickly as her aging legs would take her. She picked the little girl up, holding her close to comfort her.

"There, there, child, it certainly can't be as bad as all this!" She tried to soothe Katharine's tears away, hugging her, wiping at her eyes, and smoothing the wispy blonde, shoulder-length hair away from them.

Constance had by now regained her footing, and walked slowly back towards them and the veranda, empty wine glass in hand.

"My goodness, Mrs. Abernathy; what could possibly have happened? I was only inside the house for a few minutes!"

Constance, by now, had also regained her regal composure. She only haughtily replied, "Oh, nothing much! When I went over to try to get her to come up for her snack, I must have surprised her a little, and she stumbled and bumped her head a bit on the birdbath. I'm sure she's just fine by now. She is just enjoying the little tantrum she is having. That's all!"

Aggie surveyed the woman, slightly dismayed at Constance's apparent apathy. But, since she hadn't seen what had happened, she accepted what Mrs. Abernathy had told her, not noticing the wine stains on her mistress's dress. She carried the calming and quieting Katharine up to the veranda. By now, Katharine was just crying softly, and wiping at her eyes with her chubby fists, and soon Michael joined her and Aggie and the tray of goodies.

It wasn't long before Katharine forgot her reason for crying, and she picked out a cookie while Aggie poured her a little drink. All was well again, at least for now.

Up at the double French doors that led into the house, Constance eyed the little group with spite and disgust, and then went inside to change now that her garment was ruined.

She mused quite angrily while she poured herself yet another drink. She did not like these children, especially that little witch of a girl, and did not understand exactly what invisible force it had been that had pushed her, causing her to have suddenly fallen backwards.

That night, Constance cuddled up to Edward in their bed. She was still rather dismayed with what had happened in the arbor garden, and she had an odd craving for some reassurance of some kind, but exactly what, she was not sure.

Later, while she watched her husband as he peacefully slept, his face kept being replaced with tiny, glowing, angry looking specters.

The butterflies back in the garden by the arbor whispered to each other, "Poor child! We must watch over her and protect her. The king and queen of the butterflies have spoken to us. They saw what happened through her magical locket! We will take care of her!"

Family Christmas

Months passed, and Christmas was approaching. Michael was now enrolled in the local Catholic School, in second grade. Edward Abernathy was still quite thrilled about his newly enlarged family, and was looking forward to bestowing many gifts on them for the coming holiday. He had always wanted to celebrate an old-fashioned Christmas, at home, with his family. By now both the children loved him very much, and both of them called him Daddy.

Constance, on the other hand, didn't really have a name as far as the children were concerned. She wasn't around much, and when she *was* home, she still avoided them like the plague, much to Edward's dismay. She rarely lifted a finger to even help with the children, and left all of those duties to Edward, Aggie, or one of the servants. She was also extremely annoyed even now at the sound of children, and subsequently, they were extremely careful to be quiet if Constance was home when Edward wasn't.

Katharine especially did not want to raise the woman's wrath again, after what had happened by the flower garden out back. She was now fully potty trained, growing like a weed, and beginning to speak more and more to those who cared for her.

However, she still rarely said a word to Constance, in an effort to avoid her.

Even at her young age, Katharine was frightened of the woman after what she had done to her that day. Although now she only vaguely remembered it, Constance's abuse remained etched deep within her memory. Her subconscious instinctively knew that she should be wary around the woman.

Christmas morning dawned, with a couple of inches of fresh snow that had fallen overnight. Aggie had been given the day off, as had most of the other servants. Only Rosie remained to cook their meals and eat with them also, since she had been kind enough to stay to help that day.

Edward's parents were there, visiting with all of them for the holidays. Constance's father had passed away several years ago, and she did not get on well with her own mother, so they were the only relatives staying with them to share their old-fashioned Christmas.

Around seven in the morning, Katharine awoke to Michael shaking her slightly, and telling her excitedly, "Katharine, it's Christmas! Let's get up and see what Santa's brought us!"

Both children ran with enthusiasm downstairs, to the gigantic Christmas tree in the huge living room to find Edward and their grandparents already waiting there with big, happy smiles. Edward's parent's loved and doted on these children too. Just like their son, their family was all-important to them, and they simply loved visiting with their new grandchildren.

"Oh, Daddy, oh Daddy, can we open our gifts now? Please?" they implored eagerly.

Edward had planned on waiting until Constance was awake, but the children were so very anxious to open their gifts now, and Constance would probably be in bed for hours yet!

Whenever Constance doesn't work, she does whatever she pleases, and since today is a holiday, she could quite possibly stay in bed until noon! Edward reflected. *After all, she is not used to getting up early on a Christmas morning so children can open their gifts!*

"Sure children, why not? Go right ahead!" Edward sighed, and relented then, and they excitedly tore into every gift until every single one was opened, with plenty of noisy exclaiming about each and every one. Edward just chuckled to himself. All those hours he had spent shopping to find just the right gifts for the children, and all of the hours that he and the servants had spent wrapping and preparing just for this day! Now, everything had been torn through and opened in just a matter of minutes!

As Edward had feared, Constance didn't make her appearance downstairs until nearly eleven-thirty in the morning, and he was glad that he hadn't forced Michael and Katharine to wait that long. By then, all the wrapping paper mess had been cleaned up, the children had sorted their gifts into their own huge piles, and then had arranged most of them neatly back under the tree. They were quietly playing with some of them near the older folks while Edward and his parents sat, softly conversing.

After Constance had taken her time eating her small breakfast in the dining room, she finally came into the living room, and surveyed the happy, picture-perfect scene with a look of disdain on her beautiful face.

"So, you children couldn't even wait for me before you opened everything that Santa brought! Well, Edward, I certainly hope all of you are very happy in here!" she commented rather sarcastically.

By now, Edward had a huge fire crackling and popping in the elegant fireplace. He rose from his chair nearby and said, "Oh, Connie, please come here and enjoy the coziness of the fire with us! I still have a few things for you to open yet, and so do Mom and Dad. And it is such a *lovely* Christmas morning!"

After a slight hesitation, Constance reluctantly joined them for awhile, and opened the expensive gifts that Edward and his parents had given her. She gave them all a few fine things to open also. She relaxed slightly, and began to enjoy herself somewhat.

The grandparents opened their gifts too, while the children continued to quietly play with everything Santa had brought them.

After lunch, Edward announced that since there was a little snow on the ground outside, they should all go sledding. Constance, of course, declined. An activity of that sort was much too cold and dirty for her. She went off with the in-laws to visit in the den and drink wine for a while.

Edward and the children changed excitedly into winter coats, hats, boots and mittens, and went outside and sledded in the snow for a couple of hours until everyone was exhausted and rosy-cheeked.

Edward doted on the children all day, much to Constance's resentment. She spent most of the afternoon and evening drinking her wine, eating occasionally, and paging through fashion magazines and books, and talking with Edward's parents.

She was feeling quite bored with all of the day's nonsense, and rather jealous of all the attention that Edward was paying to the children. In years past, she had spent holidays with Edward in Paris and other exotic places, and she was also feeling quite left out.

That evening, before bedtime, both Katharine and Michael were playing quietly together after their baths. They had each selected a couple of toys, and sat in front of the Christmas tree near the warmth of the roaring fireplace. The grandparents had retired to their room upstairs a short time earlier. Rosie had left a couple of hours before, after serving a delicious Christmas dinner for everyone's enjoyment and then making sure the kitchen had been cleaned up.

After a bit, Michael began gathering together a few small items that he wanted to take up to his room, and soon ran off excitedly to take them up there. Edward was upstairs somewhere getting ready for bed himself, and Constance was in the nearby den, reading a book. She rose, stretched slightly, and then went to get another glass of wine from the small bar in the room. She was tired, and considered joining Edward upstairs.

As she poured the glassful at the bar, she happened to look through the French doors that led into the living room, and saw Katharine sitting in there by herself, in the glow of the Christmas lights from the tree and the fire. Irritated, she wondered to herself why those children weren't in bed yet. *Edward spoiled them all day, and yet, here is the little girl, still playing down here with her toys when she should have been in bed a couple of hours ago! I don't like this little girl!* thought Constance. There was something about her that disturbed Constance. She just wasn't sure what it was!

The boy seemed relatively harmless, even if he was still a brat. Almost as though beckoned, he returned to Constance's view, digging through his pile of toys near where Katharine was playing, wearing his pajamas. She waited and observed, as he dug through them one more time. Then, satisfied with whatever little treasures he now was holding, he said goodnight to Katharine, and ran back off up to his room.

Where is Edward, anyway? Constance wondered to herself with aggravation as she took another sip from her glass. She decided that if this child was going to go to bed anytime soon, that she would have to take care of it herself!

She set the glass down, and then quietly opened the French doors, and silently padded across the luxurious, thick carpet in robe and soft slippers toward Katharine.

The little girl was engrossed in a large picture book that Edward had picked out especially for her. It contained elaborate drawings and descriptions of each and every butterfly known to exist. Even though Katharine couldn't yet read, the pictures were absolutely beautiful, and so very colorful, and she didn't hear Constance come in.

Now that she was near to Katharine, Constance harshly and sharply scolded her, saying without warning, "Time for bed now!" scaring Katharine from her reverie and causing her to drop the book.

Extending a hand toward the little girl, she again demanded, "Come along now, let's go! Time to head upstairs!"

Katharine, always leery of the woman, and always obedient, immediately rose to go up to bed, but quickly leaned back down to pick her picture book back up.

Constance became instantly enraged, and took a hold of Katharine's shoulder, roughly jerking the child back up into standing position before she could grasp her book.

"Why won't you listen to me, you impudent little brat? I told you, it's time for bed! You should have been in bed a couple of hours ago!" she hissed derisively.

Tears were now beginning to form in Katharine's eyes, and her lower lip began to quiver. She didn't understand why this woman treated her so badly, when she *was* getting ready to go up. After all, Michael had taken several of *his* toys upstairs with him, and all she wanted was to take her pretty book up to her room too!

"You stupid little good-for-nothing; get up the stairs, now!" Constance spat out in a low, menacing voice. Then, leaning over in her rage, she spitefully scooped the book up and tossed it directly into the burning fire, and then gave Katharine a rough shove in the direction of the stairway.

Katharine began crying loudly at the loss of her precious treasure and clutched at her locket, which had flown up toward the collar of her pajamas and gotten stuck there.

Without warning, the logs in the fireplace collapsed, strewing ashes and hot burning coals all over the hearth. They landed on the marble tiles on the floor in front of the fireplace, along with the picture book. Some of the fiery embers reached Constance's slippers, causing her to back away from the smoldering, scorching mess as quickly as possible.

Then, suddenly, an invisible energy lifted her slippered feet off the marble tiles in a split second, tipping her over. Screaming, Constance fell hard, first on her rear end, and then on her shoulder, nearly causing her to bang her head on the raised ledge in front of the fireplace.

As she lay there in stunned and pained silence for a moment, she gazed dazedly above her as a bright, angry-looking and rather iridescent specter materialized directly over her. *It almost resembles one of those blasted butterflies in the little brat's book!* she recalled vaguely.

By now, Edward had heard Katharine's crying, and his wife's screaming. He reached the downstairs, and ran into the living-area. He observed the mess in front of the fireplace, saw his wife lying there, and quickly ran over to help her up.

Thinking fast, he then stomped on the still-bright coals lying all around on the floor with his leather slippers in order to extinguish them. Some were dangerously close to the elegant carpet.

"Darling, are you all right? What happened?" he asked his wife in a panicked voice. Katharine just stood there looking up at him with wide, streaming eyes, so upset that she was shaking and couldn't speak even if she tried.

Constance, standing on shaky feet, reached down and began vigorously shaking off and wiping briskly at any live embers that were still on her robe, while Edward helped her.

"*Oh*, my arm!" she cried out in surprise, reaching for it with her other hand.

Again, Edward implored, "Connie, what happened?"

By now, Constance had had some time to gather her thoughts, and tears began forming in her eyes. Adeptly, one sprang out of her eye, and ran down her cheek in the hopes of creating some pity toward her within her husband's mind. Frankly, she *was* in pain, and felt like crying a little anyway.

Finally, she spoke, whining, "Oh, Edward, I was just telling Katharine here that it was time for bed when the logs in the fireplace suddenly collapsed. In an effort to get away from the hot mess here I fell, and it scared poor little Katharine. I think some of the embers got on her picture book too!"

Edward took Constance in his arms gingerly, in an effort not to injure her bruised arm further. After a couple more minutes of consoling his injured wife, he released her. He then picked up the picture book, dusted a few ashes off of it, and looked it over.

He pronounced to Katharine, who was now just sobbing quietly nearby, that her beautiful little book was just fine, untouched in fact! Placing it on a nearby table, he then went over to Katharine, picked her up with his back slightly to Constance, and asked her, "Are you all right, honey? Your mother had quite a scare there! You didn't get hurt too, did you?"

He looked her over with concerned eyes, and Katharine glanced at Edward first. She could see that he genuinely cared about her. Then, she looked at Constance, who was now eyeing her back, with venom. Still feeling frightened of her "mother,"she only looked back at Edward with wide, red, swollen eyes, and shook her head no.

Katharine was still slightly quivering from being so upset. Edward turned and faced Constance now, and said, "Since Aggie isn't here tonight, I'll just take her upstairs and get her tucked into bed now. Are you feeling better now, sweetheart?"

"Yes, dear," Constance replied, rubbing her sore arm gingerly, "but my arm and backside are hurting terribly. I'll wait down here until you get her into bed, and then would you please come back down here and help me up the stairs? I'm afraid I'm going to be quite stiff and sore in the morning!"

"Certainly, darling." Edward replied, and then headed toward the staircase carrying the steadily calming Katharine.

While she sat waiting, Constance began to feel a niggling sensation of genuine fear. She was an extremely intelligent woman. Being so, she understood that twice now, when she had tried to reprimand that insolent little brat upstairs, she had fallen and gotten hurt, while the child had remained relatively unscathed.

She could also have sworn that after she had fallen both times that she had seen some form of bright, iridescent apparition moving around above her! *Maybe I had bumped my head a little, and had seen stars. Then again, perhaps the impudent brat is a witch,* she decided to herself.

She should certainly at least be more careful in the future.

What if Edward had walked in and seen me yelling at the child, shoving her, or throwing that blasted book into the fire? And what if I had banged my head on the stone ledge in front of the fireplace?

Something had actually lifted me off the floor, she vaguely remembered, *just like that day out by the little garden when something had forced me backwards away from the little brat!*

Soon, Edward returned to his languishing and rather distracted-looking wife. He sat down beside her and asked solicitously, "Connie, are you sure you will be okay? Maybe we should call the doctor and have him come look you over and make sure nothing is wrong!"

"Oh, Edward, don't be ridiculous! I'm fine, only a little bruised, and I will probably be a little stiff and sore tomorrow. But I'll be all right!" Constance replied, with a bit of an edge to her voice. "Let's go upstairs to bed now. It's been a long and exhausting day!"

Edward couldn't argue with her there, so he rose and closed the screen and glass doors on the front of the fireplace so there would be no more likelihood for "accidents."

He took his wife's arm and slowly directed Constance toward the staircase, then gradually up it, and then finally they made it to the bed. He gently helped his wife get in, and while she was still sitting, she asked him if he would please pour her a glass of wine to help ease her pain, dear.

He complied gladly, handed it to her, then went over to the other side of the large bed and turned out his light on his nightstand and got in himself.

Edward leaned over, and said to Constance, "Well, goodnight then, darling." He kissed her, and then scooted down into the covers. He rolled away from her, got comfortable, and then fell quickly into a deep, contented sleep. It *had* been a long, but mostly happy day.

It was quite some time later that Constance finally finished her wine in the chill of the large master bedroom, after pondering the events of the day. The anger that she had felt earlier at Katharine began to increase. *I didn't enjoy my Christmas at all,* she observed adamantly and selfishly. She then made a mental notation to herself that next year she and Edward would have to plan something without those bratty children, far away in perhaps a warmer climate for the holidays! She had enjoyed visiting a little with the in-laws, but did not appreciate spending a whole day around those little "brats," and did not wish to repeat that same mistake again next Christmas!

Finally, the exhaustion of the day was beginning to claim her somewhat too, so awkwardly, and more than a little painfully, she slipped down into the warm covers herself. In a few moments, she was sound asleep just like her husband beside her.

Many times during the night, however, she tossed and turned in a fitful sleep, partially because of the pain she was in, but mostly because of the angry apparitions that kept haunting her restless dreams.

Unhappy Birthday

Constance was indeed stiff and sore the next day, with several nasty bruises in shades of dark purple, black and blue.

Partly because she was in so much pain, and, to a degree, just because she wanted to make others feel sorry for her, she spent the next five days in bed sipping wine. She was pleased with her own ingenuity, and it was also an excellent way to avoid being around the children!

She was still having trouble dealing with the events surrounding her and Katharine, and used this time to mull everything over. Edward and the servants were especially solicitous of her, while her bruises healed, and she enjoyed their meticulous attention, but she *was* rather bored just sitting in bed all day.

After much thought, she decided it would be best if she just avoided both children as much as possible, letting others worry about their care.

At the same time, however, she began to question if it wasn't just her imagination that someone or something had been responsible for her falling both times that she had reprimanded Katharine. Pondering the half-filled glass in her hand questioningly, she wondered if perhaps she should try to ease off the wine somewhat in the future.

Quickly enough, however, she was back to her old self once again, and went back to Abernathy's to again take charge of her department. As usual, her poor employees received the brunt of her hatred and spite.

Edward, on the other hand, was beginning to wonder if there wasn't something *wrong* with Constance. She seemed to have no maternal instinct whatsoever, and avoided the children every chance she got. He was saddened by her lack of care for either of them, and was beginning to realize that his dream of having the perfect family was never going to happen. At times, Constance seemed to even avoid spending time with *him*, and he was lonely for what they used to have, and feared that they might never have that special closeness again.

Several months passed, and the children kept growing like weeds, becoming taller, and learning many new and different things with each passing day. Michael was now eight and getting ready to enter the third grade, and Katharine's fourth birthday was approaching.

A party was held in June for Michael's birthday, with special friends and family members all attending, and now Edward was in the planning stages for Katharine's special day.

Constance, of course, was not interested in any of that nonsense, so Edward simply worked with the servants to get it all arranged.

As with Michael's party, the house was cleaned from top to bottom, and the yard mowed with care, the gardens all carefully weeded, and so on. Rosie the cook had been busy in the kitchen for days, preparing what could be made ahead of time along with several of her workers, and there was already an abundance of food ready for the party.

Edward had taken both of the children to Abernathy's for new outfits for the special day. The dress that he had selected for Katharine was gorgeous, white with frilly lace, a full skirt, and a small floral print all over. It was very feminine.

Edward also purchased lacy ribbons to match the dress for her wavy blonde hair, which now reached to nearly the middle of her back. He secretly congratulated himself. *Katharine is going to look like quite the princess for her fourth birthday!* he thought to himself.

By Katharine's birthday-party morning, the entire estate had been groomed to perfection. It was going to be a supreme summer day, with blue skies holding only a few puffy white clouds floating lazily aloft here and there.

Large, white, elaborate tents were being set up all over the back lawn. Huge, pastel-colored balloons drifted lazily above the tents with curly streamers dangling nonchalantly from below them. Rows of long tables and chairs were set up in all the tents. They were decorated with long white tablecloths, streamers and balloons, candles and floral centerpieces.

In the main tent, a large, multi-tiered, and elaborately embellished cake and crystal punch bowl with numerous little matching cups were placed. There was another long, large table nearby where all the plates, cups, and silverware, and all the carefully prepared food would be arranged as party-time grew nearer. A smaller table was set up not far from the food table to serve as a bar. There were also several tables in the tent for the guests of honor, such as immediate family, special friends and such.

Game areas were set up under shady trees, where children could play pin the tail on the donkey, have races with eggs on spoons, dunk for apples; hold gunny sack races, and so on. The whole lawn bustled with activity for hours in preparation for the party.

Both Katharine and Michael ran around on the lush green

grass, near Edward, who had told Aggie that he would keep an eye on them both. They were awestruck and excited over the fancy decorations, and everything else going on around them.

Edward was busily and proudly strutting around outside, seeing to it that everything was perfect.

Constance was hiding inside, lounging around somewhere, away from the hustle and bustle and aggravation. She sipped at her standard umpteenth glass of wine, and paged through a fashion magazine. Preparing for large parties always made her rather nervous anyway, so "let the others do all the worrying about them," was her motto.

After several hours of that, though, she became bored. She could hear all of the contagious cheerfulness going on outside! After pouring another glass of wine, she abandoned the coolness of the mansion momentarily and finally ventured out a bit to walk around on the veranda, and observe all the merry goings-on.

Constance was ready and dressed for the party in a light, form-fitting dress with short, layered, frilly sleeves and hem. It was a designer gown, made out of a pretty, pleated mauve-colored crepe. It had matching, tiny delicate high heel shoes of the exact same shade, and she looked quite the fashion plate. Her dark brown hair had been swept up into an elegant French twist in preparation for the party, and diamonds dangled from her earlobes.

From all outward appearances, to her it looked as though everything was just about ready, except for the food being brought out, and she knew that in about an hour that the servants would begin taking care of that as well.

Constance could see Edward way out there on the lawn, speaking with one of the servants, and decided to venture across the green expanse to join him for a bit. There was an air of excitement all about, and even though she was usually in a sour mood, she began to feel unusually cheerful, not only at the beauty of the day, but everything else that was going on.

On her way to talk with Edward, she saw the large, ornate fountain over in the slight clearing splashing happily and crystal-clear, and it looked so cool and refreshing that she decided on impulse just to walk over there for a bit.

Her tiny high heels kept sinking into the soft earth beneath the lush green grass, making it hard for her to walk. So, she stopped to remove them on an impulse until she got back up nearer to the house.

As she removed them, she happened to look out in a different direction, and noticed Katharine wandering way out back quite far from the goings on, by one of the large flower gardens.

Michael was nowhere in sight out that way; and neither were any of the servants. *Katharine is probably conversing with those blasted butterflies of hers again!* Constance mused. *But really, the girl is too far away from the house, and could get lost way out there! Edward really should be more careful to make sure that Aggie watches over her.*

Constance glanced back to where she had last seen Edward talking with the servant, but now they had both disappeared. Deciding that it would probably be simplest if she just attended to the matter herself, she made her way over to the garden. *Where is Aggie at, anyway?*

This particular garden had always been one of her favorites. The groundskeeper perpetually took painstaking care to keep everything in it in excellent condition. There were two sections to this garden, both a sunny area, and a shady area under a large, ancient oak. Brightly colored, appropriate flowers were planted all throughout, and a square, concrete pool sat in the shaded section with ornate concrete benches nearby. The pool was several feet deep, and contained bright orange goldfish and water lilies that were blooming in profusion.

There was a sense of peace about the area, with birds chirping brightly and fluttering from branch to branch, as if they had not a care in the world. Other than the chirping of the birds, however, there were hardly any other sounds because of the distance this garden was from the house.

As Constance got closer, she could see the little brat now, standing near the edge of the pool, leaning over and looking in at all the goldfish in the water, and giggling cheerfully at their antics in the pond below her.

Hatred and contempt swept throughout Constance as she observed the beauty of the child. Not only was she jealous of how innocent and adorable Katharine looked, with her long blonde hair and thick, dark eyelashes framing sky blue eyes. But also, she was spiteful of how much Edward doted on her, many times favoring the child over the rest of the family. Katharine looked pretty as the dickens in her party frock and hair ribbons, and was so busy watching the swimming fish that she never saw, nor heard Constance approaching on the soft grass.

She was completely startled out of her preoccupation with them, when quite suddenly Constance loudly and sharply scolded, "What are you doing way out here?"

Katharine jumped, so frightened was she at this unexpected interruption that instantaneously she turned around to face the approaching Constance. With wide blue, fearful eyes, she now just stood frozen, unable to speak in her surprise and fear. Constance appeared to enjoy scaring the daylights out of her, it seemed!

"Well? Answer me, you spoiled brat!" Constance hissed, then reached out to yank the child toward her, and missed. Katharine, out of protective instinct, had taken a quick step or two backward, forgetting completely that the edge of the pool was just behind her. Then, too late to regain her balance, she tumbled backward into the cool, dark water with a loud splash.

Constance, in her enmity for the child, simply stood there and observed with detachment the now panicked and splashing Katharine, who did not know how to swim. A couple of minutes passed, with Constance still standing and just watching. She stood, unmoving, chin held high and eyes full of hatred and vindictiveness, at what was now taking place in front of her. *Perhaps the little witch will drown,* she hoped to herself, and indeed, the water was at least a foot deeper than Katharine was tall!

Katharine, in her turmoil, could see Constance's venomous eyes watching her. Her heart and eyes filled with dread. She knew that this horrible woman hated her, and could see now that Constance had absolutely no intention of helping her out of her awful quandary. Even in the innocence of her young age, she knew that her life was in horrible danger.

A large, extraordinarily beautiful moth suddenly swooped down from someplace high up in the trees, fluttering momentarily between Constance and Katharine. Then, it soared aloft again, fading from sight. It went unnoticed by either of them in the horrid quandary that Constance continued to allow.

"Daddy, Daddy!" Katharine began to scream, betwixt all of her choking and sputtering. Unfortunately, Edward was nowhere near.

Still the sick, twisted spectator, Constance continued to wait, while nearby, colorful butterflies rose from their nectar lunch as Katharine thrashed about in the water. She was beginning to lose her struggle, and grasped at her choking throat, touching the antique locket in doing so.

Instantly, the delicate, winged creatures were alerted to Katharine's predicament. They soared toward the help of other people walking about some distance away. There was the poor child's father, they knew instantly!

Wasting not a moment, they soared toward him, and then flew round and round his head, their delicate bodies intermingled with several tiny, bright, rainbow colored lights. They circled for just a few seconds, right in front his face while he was conversing with a couple of servants.

Butterflies! he observed subconsciously. Then, reality struck! *Oh my!* his mind screamed. *Where has little Katharine gotten off to?*

Suddenly, fear gripped Edward's heart. For no explainable reason, he knew with a horrible dread that something was terribly wrong!

He looked around to see where the children were, saw Michael pushing a bulldozer around in the sandbox in the play yard, and he realized that he did not know just where Katharine had gone. He had seen her just a few minutes ago playing happily by the garden with the pool, but he had gotten sidetracked with the preparations for her party. Now, he was on the other side of a large tent and there were trees blocking his view, and he couldn't even see that garden from here at all!

Without any explanation whatsoever to the servants, he immediately left them and began to run toward the garden as fast as his legs could carry him. As he neared it, he could see his wife standing with her back to him, near the pool, and his fear eased slightly. *Perhaps she is watching over Katharine while she looks at all the flowers and the butterflies*, he hoped. Edward knew that his daughter loved them so.

He flew across the lawn and down the slight incline toward the garden. Perhaps everything was all right after all! As he neared, he was feeling quite out of breath from his exertion.

To catch his breath, he slowed to a walk. Then, at first stunned, and next, totally sickened to his core, he realized just what was going on!

There stood Constance, casually observing their splashing, drowning, gasping child as if she were examining every detail of a fine quality painting in an art gallery! His wife never once moved even though there was an emergency going on right in front of her. Instead, she just continued to stand there coolly, sipping from her wineglass as if to enjoy what normally would have been the tranquil peace of the garden. He couldn't believe his shocked eyes!

"Connie!" he screamed hoarsely, still trying to recover his breath after running so hard. He was astounded at the scene taking place before him. He began running toward them again. The sound of his voice shocked his wife out of her bizarre detachment and into sudden movement, and she turned her face toward him in total surprise.

"Oh, Edward, thank goodness you're here!" she hastily said as she recovered, and then, "Please, help, Katharine just fell into the water!"

For the moment, he forgot the look of pure contempt that had resided on her face and the total hatred he had seen in her eyes as she had turned toward him. He quickly ran past her and jumped into the water, suit, shoes and all! Landing in the water next to the sputtering, flailing Katharine, he grabbed a hold of his nearly-by-now drowned daughter, and quickly set her up onto the ledge of the pool.

"There, there, sweetheart!" he soothed the coughing and nearly delirious girl. He climbed out of the water and patted her quite soundly on the back of her ruined party dress to help her cough up all of the water that she had swallowed.

Panting quite hard, Edward now looked up at his wife, who actually had the grace to adopt a slightly mortified, embarrassed look on her beautiful face while she remained standing.

Not once however, did she offer any help or comfort to either of them, and that was not lost on Edward. Instead she stood meekly, with a look of consternation on her face at the realization that her husband had probably observed her total lack of concern or help regarding what had just happened to Katharine.

Meanwhile, as her husband continued to comfort Katharine, he began to see his wife in a totally different light. He had heard employees at Abernathy's gossiping amongst themselves from time to time, and sometimes the servants also, about how cruel Constance could be. However, he had never actually observed her doing anything of the sort until now. *Why, she had just been standing there, and still was!* he realized with increasing irritation and anger to himself.

Right in front of her, their beautiful daughter had almost *drowned*, and just as well *might* have, had he not happened along when he had, and she had not even twitched one of her fingers in what could easily have been a helping hand to pull Katharine out of the pool!

Now, he just sat there, holding the barely calming, yet tremulously sobbing girl in his lap. He gazed with veiled inquiry at Constance, wondering just what exactly had been going through this woman's beautiful little head while all of this had been going on!

He couldn't believe that he had been married to her all of

these years, and never observed this horrid, spiteful side of her personality before!

He already knew that she didn't care much for the children, and never really paid them any attention at all. However, with new realization, it was now beginning to dawn on him that perhaps she had no feelings of affection for them at all, but rather, *hated* them instead.

There *had* been a couple of other incidents involving Katharine and Constance when no one had been around to witness anything. He had seen that horrible, spiteful look in her eyes as she had turned her face toward him, and now it resounded through his head, pounding as if in waves, reverberating over and over again.

At just that moment, the two servants with whom he had been discussing the party preparations were now hurrying toward the hapless-looking group, finally catching up.

Edward was still sitting there, on the wet ledge of the pool, holding Katharine, and both he and the crying child were soaked to the bone.

"Mr. Abernathy, oh my God, what happened!?" the male servant exclaimed, while the female servant just stood there out of breath, taking in the entire crazy scene.

Constance, at this point, was quite worried about what her husband was thinking of her at that very moment. He just kept sitting there with that careful, questioning, evaluating, and now almost challenging look in his eyes.

She finally broke the silence, saying, "It's all right, Simon. Katharine had just fallen in when Edward happened along, and before I could even help our little birthday girl out of the water, my hero of a husband jumped in and dragged her right out! She's just fine, just a little shaken is all, and was only in the water a few moments. Why don't you and Rebecca take her on up to Aggie? Wherever is that awful, irresponsible woman? She was supposed to be watching over the children! See to it that Katharine gets changed into something else suitable for the party."

Just how much has my now rising husband seen anyway? Constance wondered silently and seriously as he stood and handed Katharine over to Simon. *There had been so much noise from that blasted little urchin splashing about in the water, coughing and choking, that I didn't hear Edward approach at all until he yelled my name.*

The two servants hurried quickly back up toward the house with poor Katharine, who had now resumed crying for the want and comfort of her much-loved daddy. Edward stood rooted to his spot for a few moments more, tears building up in his eyes as well, while he sized up his wife.

Constance stared back at him with huge, cautious, beautiful brown eyes.

Finally Edward spoke, with contempt overwhelming his voice. "Just what was going on here, Connie?" he demanded. "Haven't I always been the best husband I could possibly be to you? I have given you everything here that any woman could possibly ever dream of, or want for! Funny, how in the rare moments that Katharine is alone with you, something terrible always seems to happen! How convenient when no one else is around!"

He continued, his voice steadily rising, quite tremulously. "I saw you, several moments went by, and you did nothing at all to help our daughter out of that water! You just stood there, sipping at your wine as if you had all the time in the world! This pool is deeper than her, you know! How could you *not* know? What's the matter, were you afraid you were going to spoil your expensive dress? I knew you weren't very happy about being a mother, but I haven't complained about it at all to you, ever! I don't make you do anything pertaining to their care, so *what's the problem?* Do you have so much spite toward me or the children for my simply wanting a family like any other normal man would, that you would let harm come to them if you could? What on God's green earth is the matter with you?"

He was shouting at her now, and Constance genuinely felt fear expanding insidiously in her heart. So, Edward *had* seen the whole thing after all, or at least enough of it to know exactly what her intentions had been toward Katharine. In all these years that they had been married, he had rarely gotten angry with her, and never to the point where he had shouted!

Suddenly, he reached out to her with both hands, and angrily took hold of her shoulders and shook her hard for a few seconds.

Constance just gaped back at him now, wide-eyed with fear and feeling slightly disembodied from the entire scene. Stupefied into silence for one of the few times in her life, Edward continued to shake her in his tempest.

Finally, the delicate high-heeled shoes that she had been holding all of those long moments, along with the nearly empty wine glass, came loose from her fingers. The shoes landed near the ledge of the pool with a thud. One shoe bounced into the water with a splash, and the other landed on the ledge, both in an odd slow-motion effect within her mind-disembodied state. The dainty wine glass followed closely, nonchalantly spilling and then shattering all over the shoe that remained.

"You disgust me!" Edward spat at her menacingly, and after giving her shoulders one final rough shove, he promptly strode away. His forlorn wife was left just standing there, shaking tremulously, and knowing with the utmost certainty in her heart that Edward would never look upon her with loving eyes again.

Daddy is Gone

Despite the earlier disaster with Katharine in the pool, the rest of the day went off without a hitch. The servants, always professional in their jobs, did not utter anything about the incident between either themselves or to any of the guests that day. They waited until much later to gossip quietly about Constance's apparent involvement and Edward's rather cloaked and distant behavior toward her that had followed the near-tragedy.

Katharine was cleaned up and changed into another pretty dress, soon forgetting the awfulness of the earlier afternoon when the guests began to arrive.

Constance hung around the party for a while, struggling to maintain an elegant, calm attitude and socializing. However, she couldn't help but glance over at Edward now and then beseechingly. He, of course, had changed his suit and now looked even more dashingly handsome than he had earlier. When he didn't totally ignore her, he looked at her with indifference.

After a couple of hours of her deserved treatment from him, she finally claimed that she had a terrible headache, and retired to their room, to wait and worry about what would happen when he finally came up there.

She attempted to take a nap, but there was so much noise and revelry from down below that she could not settle down, and she became increasingly more anxious as the day turned into evening.

Actually, by now she *had* developed quite a severe headache, so she poured another glass of wine to ease its pain.Evening turned into darkness, and finally the guests began to leave. Still upstairs, Constance waited, with growing headache and anxiety. Finally, after many hours and many more glasses of wine, she succumbed to an uneasy, restless sleep haunted with butterfly-like apparitions and Edward's insolent face.

Edward never did join her in their bedroom that night, nor any night thereafter. Instead, he slept in a room quite far down the long hallway.

He began having hushed meetings in his library downstairs, with the trusted family lawyer, Thomas Mortimer.

And Constance's anxiety only grew with each passing day, though she went to Abernathy's to keep busy in an attempt to keep her mind off the problems at home. Her nasty temper at the store was now relentless, and she even fired one employee that had been with the store since its inception.

That evening, Edward came home to confront her about the employee's firing soon after she herself had arrived home. "How dare you fire Mrs. Rowcliffe!" he yelled. "She has been one of our most trusted employees for nearly eight years now! All of the other employees are totally up in arms over this, and are wonder-ing who you'll have it in for next! I have already called this poor woman's home and told her that you were mistaken, but she is so upset right now that she won't hear any of it! *What were you thinking?*" he demanded.

"Well," Constance replied haughtily and defensively, "there was money missing out of the register that she could not account for, so I simply let her go, as we have always done with any employee that steals from us!"

Of course, unbeknownst to both Edward and Mrs. Rowcliffe, Constance had simply removed fifty dollars from the register before accusing the poor woman. She had never liked the old bag anyway, so what was the big deal?

Edward stood there several seconds more, eyeing her with obvious contempt, and then quietly and menacingly said to her, "I want a divorce, Constance! Of course I will see to it that you are taken care of financially, but I am going to order the servants to begin packing your things. I can't stand the sight of you anymore!" At this point, he had begun shouting again. "I have already started making arrangements with our lawyer. You would be wise to start looking for a place of your own to live!"

Constance just stood there at first, her mouth agape, and then finally, she stuttered, "B-b-but Edward, surely you...you can't mean that! The woman stole from us! And as far as the children are concerned, I promise I will make *every* effort that I can in the future to treat them nicely. Perhaps in time they will warm up to me if I try! I love you, Edward. Please don't do this to us! *Please!*"

"Too late, Constance." Edward coldly replied. "If you have a heart at all, it's made of ice, and frankly, I simply do not love you anymore!" With that, he strode away from her, leaving her wallowing there in regret and confusion and tears.

In the ensuing days, servants began packing her things, but Constance refused to look for another place to live. She and Edward argued again over that. Edward had spoken to several of his most trusted servants. Constance was no longer allowed to be anywhere nearby the children, only downstairs to the kitchen three times a day apart from the rest of the family for meals. She spent the rest of her days and nighttimes in her bedroom drinking and in tears.

Finally, out of frustration, Edward asked Thomas Mortimer to begin looking for an apartment for her in a very exclusive part of the city. Still, Constance was refusing to leave, arguing with Edward every spare moment he had; trying to wear him down.

She had begun to quit caring about her appearance, had stopped going to work, and was threatening suicide. Edward would hear none of it. He was fed up with her, and soon, his lawyer informed him that he had found a place for her to live.

Finally, one late afternoon after Constance had eaten an early dinner by herself in the kitchen, Edward happened upon her. She was still dressed in her filthy nightie and on her way back upstairs.

He informed her that her new apartment was now ready, and had been cleaned, furnished, decorated, and stocked with food and most of her belongings. He also said that he had hired a permanent servant to help her with whatever she might need. She was to be driven over there in their limousine after the rest of the family and servants had eaten their dinner.

Flying into another angry rage, with hair disheveled, she screamed to him at the top of her lungs that she was not leaving, and ran up to what had formerly been their shared bedroom, slamming the door in punctuation and locking it.

Edward strode determinedly toward the elegant curved staircase, and then up it, and when he reached the bedroom door, he discovered it locked. Unable to open it, he began pounding on it in fury and frustration. "Constance! Constance! You come out of that room now, or I will call the police and have you physically removed!"

None of the servants were around at the moment, and he angrily shook the locked doorknob in an attempt to enter the room.

"Go away, you mongrel! Leave me alone!" Constance screamed from within the confines of the bedroom. "Go away!"

By now, Edward had lost his temper, and out of anger he backed up as far as he could into the hallway. Then, using the full force of his body weight, he slammed into the bedroom door with all of his might.

"Constance, open the door, now!" he yelled, slamming into it again as hard as he possibly could.

This time the door gave way, and Edward just stood there for a moment, in an angry rage, with fists clenched, surveying this object of his anger with an ever-increasing fury.

She gazed back wildly, breathing heavily, with messy hair and dirty gown and a crazy look in her eyes. She stood shaking, surrounded by a bedroom filled with a disarrayed mess. She had been reduced to just screaming wildly and unintelligibly now.

He purposefully walked over to her, grabbed her arm, and shook her. "Change into something presentable, *now!*" he ordered loudly.

She kept screaming and refusing and trying to pull away from him, but Edward, being the stronger of the two, wouldn't let go. Finally, in her desperation to be free of his grasp, she swung wildly with her right hand at his handsome face and slapped him soundly across his cheek, leaving a bright red hand print in its wake.

Edward let go of her temporarily, stunned that she had actually *hit* him! In all of his life he had never laid a hand on any woman! He had been raised to believe that men should never hit women, and now he couldn't believe that she had actually found the nerve to slap *him!*

"Why, you insane harpy!" he roared, grabbing her again and pulling her toward the staircase, since obviously she was not going to be gracious in any way about this. He would haul her into the car himself still dressed in her nightie if he had to!

She kept battering his face with her free hand, and then, at the last moment, with a horrible, nasty expression on her face, she attempted to rake her nails across his eyes. Edward saw it coming, and in the split second that her long, perfectly manicured nails moved toward his eyes, he let go of her other arm and backed up just enough to avoid them.

Constance, perversely seeing the split-second opportunity that presented itself, gave Edward a mighty shove backwards over the edge of the staircase. Then, too late, with what little conscience she still possessed, she realized with enormity what she had done, and sobered instantly.

She screamed, *"Edward!"* as she watched him, almost in a macabre slow motion dance, fall backwards head over heels. The surprise and reality of what she had just done was evident on his handsome face. Screams of agony could be heard coming from him as he kept falling.

Parts of him occasionally connected with an oak stair-tread on his way down, bones snapping and twisting. Finally, there was silence after he landed at the bottom on the hard marble floor, his neck and body contorted grotesquely. With his eyes wide open, and blood beginning to ooze from his ears, he stared at his wife. She stood transfixed, still up near the top of the staircase. He glared at her with what would be his last accusatory look at her ever, and then, finally, he just closed his eyes.

Edward's Last Wishes

Edward Abernathy's funeral was a heart-wrenching, solemn event. Since he had been loved by so many, including family, friends, and employees alike, the funeral was held at their large, beautiful Catholic Cathedral. It was attended by an enormous throng of acquaintances. It took hours for everyone that had known and loved this dear man so well to pass through the colossal building.

Katharine took her father's passing especially hard. She had loved him so very much, and Michael was also greatly saddened too.

In the moments before Edward's death, several servants had heard all the commotion. Being busy with their duties, and rather used to hearing arguments between their employers lately, however, they did not pay it much heed.

Of course, no one had expected Edward to die, not even Constance. Edward had already warned most of the help that he felt that she could be violent, and was capable of harming the children, and that they were not to let her anywhere near either of them anymore.

Rosie had been in the kitchen preparing the evening meal, and had heard the argument when it began downstairs. "My land, what is goin' on in there!" she commented to some of the other kitchen help. "Sounds like all of heck risin' up ta me!"

Nettie, in housekeeping, had been folding some laundry, and heard the yelling, but also didn't pay it much attention. Edward and Constance had been yelling at each other quite a lot lately.

Aggie had been off with the children in their playroom upstairs, reading them books and watching them color. Later, when the argument began, she simply got up to close their door with no comment to the children when she heard all the commotion downstairs.

But their Butler, Charles, had actually witnessed nearly the whole thing. He had been just outside of the kitchen, near the dining room, seeing to arrangements for the evening meal when the argument began. He had been one of the trusted servants that Edward had instructed to keep an eye on Constance and make sure that she didn't get near the children.

When Charles heard all of the commotion going on near the stairs, he opened the door leading to the dining area slightly. He peeked through and listened, first to make sure the children weren't around, and then, as things became more interesting, simply because he was nosy.

That horrible woman that Edward has called his wife for so many years has apparently lost her marbles! Charles had thought to himself. *Why look at her! She has always been so careful about her appearance, and now there she stands, in a drunken rage with her hair looking as if she hasn't brushed it for days, and she's still in her dirty nightie at this time of the afternoon!*

Well, none of the servants have ever cared for her anyway, he mused. They all gossiped about the dreadful woman between themselves constantly, just going about their jobs as professionally as possible, and staying out of the viper's way!

As the argument had progressed into total rage on both Constance's and Edward's parts, he had opened the door slightly further, and could barely believe his ears. In all of the years that he had been employed by Edward Abernathy, he had never even heard the kind man raise his voice at anyone until just a couple months before. Then, it had become obvious to everyone around that Edward and Constance were indeed having marital problems.

Even then, Edward had seen to it that most of their arguments had taken place in Mrs. Abernathy's room, since she was hardly ever allowed out of there anymore except to partake of meals. And, for even those she was sequestered from the rest of the family.

But, when he observed Edward break open the door of her room, and storm angrily in there, to come out of it pulling Constance firmly by the arm toward the staircase, Charles opened the downstairs door wider, and watched. He was almost entranced at the horrid scene going on before him.

Never had he witnessed either of them become violent before. Constance was slapping his face, and Edward was pulling her along toward the stairs. Even though Constance had always been hard to work for, she had never exhibited anything of the kind that he was witnessing at this moment.

Charles had become quite alarmed, actually, and was considering calling the police at just the very instant that Constance had tried to scratch Edward and then shoved him backwards out over the staircase.

He had watched, transfixed at the grim scene; that still played out in slow motion over and over in his head every night when he tried to sleep. *But then, after all,* he kept telling himself, *there was no way that anyone could have possibly known that their horrid argument would have come to this, or any way that anyone could have helped poor Edward!*

So, that had been what he had told the police as soon as they had arrived after he had run and called them and an ambulance in a panic, hoping that Edward could by some miracle still be saved.

When the medical personnel had arrived, Edward had been carefully and promptly taken off to the hospital on a stretcher.

Charles could still see the wickedness in Constance's eyes, when slightly later, after surveying the entire mess and interviewing several of the servants, the police officers walked her past him, and out the door.

She had eyed Charles then with what he could only have perceived as some sort of perverse accusation, and remembered the cold chill that had run down his spine when he had witnessed that! The woman had to be insane, totally insane. He knew that now with absolute certainty. Never in his life had he encountered evil of such intensity, and it still shook him to his very core.

Edward's attorney, Thomas Mortimer, had taken care of all of Mr. Abernathy's funeral arrangements, and had discussed the case with the police often in the days following Edward's horrible, unexpected death.

Apparently Constance's behavior had been just as appalling at the police station, and it had finally been determined that Constance was, indeed insane. She had subsequently been committed to a mental hospital in the country.

Edward had found the foresight, in his final days of life, while discussing the divorce proceedings with Mr. Mortimer, to have the attorney draw up a new will for him, after he had suggested it.

After all, there were the children to consider now, and a divorce appeared to be imminent. His will certainly did need updating. Thomas Mortimer had been appointed as his executor.

In the will, Edward had left Constance a small monthly stipend, still extremely generous by most standards in those days, which would now be directed toward her care at the mental facility.

The rest of the sizable estate had been put into a trust, divided evenly between both children, with monthly allowances for both Michael and Katharine. The mansion, other properties owned by Edward, and Abernathy's was to be held in trust until both children were over the age of twenty-one.

Several of the most trusted servants currently employed at the mansion, and the employees that had been Edward's most reliable helpers at Abernathy's, were to be allowed to remain in their positions until they left of their own free will, retired, or passed away, whichever came first.

The will also stated that if Edward should die before the children were twenty-one; that they were to be given into the care of his older brother, George, and his wife, Madelyn. It was also his wish that the children would attend private schools; and then college when they were old enough.

A good part of their monthly allowances were to go toward their educations.

The will also stated that Constance was not to be allowed to have any further contact with them until, and then, only if they wished, they were over twenty-one.

Since Thomas had known about Edward's plans to divorce Constance, the apartment that had been meant for her was leased out, and all of her unnecessary belongings were sold at auction.

Aggie, who was getting up slightly in age, was left a generous retirement fund. Edward had very much appreciated her conscientious caring for the children, and she *had* been a wonderful nanny, even if only for a short time.

Two weeks after Edward's funeral, George and Madelyn Abernathy came to pick up Michael and Katharine. All of the children's things had been packed carefully by the servants, who would miss them terribly.

Both children were quite subdued. So many changes had taken place in the few short years of both of their lives, and they had both loved Edward so. The pair of them understood now, even the young Katharine, that they would never see him again.

As their new parents drove them slowly away from the beautiful Victorian mansion that had been their home for only a little over a year, both children stared out the back window of the car at it until it disappeared. Watching it swimming slightly in the tears they both quietly shed as it faded from sight, they then turned forward, and quietly began the long journey toward their next home.

Starting Over

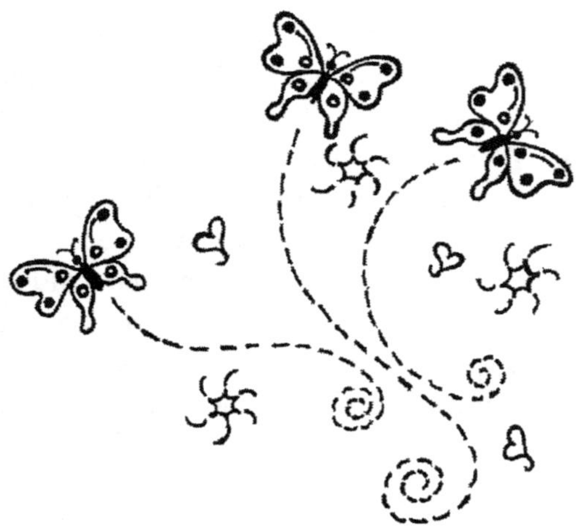

George and Madelyn Abernathy were kind, patient parents. They were both several years older than Edward, and had plenty of years of experience with parenting behind them. They were practically empty-nesters, with three children of their own. The eldest of their children had just started attending college, a son named Henry. They also had two daughters named Katie and Erica, who were fifteen and thirteen respectively.

All three of their children were good kids, very intelligent, and excelling at school. They were, however, enough older than Michael and Katharine that it was difficult for the younger children to truly bond or play with them. Henry, of course, lived on the campus of the college that he attended, and was not at home often. Katie and Erica were both at the age where friends and boyfriends were starting to become very important. Although neither of the girls was officially allowed to date until they were sixteen, they still had plenty of social events to attend which allowed them to socialize with the opposite sex. They also attended public schools, their parents being of much more modest financial means than Edward had been.

Madelyn instantly fell in love with little Katharine, and her adorable, wavy, long blonde hair and blue eyes. They both shared a love of nature and butterflies, and gradually Katharine grew to love her just as much in return.

George was a very amiable man, even though he worked many long hours at his modest automobile repair business. Both children, especially Michael, who had always had an affinity for anything with a motor and wheels, grew to love him too.

George had a terrific sense of humor, which, once the children got used to, they truly enjoyed. For the first time in their short lives, they felt secure with two loving parents who they knew had only their best interests at heart.

With the generous monthly allowances that Edward had left them for their care, in time George began to realize that perhaps he didn't have to work quite so many hours for himself and Madelyn to be comfortable. He relaxed his work schedule somewhat.

Michael was not enrolled in a private school for approximately two months after he and Katharine arrived, to allow him time to adjust to his new surroundings. Katharine, of course, was still not old enough to attend school, and would be enrolled the following fall.

Christmas arrived quickly, and with it all the preparations and gift-buying that accompany it. Katharine and Michael were encouraged to help in the decorating of the tree. They made long strings of popcorn to grace it, along with helping to hang all of the glass ornaments. They helped place the pine garland over the fireplace, and another up the considerably smaller and much less graceful stair railing than had adorned their home with Edward.

Time, and loving parents were beginning to heal their wounds, and both children began to feel a true sense of peace, even though they both still missed Edward tremendously. The family Christmas they celebrated with George and Madelyn and their older children was a magical time of wonder and love. Even though it was considerably smaller than last year's Christmas had been for Edward's two children, everyone enjoyed it tremendously.

Soon afterward, Michael went off to a boy's private school, where he would live for the rest of the school year. Katharine missed him terribly. Summer came and went, with Michael home for the break. The two happily played outside in the warm weather often.

Katharine also often helped Madelyn care for her flower gardens, with the butterflies always silently watching over her. They were overjoyed with the knowledge that Katharine was completely safe in this place.

The following fall, Michael went back to the private school and fourth grade. Katharine stayed home with George and Madelyn one more year while she attended kindergarten half-days at the same public school their three older children had attended. The following year, she would be sent to a girl's private school.

Her kindergarten year was the happiest that Katharine had ever known. She loved making new friends at the school, and her teacher adored her. Kindergarten passed very quickly for little Katharine, and the summer after that, when again, Michael joined her back at home to enjoy playing and gardening with her once more.

Katharine was growing up quickly. George and Madelyn often talked about her quietly amongst themselves, and they were saddened that the time was coming, and soon, when she also would be going to private school. She would be missed tremendously.

Her aunt and uncle decided one day before she began private schooling to tell her about her adoption by Edward and Constance. Katharine was six years old now. Edward had always felt that he should wait until she was old enough to understand fully what adoption meant.

He had told George and Madelyn that the orphanage that they had adopted her from had known nothing about her origins, only that she had been abandoned near the Blue Ridge Mountains, and that when she had been discovered, she had been wearing the antique butterfly locket.

Although Katharine no longer remembered her days at the orphanage, she had always had a vague sense that Edward had not always been her daddy.

When George and Madelyn told her about her adoption, she seemed slightly saddened and confused, but didn't say much at first. Finally, she asked them who her real parents were, then.

"We're sorry, honey," was all they could really say. "Your daddy told us that the orphanage did not know any more than that. They only knew that you had been found in a small, mountain town."

Fall seemed to come early that year. It was a cool, crisp autumn day when they drove her off to the girl's Catholic school where she would now spend most of her remaining growing-up years. Katharine did not want to go at first. She loved her new mommy and daddy and was scared at the prospect of living somewhere else, yet again.

She was crying when they hugged and kissed her goodbye for the final time, once she was settled in with her things. Katharine would be living in a room with two other little girls, whom she had not yet met. A nice woman that watched over the dorms assured her parents that she would be fine as they both left her, with tears in their eyes also.

Saint Mary's Academy for Young Women consisted of several huge, daunting brick buildings. It had a large playground, baseball diamonds; basketball and tennis courts. It was graced with endless, lush green grounds, beautiful garden areas, and of course, a chapel. There, the students were required to attend religious services each Sunday, and morning Mass each day.

Days passed quickly, eventually her sadness and fear began to fade, and she made friends with not only her roommates, but many other girls in the school as well.

Katharine developed a very sweet, helpful personality that most of the other girls appreciated, and her beauty seemed to grow more with each passing season.

Most of the students at St. Mary's were nice, and the teachers, although strict, treated the girls well.

However, there was a small clique of slightly older girls that liked to be rude and mean to the younger students when the teachers were not looking.

The ring-leader of the clique was a rather tall for her age, and more than slightly plump third-grader named Ingrid. Ingrid was not the brightest or most attractive of girls. She had freckles all over her plump face, and long, frizzy red hair that no brush or braid could tame. When she smiled, which wasn't often, more of her gums than teeth were revealed. Her tiny, disorganized teeth were rudely stained a nasty yellowish tinge, and she had horrible breath. Ingrid also liked to pick her nose, often eating any green "morsels" that she came across. She would threaten to beat up anyone who remarked about her nasty habit.

She was the leader of the clique simply because all of the other girls in it were afraid of her. As is typical of such groups, they also were insecure and needed someone to tell them what to do and give them approval when they did it.

Oftentimes, on the playground, the attendants were busy gossiping amongst themselves and not paying as much attention to what was going on out there as they should have been. Then, Ingrid and her group would harass and sometimes hurt other girls, depending on how much they were able to get away with. They particularly liked to bother the younger girls, to find out which ones would be the best scapegoats.

One afternoon, when she was in the third grade, Katharine and a group of her friends were playing four-square, bouncing the ball back and forth to each other, and giggling. Ingrid and her group approached.

"Our turn!" Ingrid interrupted rudely, while they were still in the middle of their game.

Katharine, not realizing how nasty Ingrid could be, said pleasantly, "We'll be done here soon." and bounced the ball over to her friend Emily. The other girl giggled, and then Ingrid scooped her plump arm and hand around Emily and the ball, wrenching it away from her.

"Hey!" Emily exclaimed. "Give that back!"

Ingrid just stolidly stood there, and said, "Make me! I said, it's our turn, and that means now!"

By now, Katharine was standing in front of Ingrid. "Please let us finish our game, we were almost done, and then you can have a turn," Katharine implored.

Ingrid only laughed loudly at her, looking at her clique and saying boisterously, "Well, what do you girls say? Should we give back the ball? It's our turn, right?"

The wide-eyed other girls agreed with Ingrid, taunting, "Yeah, it's our turn!" They stood, waiting to see if Ingrid would hold her ground.

"Listen, you little babies," Ingrid said sarcastically, "it's time to go get your diapers changed. Run along now!"

Katharine still stood in front of her, looking at her own group of friends, and not quite knowing what to do.

Now, Ingrid observed Katharine's delicate, lustrous locket. She snorted derisively. Then, without warning, she reached out to grab it and yank the pretty, little offensive thing off of Katharine's dainty, little, feminine neck.

Honestly, the girl resembles a porcelain doll, thought Ingrid as she was consumed by sudden, overwhelming jealousy, and an intense desire to smash her.

Katharine moved her face and shoulder away, instinctively trying to avoid Ingrid's sweaty grasp. Ingrid's chubby hand clamped onto her necklace anyway, and gave it a sharp tug. The delicate chain gave way, and Ingrid grinned at her triumphantly, holding the tiny trophy high for everyone that stood by watching to see.

"Ha, ha, you stupid little twit!" she exclaimed triumphantly, and then contemptuously she threw the locket and broken chain on the ground into the dirt. She spat in the direction of the forlorn broken thing for punctuation.

"Get out of here now and leave us to play!" she commanded once again.

Katharine had tears forming in her eyes now. She leaned over to pick up her locket, and Ingrid gave her a nasty shove, pushing her into the dirt near where the locket still lay, skinning one of Katharine's knees and dirtying her dress.

A large, mysterious, pale green moth floated delicately between the cluster of girls, hovered briefly, and then drifted off. None of the girls paid it any attention. They disregarded the abnormality of seeing such a moth in the middle of the day, and in the bright sunlight at that. Only Katharine's mind registered the sight of it subconsciously, loving such creatures as passionately as she did.

Now, Emily, only wanting to defend her sweet friend Katharine, tried to pull Ingrid away from her, yelling, "Stop that! Leave her alone!"

Ingrid swung her huge, pudgy hand toward Emily's face and slapped her as hard as she could, leaving a bright-red handprint. Afterward, she pointed at Emily and taunted and laughed at her.

Finally, Katharine, having endured enough of this nonsense already, picked up her locket off the ground, and stuffed it unceremoniously into her pocket. Then, after standing up, she gave

Ingrid an extraordinarily strong shove to the ground that she herself had just occupied. Ingrid was, after all, almost twice her size.

Tiny glowing apparitions appeared out of nowhere to swarm around Katharine while she shoved Ingrid, but only for an instant.

Ingrid landed hard on one elbow and knee, skinning both of them deeply, and then began screaming and crying loudly in pain.

Of course, after all that had happened, the attendants only now decided to look away from each other and the gossip session they were holding just in time to see Katharine shove Ingrid.

"Help, she pushed me!" Ingrid caterwauled, pointing at Katharine, and then she screeched, "She started it! She was fighting with me!"

The other girls in Ingrid's bunch were by now chanting, "Beat her up, beat her up!" when finally the playground monitors came running over. "What's going on here?" asked one of the women sternly.

The large Ingrid struggled up onto her feet, rather slowly. "These little brats over here wouldn't give us a turn at four-square!" she proclaimed indignantly, brushing off her dress. Tears streamed down her face; partly from the injuries she had received. Mainly, however, it was in an effort to make the school matrons feel sorry for her.

She pointed at Emily, and said, "This girl shoved me, and so I slapped her to get her away from me. Then, this other girl pushed me really hard and knocked me over and now my elbow and knee are all scratched up!" She was now pointing an accusing, fat finger at Katharine.

Meanwhile Katharine, and Emily also, who had the red handprint still visible on her cheek, had both began crying all over again. Both of them protested, each saying "No, this girl is lying! She started the whole thing, then slapped Emily and shoved Katharine!"

The matrons looked at all the girls, sizing them up and trying to determine who was lying. Finally, one of them just said, "All right girls, all of you are required to come with me to the dean's office. We'll let all of you tell your stories to her, and she will determine who did what!"

The dean was a kindly older woman who knew Ingrid and her bunch quite well, but since the monitors had only seen Katharine shoving Ingrid, she sat them down and questioned them all.

Naturally, the girls that were friends with Katharine all agreed that Ingrid had started it, and the girls that were Ingrid's buddies agreed that Katharine had started it.

Ultimately, the dean decided that since no one was going to change their story, that all three girls that had been involved in the fight would get two-hour detentions after school that afternoon. Once the dean had spoken, the girls were released to their respective classrooms to finish out their day.

Katharine and Ingrid were both sent to the nurse first, to have their skinned elbows and knees attended to. While in the nurse's office, Ingrid glared at Katharine with contempt, although she said nothing more.

Back in class, Katharine and Emily whispered distraughtly between themselves about what had happened, and the unfairness of it all. They were getting punished just as much as the girl that had started it! Ingrid had thrown the first blows, and now they were in just as much trouble as she!

Once school was finished for the day, all detention students were to meet in classroom 101 to serve the next two hours of their day sitting at their desks, with nothing to do but watch the clock slowly crawl along.

It was the most boring two hours Katharine had ever spent in her entire life; and rather scary at times too. When the detention matron wasn't looking, Ingrid consistently gave both her and Emily the evil eye. In between her nasty glares, she picked her nose and snacked on the foul green "delicacies."

Katharine just knew that this wouldn't be the last of her troubles with Ingrid. *Why is that girl so horrible to us anyway? She doesn't even know either of us!* she wondered.

Walking away from room 101 after detention, Emily whispered to Katharine, "Did you see the way that big girl kept looking at us? She's going to try to get us again. You just watch!" Katharine only nodded tiredly. She already knew that what Emily was saying was true.

Katharine was not only tired physically, but her spirit was weary now too, and she just wanted to eat her dinner and go to bed. *Why am I so often the one that other people pick on?* she wondered to herself. *It's not fair!*

Her dreams that night consisted of odd forms in the night. Katharine slept restlessly through these. Sometimes, she could have sworn the forms were Luna moths, but she could not quite make them out. Something about them disturbed and chilled her sleep, however, and she tossed and turned about throughout the night.

The next day, one of the maintenance men from the school kindly mended the chain on Katharine's beloved locket, and all was well again, at least for now.

Weeks passed, with the memory of the eternal detention still on all the girls' minds. Ingrid taunted and teased them occasionally, with a menacing look in her eyes, but did not bother them again for quite a while. Instead, she chose to entertain herself and her little group by picking on other students they hadn't annoyed for some time.

One day, however, everyone was in the gymnasium on a cold, rainy afternoon watching a movie. A large, white screen had been set up, and students sat watching a silent, old-fashioned picture show. A projector shined the movie by way of a long, narrow light through the darkened room toward the screen. The movie was a comedy, and the girls giggled and laughed at the antics going on from time to time.

It was their normal afternoon recess time, and since the weather outside was so nasty, the teachers had all decided that they would show the girls a movie to keep them occupied.

Metal chairs had been neatly arranged in rows, and Katharine, sitting toward the back of the room, had been unfortunate enough to have the detested Ingrid sit directly behind her. Ingrid spent a good deal of the movie kicking the seat of Katharine's chair in a constant, rhythmic thump, thump, thump, and wiping boogers onto Katharine's long, blonde braid. It was impossible for Katharine to concentrate on or enjoy the movie with all this going on.

"Stop it!" Katharine finally exclaimed in anger, turning around after quite some time of putting up with this treatment and whispering loudly to Ingrid in the hushed room.

Whispering from the troublemakers behind her could then be heard for several minutes while the thump stopped momentarily, and then resumed with even more forceful gusto.

Again, Katharine turned around after several more minutes of this annoying treatment, saying, *"Stop it, now!"* sharply to Ingrid again.

Ingrid, finger digging deeply into her nose, just gave her a rude, twisted, sarcastic-looking smile, exposing her disgusting teeth, and kept right on kicking.

Katharine heard more whispering, and quite a lot of giggling, and in defeat, she turned around to face the movie screen with a sigh, frustrated with what Ingrid would not stop doing, and not knowing what to do to make her stop.

Thump, thump, thump!

She looked over at Emily, who glanced back at her with sympathy. There were only two teachers up at the front right side of the huge, dark room, sitting and watching the movie together.

Suddenly, Katharine's long, blonde braid was yanked hard, jerking her head back violently and hurting her neck. She screamed, and Ingrid yanked again, even harder this time, pulling

Katharine's chair directly over backwards and right into Ingrid and her group of bullies.

The chair was flung aside, and the whole group immediately congregated in a dog-pile on top of Katharine, who could barely be seen underneath. Fists pounded, hair was pulled, nails scratched and legs kicked in an angry mess of about half-a-dozen screaming girls. A teacher ran toward the flailing group in order to break up the fight.

At the bottom of the pile, Katharine could barely breathe. She was being choked hard by the big, chubby hands belonging to her nemesis. Her left eye was burning awfully, since Ingrid had already punched it, and hard. Now, Ingrid was pulling on her locket again, and she reached to try to swat away Ingrid's fat, sweaty hands. Finally, she was able to pull the locket out of Ingrid's grasp.

By now, every girl in the room was on her feet, straining to see what was going on in the dark room. Some of the feistier ones that were shaking their fists high were yelling, "Fight, fight, fight!"

Emily, along with Katharine's other dumbfounded friends, did not know what to do to help her, and simply watched and yelled for the other girls to stop. As they stood there trying to get the mean girls to quit hitting Katharine, they saw glowing, bright rainbow-colored specters materialize out of nowhere around the fight, circle for an instant, and then swiftly enter the pile. Then, without any warning, all the girls on top of Katharine were violently raised off the poor child. They were flung aside inexplicably, inflicting pain where their bodies hit surrounding chairs and students and even the teacher as they flew.

Emily's friends, and some of the other girls, had also seen the odd lights, and had watched, unbelieving. The glowing specters appeared to enter the pile of flailing arms and legs, and then perceptibly lift and fling all those girls off of her. The lights circled again, delicately almost; over Katharine as if to make sure that she was okay. Then, they floated away up towards one of the windows high in the gymnasium, and disappeared.

Everyone that had been close enough to observe the peculiar sight stayed glued to the spot where they had been standing, gasping at the uniqueness of the whole thing for several moments.

The teacher that had not been knocked over had run out of the gymnasium for help, and several more teachers had now arrived, with the dean in tow. The dean now stood there sternly, hands on hips, scolding the girls, and yelling harshly, "What on earth are you girls doing? To my office, now!"

Banged up and bruised, but not very seriously injured, they all began standing, straightening dresses and hair amidst much loud crying and groaning.

Katharine slowly, and with pain, picked herself up off the floor. She had an already-blackening eye, and was sobbing and shaking quite uncontrollably. Nevertheless, she was not seriously injured. There were finger marks around her neck from where Ingrid had choked her, also.

To the office she, and Ingrid and her cohorts went again, to be sternly reprimanded by both the head-mistress and the dean this time. The entire group was sentenced now to an all Saturday detention, along with all week after-school cleaning duty, sweeping classroom floors and washing chalkboards, and the like.

Letters were also being sent home to the girls' parents, informing them of what had taken place, the dean informed them. Katharine could do nothing but sit there and cry. It was only her word against all of these bullies. The adults in charge were not interested in who had started what. Katharine was given a cold cloth containing several cubes of ice to put on her sore eye, and then sent off to her next class.

Later, back in her dormitory, the other girls tried to console her, but she did not want to talk to any of them right at the moment. She was upset about what had happened, and the punishment that she would have to serve for it. She had noticed, however, that every time someone was trying to do harm to her, that she would see glowing lights resembling kind-faced butterflies that helped her.

Perhaps it was just her imagination, but whatever it was, she was grateful for it. Sometimes, however, she just wished she knew who her real parents were. If ever she needed them, it was at times like this. There had always existed an aching and longing within her, when she thought about it. She missed the closeness that she had once had with Edward.

Although George and Madelyn had always been very kind to her, and she loved them for it, there was still a void. All of the other girls knew who their parents were, even the detested Ingrid, who liked to throw that in her face from time to time, too. Without even going to the cafeteria to eat her dinner that night, Katharine simply went to bed and succumbed to the soothing peace and serenity of slumber.

That night she dreamt of endless, hilly green fields full of wildflowers and deep green valleys with lush streams. She was there, running through them and laughing and floating with butterflies. Off in the distance, faceless, nameless strangers stood waiting, but no matter how hard she ran, nor how far, she could never quite reach those that she just knew she belonged to.

Ingrid, in her bed later that night, along with all the members of her clique, had strange, rather frightening dreams involving weird apparitions that resembled butterflies with angry faces. All throughout the night, they were haunted by them, and slept restlessly.

Private School

The eternal Saturday detention was served uneventfully, along with the cleanup duty after school, and everything began to get back to normal. Katharine did not look once at Ingrid's face during this detention, even while the detestable girl picked her nose, examined the green glop meticulously, and then licked her fingers and snacked on it endlessly. Even during the cleanup duty, she chose to ignore the girl and her friends, hoping that if she left them alone, perhaps they would return the favor.

On the playground, at recess time, Katharine's group of friends all tried to avoid the miscreant bunch. After all, those girls spent the rest of their days in entirely different classrooms from Katharine and her friends. Apparently, most of them had received harsh scoldings from their parents regarding their parts in the fight, as had she. Now and then, she had to deal with small confrontations from the older girls, but things never got out of control, as they had in the past.

After the big fight, years passed without Katharine again having significant trouble from "those" girls. Ingrid started looking for other, younger scapegoats, and though she would never admit it to anyone, she was still slightly frightened by the strange specters that she had seen that fateful day. She did not quite understand exactly what had taken place, and was more than a little afraid of Katharine because of them.

School years passed, with Katharine still going home over long breaks for Christmas, Easter, and summertime, of course. Those times were the happiest for Katharine, as she was able to spend them with Michael and her new family, who were now beginning to feel like old friends. She always felt safe with George and Madelyn. Still, there were times when her heart ached to know who she really was.

Spring had arrived, and for the most part, Katharine was enjoying school. She was in the sixth grade now, getting high grades in all of her subjects.

She especially loved art class. Often, with whatever kind of project that the class worked on, it gave her an opportunity to create the forms that so often had captured her imagination over the years: butterflies. Regardless of whether the class worked with crayons, paints or pencils, she would draw or paint them. If clay was to be used, she would form them with her bare hands. Her friends admired her artwork, and she surprised herself too, she was actually quite good!

One class she did not care much for, however, was physical education. Her body just never seemed capable of doing most of the things that the instructor taught them. She was usually one of the last girls to be picked when the instructor designated girls to choose teams. To Katharine, those were the most humiliating moments of all.

So, one day, while yet another new pair of team captains chose from the girls who would form their respective teams for softball, she again stood waiting near the ball diamond for what seemed like an eternity before her name was called.

Finally, when there were only two other girls left standing with her, she was chosen. As she joined her "team," several girls in her class groaned and complained. They had not wanted her to be with them.

Their instructor, Miss Stutz, was a rather mannish, unmarried woman in her late thirties that did not like having girls in her class that did not excel at athletics. It was her opinion that those types of students were simply not trying. Miss Stutz also did not stop girls from picking on or saying rude things to each other either, erroneously thinking that it might make poor athletes try harder.

Soon, players from both teams were in their respective positions. Katharine sat warming the bench for a very long time, waiting for and dreading her humiliating turns at swinging the bat.

A couple of innings went by, with her still either warming the bench, or stuck way back in the outfield where she could do no harm. Finally, she got a turn at bat, and, as usual, it wasn't long before she had struck out, to return to the bench amidst jeers from girls on both teams. Her closer friends remained silent, but that didn't do much to cheer up Katharine. She just wanted this torture to be over.

As the innings went by, more time was spent by her on the bench, and again in the outfield.

The game was drawing to a close now, with both teams tied up, and her team's turn at bat. As fate would have it, Katharine was to be up next. The girl at bat now was a very athletic girl named Lisa, who had glanced Katharine's way before she went up to bat. The snot had said rather rudely and confidently to her,

"The bases will be loaded after I get done here. Don't you dare screw this up!"

Katharine didn't reply, she just wondered silently to herself why things always ended up turning out this way. Why did so many games' successes hinge on her performance, which almost always turned out to be lousy? She prayed silently that Lisa would be called out, and knew that if that happened, it would be the third out for the inning. Then, the game would simply end tied if she got lucky. Their class time was close to being done for the day as it was.

The pitcher threw the ball, and Lisa swung the bat.

"Strike one!" yelled Miss Stutz, glancing at her watch. The pitcher tossed the ball to Lisa again, and she swung, whacking the ball soundly with a loud crack, way out into right field. Lisa took off running as hard as she could, making it to first base before the ball could be returned to tag her out.

"Yes!" all the girls on Katharine's team cheered but her. *Oh, no*, she thought silently to herself. *Now it's all up to me*, as usual. Tears began to well up in her eyes as she became choked up with the dread of what would most likely happen now. Please God, she prayed silently, please let me at least hit the ball! Please!

She slowly walked over with fear and picked up a bat. The pitcher was a particularly athletic, rather nasty girl who was jealous of Katharine's grades and always made fun of her when she failed. She looked down her nose at Katharine with a sneer, and then sniped triumphantly at her, "Looks like our team's going to win *this* game!" Katharine's face reddened slightly. *After all, that snot is probably right*, she thought.

The pitcher threw the ball quickly and viciously toward her, and the ball smacked neatly into the catcher's mitt behind her, without Katharine having even swung at it.

"Strike one!" yelled Miss Stutz.

The pitcher smirked at Katharine as if to say, "Told you so!" and then threw the ball hard toward her again. This one flew slightly toward Katharine, causing her to step back a bit.

"Ball one!" yelled Miss Stutz.

For yet another tortuous time, the ball hurtled toward Katharine, and she swung, missing it totally.

"Strike two!" yelled the teacher. *Oh, no,* Katharine worried silently to herself. She fingered her locket lightly. Maybe it would be her good luck charm. *One more strike and I'm out!* The ball shot toward her again, and Katharine swung blindly at it, hitting it just barely, with the result that the ball bunted and bounced to the ground between her and the pitcher. Tiny rainbow lights congregated where the ball had just made contact with the bat, spinning round it briefly, and then fading away.

Katharine stood there a moment in surprise, not believing that she had actually hit the ball, before she took off wildly at a run for first base. The pitcher, after recovering from her own surprise, grabbed the ball, and threw it quickly toward first base, where the girl waiting there nearly caught it in order to tag Katharine out, but dropped it instead!

Katharine ran on, nearly stumbling over her own two feet. She had just barely avoided running into the first-base-girl who had swiftly recovered the ball from the ground and tried to tag her anyway.

She was approaching second base now, and the girl from first base had finally thrown the ball uncontrollably toward second base. It flew way over the second-base-girl's head and toward the outfield, where another girl cleanly caught it, throwing it back toward third base.

I will surely be tagged out now, Katharine worried with despair, still running toward her doom. Suddenly, several girls all congregated together near third base in an attempt to catch that ball. Tiny, iridescent specters began glowing between them. Looking skyward while reaching to catch the ball, the girls ran headlong into each other and fell, leaving the pathway clear for Katharine to now cross third.

Oh my gosh! she thought as she raced along, now picking up speed. *Maybe I can do it! Maybe I can!* In front of her face, a transparent, iridescent form of a kind-faced butterfly materialized, only for an instant, smiling at her. In Katharine's mind, she heard it whisper to her, "Keep going Katharine! You can make it! Your team will win this game because of you! Run!"

Not having the time to think about what she had just witnessed, her mind accepted the suggestion and praise. She ran toward home at a newly energized clip, outrunning the girl who the ball had just been tossed to, and safely made it across home base! She couldn't believe her good fortune! Finally, she hadn't messed the whole thing up! Finally!

All the girls from her team cheered, jumping up and down, and her friends hugged her. The girls from the other team looked on in contempt. The final score had been thirteen to nine.

Some of the girls from the other team sneered at Katharine on the way back to indoor classes, and the one that had pitched the ball to her whispered nastily to her in the locker room, "Unlucky thirteen!"

Katharine tried to ignore the comment as well as she could. She was only happy that her team hadn't lost because of *her* for a change.

The remainder of the school day passed by uneventfully, but Katharine was on cloud nine all day long.

That evening, after lights out, Katharine whispered to the other girls, asking them, "Do either of you believe in fairies?"

"Why, Katharine?" asked Emily.

"Oh, I don't know." Katharine replied shyly, a little embarrassed now. "It's just that there have been a few times in my life where something bad was about to happen, and I could have sworn that each time, I saw tiny, winged creatures with kind faces and wings. They would help me get through those bad times and sometimes even stop the bad people from doing whatever they were trying to do to hurt me."

The other two girls giggled softly in their beds. Emily said, "Oh Katharine, you have *such* a wild imagination! I suppose the fairies helped you make your home run today! We should go to sleep now, before someone hears us talking and we get into trouble. Goodnight, Katharine."

"Goodnight." Katharine sighed softly, and rolled over onto her side. Maybe it *had* all just been her imagination. She really didn't know. She was just grateful for the day's events.

Before long, she drifted off to sleep, happily dreaming about running in wide open meadows full of flowers and butterflies all night long.

Again, however, in the distance, there waited the forms of two adults whom she kept running toward. But, no matter how hard or far she ran, she could never get quite close enough to see their faces.

Insipid Ingrid

The year that Katharine turned thirteen, and was in the seventh grade, many changes took place. Their school had always been quite social with other area organizations and public schools. Often, it would host parties, picnics, and fun-fairs so that the girls could socialize with other children and adults from the area.

Thirteen-year-olds were allowed to attend occasional chaperoned school dances. Boys and girls from area public schools were also invited to attend, to socialize with them.

The girls became very excited at the prospect of their first real dance, and the likelihood of meeting *boys!* They had always heard the older girls talking about the dances, even though they had never been allowed to attend. Their only experiences with dancing so far had been during physical education classes, with their classmates.

Katharine had begun to evolve into a beautiful young woman, beginning her menses, which she detested. However, along with them, her body began to develop into a tall, willowy figure with long, shapely legs and budding breasts that made it all worth it, she decided. Many of the other girls her age had already begun to develop, too.

The loathsome Ingrid, who was now in the ninth grade, and usually did not bother her much anymore, began to notice the very attractive changes taking place in Katharine also. Her former resentment of the girl began to grow again.

Ingrid herself had not developed particularly well. In fact, her face and form hadn't really changed all that much, only grown larger. She was still taller than Katharine and had quite broad shoulders for a girl, and had developed small bosoms that were not in proportion to her otherwise generous size. The freckles were still there, combined now with a disgusting case of acne that covered nearly her entire face. Chubby arms and legs protruded from beneath the required uniform blouse and skirt of her school, and the frizzy hair had not changed one bit. Ingrid still had her following of groupies, mainly yet because they were still afraid of her and wished only to avoid her wrath.

October brought the first school dance, which was held in the large school gymnasium. The girls had spent many days in advance making decorations for the occasion. That had consisted of cutting out many leaf, pumpkin, and scarecrow shapes in colors of yellow, red, orange and brown, and then taping them all around the room. They also hung yellow, orange, and red streamers all over, along with matching balloons. Katharine had helped both in the making of the decorations and putting them up, and was feeling a mounting sense of excitement at soon being able to experience what she had only been able to hear about up until now.

The evening of the dance was rather chilly, but it didn't matter to any of the girls, as they were all going to be in the gymnasium anyway. Katharine wore a very pretty burgundy colored velvet dress with a high, white lace collar. The dress had simple lines and long sleeves with a touch of lace at the bottom, and she felt that she looked quite the grown-up. She had left her wavy blonde hair out of the standard French braid for tonight. Instead, she parted it on the side and tucked one side over her ear, and it flowed long and luxuriously to the middle of her back. Her locket was displayed proudly over her bosom.

Her roommates had also taken special care with their appearances, and they too looked very pretty.

The dance began at seven. They were all there shortly before the doors opened, to carry out trays of cookies and cups and punch bowls for refreshments. Soon everything was all set up and in order; and one of the doors was opened temporarily to allow guests inside. The lights in the gymnasium were dimmed slightly, and music began softly playing.

Ingrid and her cohorts stood off to one side, gossiping with each other, and looking in Katharine's and her friends' direction often. Katharine chose to ignore them. She was looking forward to this night and was not going to let anything or anyone spoil it for her.

Guests began filing in slowly at first, and then after a while, quite a few teenagers began showing up. Katharine and her friends stayed on the other side of the gym, avoiding the Ingrid bunch.

They, too, did some gossiping of their own, but instead about all the different faces they were watching enter the room. Some were familiar from past picnics and fun-fairs, and some brand new.

Of particular interest to Katharine was a tall, slim, handsome young man with dark hair and brown eyes. He was standing in a group of several young men his own age. She kept looking at him, and then whispering to her friends about how handsome he was.

Some of the other girls had seen boys that attracted them too, and by now, their conversation was becoming quite animated.

Eventually, Mr. Tall, Dark and Handsome noticed Katharine looking at him. He began observing for himself just how lovely *she* was.

Soon, he began to return her glances, and talk amongst his friends about her, then gaze back in her direction now and then. Katharine's excitement began to grow, and, at last, she smiled bashfully at him.

Ingrid had noticed the constant exchange of glances between Mr. Handsome and Katharine, and was growing more jealous and spiteful by the moment. Ingrid had been attending these events for the past two years already. Not once, however, had any boy ever seemed interested in her, much less asked her to dance. Ingrid had seen Katharine's new interest at these dances the last couple of years since he was *her* age, and *she* had been attracted to him as well. Knowing that she herself was certainly no beauty made it all the harder to be on the sidelines watching all of this go on.

Spitefully, she began to gossip nastily about Katharine to her clique, and they all stayed ruthlessly huddled together. They watched, as Mr. Good-looking finally got up the nerve to approach Katharine and start shyly talking with her.

"Hi, my name is Martin." he spoke rather nervously to the beautiful girl. "You're looking very lovely tonight. What's your name?"

Katharine smiled back equally nervously and told him.

"Well, would you care to dance?" Martin asked her, and she nodded shyly.

He took her hand and bashfully started to lead her to the dance floor where several other couples were already gliding around. Soon, he was leading her around on it quite expertly;

however, both of them were too shy to say much of anything at first.

However, by their third dance together, they were beginning to do quite a lot of talking. They both learned what grade each of them were in, and what schools each of them were from, and so on.

Ingrid watched everything taking place with a growing, murderous look in her eyes. It wasn't fair that a girl brand new to all of this, especially Katharine, whom she detested, had already snared the older boy that she had had her eye on for the past two years! She was going to make Katharine pay for this! She just wasn't quite sure how yet. She knew she certainly couldn't just go over and yank Katharine from Martin's grasp.

After a while, it was announced that students should switch dance partners in order to give others a chance at dancing also. Katharine and Martin glanced at each other a little sadly. They had just started getting to know each other. Nonetheless, they both went to stand back at the sidelines in the hopes that someone else would ask them to dance soon.

It wasn't long before another boy had asked Katharine to dance. She accepted and went out onto the dance floor with him, while Martin just stood by watching and waiting so that he could have another turn with her.

Ingrid, grabbing at her chance, now moved rather bashfully over to Martin, and stood nearby, trying to muster up the courage to ask him for a dance. With resentment, she couldn't help but see how obviously enthralled with Katharine he already was. He didn't even seem to notice anyone else in the room!

Closer she moved, and closer still, until finally she was standing right next to him. After hesitating briefly, she decided that if she didn't say something now, it would be too late.

With Martin not even aware of her presence next to him, she managed to squeak out, "Excuse me, uh, Martin, is it?"

Martin glanced to his left to see who was speaking. He was

rather taken aback by the contrast between the vision he had been beholding on the dance floor and the homely, large girl hovering over him now. She grinned at him shyly, revealing her uneven, yellow, plaque stained teeth.

Feeling rather shocked by the sheer sight of her, he did not speak, but stood there looking at her as politely as possible, wondering just what it was that she wanted, and pondering ways to get away from her.

Finally, out of embarrassment and not wanting to appear as stupid as she felt, Ingrid finally muttered, "Would you care to dance with me?"

Martin did not quite know what to say, but knew that he did not care to dance with this girl. He was also certain that he had detected the repugnant odor of rotten breath, coming from her. He hemmed and hawed for a few moments, then eventually said back to her, "Uh, no thanks, I've already promised the next dance to someone else."

Almost as if on cue, the dance ended, and Martin quickly gravitated back toward Katharine.

Again, Martin and Katharine danced three more dances together. Ingrid, who had returned to her spiteful group, looked on in a tempest, gossiping with a vengeance. Constantly, almost, she inserted nasty barbs about Katharine into their conversation whenever she got the chance.

"Just look at that ignorant little witch!" she said to no one in particular. "Doesn't she know she's supposed to share? I ought to go beat the snot out of her right now!"

"No, Ingrid," one of her classmates warned. "There are too many teachers around, and we would surely get into big trouble!"

Ingrid reluctantly agreed. Besides, the headmistress of the school had quite recently warned her that if there were any more incidents in which she was involved this school year, she would be recommended to the school board for expulsion. She knew she was treading on thin ice already. *That's just fine,* Ingrid thought fiercely to herself. *I'll get the little snit soon enough when no one else is around to see anything!*

So, the dance went on, with Katharine and Martin thoroughly enjoying each other out on the dance floor, joined by many other couples that also were having a wonderful time.

Occasionally, the chaperones would again ask couples to change partners, but there were always other young men waiting for her to be free. Katharine danced all night long, having a joyous time.

And, Ingrid and her insipid bunch spent the rest of the evening, standing and watching with sour, jealous expressions on their faces. Not a single one of them was ever asked onto the dance floor that night.

Rescued Again

Ingrid did not have to wait long for her chance to get even with Katharine. During the following week in the middle of school one day, Ingrid met up with Katharine in the bathroom.

Katharine had been feeling rather ill in class, and had asked to be excused. It was her time of the month, and the cramps had been horrendous all morning long.

She had been in the bathroom for several minutes, and had finally washed her hands, and decided that perhaps she would feel better if she washed her face too.

Leaning down into the sink slightly and splashing cool water against her face, and then rubbing it in with her hands; she was not paying attention when Ingrid walked through the bathroom door behind her.

Ingrid knew that it was Katharine right away, however. She had recognized the tell-tale French braid and willowy figure, and took the opportunity of Katharine's being off guard to stride immediately over to the sink and attempt to smash the pretty little snot's face right into it.

Pictures of the enchanting Katharine and handsome Martin dancing together swam angrily around in Ingrid's mind. *Let's see if we can't fix her so neither Martin or any other boy for that matter will ever want to gaze her way again,* she thought evilly to herself!

Almost to the sink now, the bent-on-revenge Ingrid reached out a fat, chubby hand toward Katharine's pretty head.

Suddenly, an angry, glowing apparition appeared swiftly from where Katharine was also now rubbing at her neck with the cooling liquid. The phantom being flew angrily and speedily toward Ingrid, becoming white-hot and then vivid with color in a flicker of an instant.

She never had a chance! The fierce specter soared indignantly right into Ingrid's fat face, and then, with an unexplainable burst of energy, Ingrid was knocked off of her feet with a tumultuous force. Her entire large body lifted off the floor for a split second before she landed solidly and very painfully on her rump, shattering her tailbone on the hard, tiled bathroom floor.

"Ohhh!" Ingrid moaned loudly. Just then, Katharine was turning to see what had happened behind her, face and neck still wet.

Again, "Ohhh!" Ingrid caterwauled even louder, tears filling her eyes quickly at the knife-sharp pain in her derriere, painfully shooting like fire into her plump legs.

She glanced woefully up at Katharine, who was totally dumbfounded as to why Ingrid was sitting on the floor, holding her big butt. Always preferring to deal with the ignorant girl as little as she possibly needed to, and quite fed up at this point with the rude treatment that she had received from her so repeatedly over the years, Katharine frankly scrutinized Ingrid coolly.

She then reached for a couple of paper towels, taking her sweet time wiping her face, neck and hands off while the whining Ingrid stayed, seemingly glued to the floor. Katharine set the damp towels carefully into the wastebasket, gave Ingrid one last disdainful glance, and sauntered her way on out of the bathroom.

Ingrid was not found until after the class period had finished, when between classes, as usual, many girls made their way into the bathrooms, and discovered her then. Ingrid was still sitting on the floor crying, and holding her enormous rump. That would be the last time that Ingrid was ever to attempt to bother Katharine.

Seventh grade passed quickly. Several more school dances were held that year, when Katharine regularly danced with Martin. She now considered him to be her boyfriend, although those were the only chances she ever got to see him. Once, she and Martin had even snuck off together into a darker corner of the gymnasium for a sweet, secret kiss.

Ingrid no longer attended dances, in fact, she had faded away from most of the usual school happenings, and Katharine did not really notice that the girl had disappeared from the school.

Then, one day, she heard through the gossip grapevine that Ingrid had been expelled. The troublemaker had gotten into a fight with another girl, and knocked out the poor thing's two front teeth during the brawl.

Knowing how horrible Ingrid could be, Katharine felt terrible for the unfortunate girl whose teeth had been knocked out.

She was, however, more than slightly relieved that it hadn't been her, but hadn't really thought that Ingrid would bother her anymore anyway.

It had appeared that Ingrid had moved on to younger and easier pickings after that incident in the bathroom.

When Katharine reminisced about that day, she really had to chuckle to herself. She couldn't imagine how on earth Ingrid had slipped and fallen, but it did really serve the big, fat troublemaker right.

Fateful Trip

Eighth grade arrived, and Katharine was developing into a beautiful young woman, indeed. Most of her friends also were blossoming attractively. Emily was pretty, and Katie and Audrey were both quite gorgeous. Katharine, nevertheless, was just plain stunning in comparison.

She excelled in all of her subjects, still enjoyed art, and, as time had passed by and her confidence grown, she had also gotten better at physical education classes.

School dances were yet held routinely, and those were the times that she enjoyed the most. She still danced with Martin at them often, but by now there were also a couple of other boys that she was interested in as well.

The year flew by quickly. Spring was approaching, and with it the promise of the history class field trip that their class was to take by train to the city. There, they were to look at various war monuments and sites, visit the local courthouse and see governmental proceedings in action, eat in fancy restaurants, and spend a couple of nights in old, fancy hotels.

Katharine's entire grade was all abuzz with the excitement of the impending trip, and she and her roommates took special pains to make sure that they packed carefully, not wanting to forget anything.

The day of their train trip dawned clear and bright. It was a gorgeous, late April morning with the redbuds and magnolias in full bloom, the grass new and green, and the air fresh-smelling after a gentle, middle-of-the night rainfall.

For the trip, the girls were allowed to abandon their standard uniforms at school, and wear street clothes instead. At the station, all of the girls boarded the train, suitcases in hand and expectations high. It was going to be an exciting vacation from the school for all of them!

There were approximately seventy girls in Katharine's grade, and the teachers took their attendance meticulously before everyone boarded the train.

They were to stop in several nearby towns along the way to the city, to pick up other passengers.

By mid-day, the train was quite full, and racing along towards the city. The girls were all served lunch around noon. The scenery that passed by while they ate was breathtaking, changing slowly from mostly flat land to rolling hills, larger hills, and then finally some mountains, off in the distance.

Many of the girls had never seen mountains before, or not at least for many years. They were enchanted by the beautiful, ever-changing landscape. It was now the afternoon, and still, the train ride continued. With their stomachs full, and the lull of the constant motion from the moving train, many of the passengers became drowsy, and hunched down slightly in their seats to nap for a while. They would still be traveling for a couple more hours.

Katharine, sitting next to the window and enjoying the scenery also, mused silently to herself, wondering if perhaps one of those mountain towns held the secret to where she had come from. She fingered her locket absently, and soon her eyes began to grow heavy. Eventually, she became one of the passengers who fell asleep.

On and on the train pushed forward, and after a while Emily, who was her seat companion, dozed off also.

Toward the city the train continued to race. And on and on it headed to the place where this story first began. For you see, in the fourteen years that Katharine had been on this earth, much development had taken place in many area towns all along the mountainous border.

Consequently, the towns and cities had grown, and the railroad had taken it upon themselves to connect all of the cities and towns together. This served to better enable residents of all of these towns to get around easier, and also allow for easier trade between all of the villages.

As the train neared the city, the butterflies in the tiny town that Katharine had been born near sensed that she was getting closer.

At first, they just whispered amongst themselves, but as the distance between Katharine and them decreased, they also began silently whispering to her, while she slept.

"Our sweet baby child is drawing near," rejoiced the king and queen swallowtails in their alternate rainbow-hued universe.

"Katharine, Katharine, come home... come home to us," they spoke to her. "You are almost a woman now. This is where your true home is! Come home..." And, as the butterflies whispered to her, her dreams began to turn in a magical, darkening spiral. Then, Katharine's slumbering mind descended into an extraordinarily deep sleep.

Dreams of her entire lifetime haunted her spirit. Starting at the beginning, she could see the tiny, mountainside town with the ornate, white Victorian gazebo that her mother had placed her in, and the sad, beautiful young girl that her mother had been.

Near the gazebo, she viewed a magnificent waterfall, with a glowing rainbow actually seeming to emerge from the misty spray that it created.

She watched the form of a huge, appallingly gorgeous Luna moth swoop directly over her mother and herself, observing the drama unfolding just inside of the gazebo, as her mother bade her farewell.

Katharine then saw herself as a newborn infant, wearing her antique locket, and next, asleep with a maidenfly on her nose. Then, butterflies and glowing rainbow lights floated joyfully above her in the gazebo as the villagers had discovered her, there in the shade, near the stream and waterfall and rainbow.

Katharine saw images of her very first train ride with the kind woman that had taken her away, as she slept.

Then, she dreamt of the orphanage. Many happy and sad memories that she had suppressed or forgotten entirely were now renewed deep within in her mind's eye.

On and on the dreams flowed in her nearly comatose state. She envisioned Edward's kind face, and Constance's closed one.

Next, she saw the day she was adopted along with Michael and taken first to Abernathy's department store.

Then, her mind traveled on to the beautiful Victorian mansion on the outskirts of the city where she would only spend about another year of her life.

She envisioned Constance's cruelties toward her. The fateful birthday, when Constance had almost allowed her to drown. There was that evasive Luna moth, again. She shivered unknowingly in her sleep. Edward saving her. The death of her beloved daddy.

The train pressed forward, along with her dreams, now of her life with George and Madelyn. Then, of her years at the Catholic

School, her friends there, and her enemies. And, yet again, an elusive, iridescent, splendid Luna moth.

Her first dance with Martin, and her first kiss…the dream progressed on and on, and continued, up until the present day.

Intertwined with all the memories were also dreamlike visions of Katharine running in meadows, on hillsides, and in valleys filled with beautiful wildflowers, and voices calling to her.

There she was, searching for the faceless parents who always waited, always just out of reach and clear sight. She happily observed the ever-present butterflies that had been as much a part of her life as all of the people that she had ever encountered. Shadows of the Luna moth were wispy and vaguely disturbing.

However, they inhabited these images as well.

The train came to its biggest stop, in the city where Katharine had lived for slightly over three years in the orphanage, and then subsequently with Edward and Constance.

Emily had left her seat only minutes before to set her luggage near an instructor while she went to use the lavatory before the train came to a stop. The conductor only moments ago had announced it approaching.

Passengers began gathering their luggage and other personal belongings in noisy commotion, many of them standing while they gathered their possessions around them.

Katharine remained slumped way down in her seat in her trance-like slumber, under the butterflies' ever-watchful eyes. She faced the window, completely unaware of her surroundings, or even that the train had halted. Passengers first disembarked, and then new ones boarded. The conductor outside yelled "All aboard!" and a few tardy travelers hurriedly got on as the train began to pull away.

Outside, in the station, Katharine's group gathered and instructors took a rushed attendance. A large city bus was already waiting to take them to the hotel where they would be spending their next three nights.

Unfortunately for Katharine, there were two other Catherines in the group. The instructors, in their haste to board the waiting bus, miscounted students and did not realize that she had not gotten off the train.

Everyone in the group began to board the bus, which was nearly full by the time the large vehicle was ready to embark. Exhausted after spending nearly the entire day traveling; the assembly of schoolmates sank quietly and gratefully into their seats. Her friends did not notice her absence.

The day had turned out to be considerably warm for later April, and it was hot on the bus. In only about another half an hour, they would arrive at their hotel, and the fact that Katharine was not with them would not be discovered until then.

Poor Katharine remained sleeping deeply, as if drugged, still dreaming of peaceful meadows and crystal-clear streams, and butterflies, always butterflies. Never once was she cognizant that an older woman passenger now occupied the seat next to her.

Eventually, in a small town not unlike the one she had been born near, that woman disembarked. Katharine was never once aware that Emily was no longer there. The train was almost empty now, and approaching the quaint town of her origin.

Katharine remained soundly asleep. Suddenly, the conductor announced loudly that their next stop was approaching, and the butterflies knew that it was time for her to regain her consciousness. They began calling to her, "Katharine, Katharine! You're home!" and she awoke with a start!

Perhaps it was a spell that the butterflies had cast upon her, or perhaps it was simply the haze one's mind is in when it's first awakened after being startled from a deep sleep, but Katharine did not realize that all of her classmates were gone. She shook her head, rubbed her eyes, and stood up and gathered her things together, stretching before picking her suitcase up off the floor.

The train slowed to a stop, and Katharine, along with two other passengers, stepped down off the train onto the platform. They all carried their luggage, and then they began to walk toward the small depot. Soon, the other two passengers had hurriedly boarded an old-fashioned, waiting horse and buggy.

Still in her trance-like haze, Katharine wondered silently to herself where everyone else was. Dazed, and without emotion, she watched the train began to move away now. It rolled slowly at first, blowing its whistle loudly, and then gaining speed, until it finally disappeared around the bend of a mountain.

It began to dawn in Katharine's mind that something was not right. This did not look like a big city. *Perhaps this is just the outskirts*, she reasoned with herself. But, then again, where were all of her classmates?

A narrow gravel road led from the depot off into the trees, where only moments before the horse and buggy had disappeared. With her brain still in a fog, she began to walk in the same direction. However, a niggling sense of worry began to pervade her mind as she did so.

Eventually, she came to a fork in the road, and not knowing which way to go, she began to cry. It had been such a long, tiring day, and she knew now that she was lost and was obviously going to have to keep walking.

There was absolutely no one around to help her, and there were no road signs. Her train was long gone. The road had changed, also. It was no longer gravel, but dirt now, instead. A couple of butterflies floated past her, oddly seeming to beckon her. She could have sworn she had heard someone whisper her name!

Choosing the direction in which they had flown, along she trudged, practically dragging her suitcase and hoping that the branch of dirt road that she had chosen would soon lead her to civilization.

She began to notice that the road had developed a gradual upward incline to it, and then eventually, it became steeper. Forward, she kept going, always hoping that soon she would find someone or something that could lead her to help.

As she walked, the trees that had at first only dotted the landscape began to thicken, and then ultimately, became forest. Birds chirped and flew between the trees in the gradually dimming sunlight, their singing echoing, and Katharine became quite fearful. *It's beginning to get dark!*

By this time, her suitcase and other small bags were beginning to feel like lead weights, and she was also becoming very hungry. *Where am I, anyway?* Silently the butterflies watched from afar, ever mindful of keeping her safe. Katharine was coming home!

The darkness increased, and with it, Katharine became more than slightly panicked. Her heart began to pound, not only from the steep, uphill hiking, but because of the unfamiliar nighttime noises that were beginning to take the place of daytime ones. An oddly iridescent, glowing, and rather large Luna moth flapped closely past her, chilling her and raising the hair on her neck. Somewhere in the distance a hoot-owl hooted, its lonely cry echoing through the trees.

Still, the road continued, upward to somewhere, she was sure, even though now it was becoming difficult to even see. She began to cry again, out of frustration, exhaustion, fear, hunger—you name it; she was feeling it. And she was beginning to wonder just how much longer she could go on!

In the darkness, Katharine did not see the wire fence just off the road that had begun at a property only a short distance back. She plodded along, about ready to give up and lay down right there on the road and surrender to the sleep that was again calling her. A large owl suddenly flew out from the trees, and then right in front of her; observing her with eerie, glowing eyes, and hooting loudly, scaring her half to death!

She let out a startled scream, and with renewed energy from the adrenaline now rushing through her veins, she began to run as quickly as possible up the road, towards heaven-knew-what. She no longer cared; she just wanted to get out of the scary, dark forest as soon as she possibly could. Her legs pumped, her breath became ragged, and onward up the road she flew.

Finally, the form of a light colored small building began to take shape off in the distance in front of her. She headed for it, running headlong into the wire fence.

Falling backwards, Katharine burst out bawling. She was tired, scared, hungry, and now hurt besides, having scraped her arm on one of the wires. As she cried, she knew that she could simply go on no longer. She had to find some place to lay her weary bones down.

Eventually, the burning pain subsided, and she began to calm down enough to wipe the tears away from her now-dirty face. *Great,* she thought as she stood up to smooth her skirt, *now I've torn my dress besides!*

Probably looking quite the homeless urchin, she figured, she picked up her suitcases and other belongings that she had dropped when she had fallen. Again, she contemplated the small building on the other side of the fence.

Glowing, rainbow specters appeared out of nowhere, marking an opening in the fence only a few feet away from her. It had once been smashed flat and never repaired, years ago, by the remnants of a fallen tree.

Too exhausted to question the lights that marked her way to what she hoped was safety, she climbed carefully through, and finally reached what now appeared to her to be a small garden shed. She didn't care; she just hoped she could get inside.

Katharine lifted the rusty latch of the old, dilapidated door, and it protested and creaked loudly with neglect as it slowly swung open on its tired, rusty hinges. In the dim nighttime light, she could see that the shed didn't contain much. One corner held an old, useless looking wheelbarrow and a couple of shovels and rakes and an ancient, worn-out broom, and the other corner held a mound of time-worn straw.

She may as well have been beholding the most luxurious bedstead in the world, it didn't matter to her! Sighing with weariness and relief, and forgetting her hunger in her state of depletion, she set all of her belongings in the corner nearest the door.

Katharine pulled the creaky door closed and latched it from the inside, and removed her dress coat from her largest suitcase and shrugged it on. She buttoned it up. It would serve well as her blanket tonight! Finally, she gave in to her weariness, and sank into the cool, soft, slightly musty smelling straw with exhausted abandon, letting the soothing peacefulness of slumber claim her immediately.

Home at Last

"Katharine, you're home. At last...Katharine...welcome home!" Katharine awakened with a start to see the sun streaming through a dirty, cobwebbed window and hear the sound of a rooster crowing in the distance.

Oddly, she had been dreaming about someone welcoming her home. *Certainly this old, rather grubby shed is not my home!*

She rubbed her eyes and stood, groaning and stretching and straightening her back. The pile of straw, although relatively soft, had not been the most comfortable bed she had ever slept on, and of course, the hard wooden floor underneath it all hadn't helped!

As she stretched to ease her stiffness, she realized that her coat was all covered with straw. She took it off, opened the shed door, and stepped outside into the chilly mountain air, shaking it off briskly.

Her stomach growled, reminding her again of the hunger

that had plagued her the night before, when she had been lost in the woods. *Where am I,* she thought, *and now what? I'm going to have to try to find someone that can help me get back to the city, with all of my schoolmates. They have got to be concerned about me!*

After inspecting her coat thoroughly to see if there was any more straw stuck to it, she decided the sun felt warm enough that she probably didn't need it right now anyway.

Debating whether she should gather all her things together or head further up the road without them to look for help, she recalled her difficulty of the night before with having to carry them all. She then decided it would be best for now to simply leave them behind. After all, she had no idea just how much further she would have to walk to reach some form of civilization.

She placed the coat on top of her big suitcase, and swung the shed door closed with a loud creak and groan, latching it once again.

It was a beautiful morning, and the sun was shining brightly. She soon felt her spirits being raised, and became optimistic that this day would turn out better than the previous one had.

Birds chirped happily in the trees, several butterflies fluttered by, and she even saw a tiny maidenfly, and thought it enchanting.

Katharine climbed back through the hole in the fence that she had come through last night when it had been so dark out, and resumed her trek uphill on the dirt road. She speculated to herself hopefully that since she had heard a rooster crowing, civilization shouldn't be too far away.

Along the dirt path, she discovered a thicket of thorny wild raspberries. The berries were large and red and plump, and oh, so juicy. She ate every one that she could reach that was ripe through the fence, avoiding the sharp thorns. Her hunger somewhat satisfied, she then returned to the dirt path and plodded on.

Thankfully, as things turned out, after only two more bends in the road, maybe ten minutes total distance away from the shed, she approached an old, ornate, rusty, wrought-iron gate.

It appeared as if perhaps it had once been very beautiful, and probably painted white. She sighed with relief as she gazed upon it. "Periwinkle" was stated across the top in an ornate fashion, with rusty metal vines and flowers interlaced along the sides and across the top. The gates themselves were thrown wide open, and from the appearance of the growth of the weeds and other vegetation around them, looked as if they had not been closed in ages.

A lengthy, winding dirt drive lay beyond the gate, with long, untended grass and tall trees growing on each side of it. Shrugging to herself, Katharine decided to see what lay beyond. Trudging along, finally, after about five more minutes, the outline of a large house began to take shape in the distance.

Again, like the gate by the road, it looked rather rickety and run down, and in need of some tender loving care and a couple coats of paint as well. It was quite immense, and Victorian in style. It also appeared as if it had once been painted white, and had a huge, covered wrap-around porch. It was adorned with gingerbread everywhere. At one corner of the front there was an enormous, ornate tower with windows nearly all the way around on three stories.

Two old, fancy rocking chairs and a small, matching table resided on the porch in the shade. Near the porch stood a rusty metal antique water pump, and a wheelbarrow and gardening tools sat next to it.

As Katharine approached the place, however, she forgot all about the house and became stunned by the beauty of the numerous flowers that surrounded it. They were everywhere! Katharine had always loved flowers, and had never seen so many different kinds, and of so many different colors! Bees buzzed happily all around, and the place seemed fairly alive with the vibration of them all. Her beloved butterflies were in abundance. Some were of gorgeous varieties that she had never before seen!

The expansive lawn sloped away from the house, which obviously resided on a mountainside. Sunlight streamed through large old oak and magnolia trees in bloom, making the whole area a vivid rainbow-colored dream. What a perfectly enchant-ing place!

Off to one side of the yard, near the edge of all of the gardens, stood a very large, ornately Victorian birdhouse with numerous little separate houses all stuck cheerfully together. Goldfinches, bluebirds and sparrows fluttered happily around it. An old, ornate birdbath sat nearby, under a magnificent, ancient looking twisted redbud that was in full, resplendent bloom.

Over at the far end of the garden, resided an ornate, antique-looking arbor that had seen better years. It was rusty, but abso-lutely covered with morning glories of several brilliant shades that were in full bloom with the morning still in its prime. The morning glories were so thick within it, that it was impossible to see through it to the other side.

At each side of the arbor was old, white picket fencing, with trumpet vines climbing up it, and behind all of that a large expanse of long grasses could be viewed. The steepness of the mountainside was quite evident there. Eventually, quite some distance off, the woods began.

Through the yard, near the arbor, and off past the picket fenc-ing, a small, cheerful creek sparkled merrily through the property, bubbling and churning with crystal clear water.

A rooster crowed again. Katharine looked over behind the house, from where the noise had come, and saw a chicken coop, with plenty of chickens and one lone rooster strutting around in front of it. All of the birds pecked at the ground occasion-ally. Not far from the chicken coop, there appeared to be a small vegetable garden.

Unexpectedly, she was startled by something soft and furry moving against her leg. She looked down, and there was an ador-able orange tiger cat looking up at her with big, yellow-green eyes. It rubbed against her now, wanting her to pet it back. "Meroww!" it implored.

Katharine had never seen a cat up close before. *How adorable*, she thought to herself, and she squatted down to pet it. The cat immediately lay down on its back with its legs up in the air so she could rub its tummy. "Oh, you're a cutie!" she said to it, and then she giggled out loud.

Without warning, from behind a group of tall, old-fashioned hollyhocks, an old woman appeared, alarming Katharine slightly.

"Well, it's about time!" the old woman then said in a rather gruff-sounding voice. "You're late! The church said they would send out someone to help me with the yard work on Monday. It's Wednesday!"

Katharine was still rather startled, and didn't quite know just what to say. Finally, she managed an "Umm, I'm sorry ma'am."

"Well don't just stand there!" the irritated old woman said. "The tools are over there by the wheelbarrow! Get to work!"

"Umm…yes, ma'am." Katharine finally replied, and went toward the wheelbarrow not even knowing what tools she was looking for. Finally, she grabbed a rake and a small hand shovel and approached the old woman.

"My name's Katharine, ma'am. Katharine Abernathy. What's yours?"

"Why, Penelope Periwinkle, of course! Didn't anyone at the church tell you anything? Humph!" the old woman snorted in annoyance. "Young people these days! No manners at all!"

Now, Katharine had a chance to observe the ancient lady a little better. Tiny in stature, with rather stooped, rounded shoulders, the greatly matured woman was wearing an old flowered frock that did not match the flowered gardening apron she wore over it.

A huge straw hat embellished with a large pink ribbon and straw flowers covered her little old head. Frizzy, unkempt gray hair stuck out here and there around a wizened, crinkled old face, and tiny round spectacles with coke-bottle lenses were perched upon her little archaic nose.

Startlingly blue eyes that radiated intelligence surveyed Katharine's startling blue eyes right back. Katharine almost felt as if those eyes could somehow see right into her very soul.

Gray whiskers stuck out here and there over tiny, pruny lips, and protruded from her minute, jutting chin.

Skinny arms covered with sagging, wrinkly skin showed from beneath the short sleeves of the woman's dress, and gaunt, rather bowed legs and diminutive feet protruded from below the hem of the old dress.

Eventually, Katharine realized she was staring, and asked, "Well…ummm, Mrs. Periwinkle, what would you like for me to do?"

The old woman directed her vaguely over to an area, and told Katharine she could start weeding there. Katharine did what she was told. The woman seemed to be in an irritable mood, and she did not want to annoy her any further. Besides, this was such a lovely old place, and maybe in an hour or so, she could ask the woman for something to eat and drink, and then for directions to get back to the city.

There was something so soothing about this place; it had such a homey feeling. After a bit, Katharine forgot about her gnawing hunger and just began to enjoy it all. There were butterflies everywhere, fluttering around her head, and birds singing.

The occasional maidenfly flitted here and there, and Katharine even found a funny old toad in the depths of the flowers, trying to hide from the fingers that were searching for weeds.

Mrs. Periwinkle doddered about the garden, here and there, muttering to herself at times, and not really even acknowledging Katharine's presence at all. Katharine just smiled to herself, sneaking a peek at the woman now and then.

She really seemed quite funny, perhaps eccentric, Katharine thought, with that silly walk of hers and all of the attention that she pays to these flowers. But then, Katharine did have to admit to herself that they *were* absolutely gorgeous.

Eventually, the woman moved up toward the house. Grasping onto the ornate railing, she then hobbled up the stairs, and disappeared inside. The orange cat came back up to visit Katharine for another tummy rub, and soon, Mrs. Periwinkle came back outside, carrying a large tray. She set it on the small table between the rocking chairs on the porch. "Lunchtime!" she proclaimed in her creaky old voice.

Oh, food! exclaimed Katharine quietly to herself. *Finally, I am sooo hungry!* She hurried up to the porch with the orange cat following close behind.

Mrs. Periwinkle motioned toward one of the rockers, commanding, "Sit!" and Katharine did as she was told. "Well, go ahead, get yourself something to eat and drink!" she coaxed Katharine, which Katharine then wasted no time doing.

Gladly helping herself to several items, Katharine had not realized up until that point just how hungry she was! She wolfed a sandwich down in less than a minute. Mrs. Periwinkle had only taken two or three bites out of hers, and she watched Katharine in amazement as the girl took a second sandwich, and finished that with equal speed.

"My dear... Katharine was it? Have I already worked you into that big of an appetite?"

"No, ma'am." Katharine managed between large bites of the apple that she was now working on. "I'm just really hungry, that's all!"

"Well, I'll *be!*" was all the astonished old woman could mutter as she watched Katharine finish a third sandwich, and then start on a cookie. The whole time that Katharine ate, the orange cat sat at her feet, just watching.

Mrs. Periwinkle finally said to her, "I see that you've already made friends with Larry."

"Oh, yes, he's adorable!" Katharine exclaimed as she wiped her mouth with a napkin and picked up her glass of lemonade. Finally, her hunger was beginning to feel satisfied. "I've never seen a cat up close before."

"Well, there's two more of them around here somewhere, that I'm sure you'll like just as well," Mrs. Periwinkle told her.

"Really?" Katharine asked.

"Yes." replied the old woman. "There's a gray and gold tabby with white socks named Curly, and a black tuxedo cat named Moe."

"The Three Stooges?!" exclaimed Katharine, laughing slightly.

"Yes!" Mrs. Periwinkle said, with crinkled blue eyes beginning to twinkle. She was starting to warm up to this girl, as Katharine was to her. "I saw them in a picture show once, a few years back. My grandson and his wife were kind enough to take me. Never laughed so hard in my life, and once you get to know these cats, I'm sure you will see how well their names suit them. Never a dull moment with cats around!"

Katharine smiled at her in return. Mrs. Periwinkle seemed like a nice woman. And this was such a lovely place to be, on such a perfect afternoon. Katharine had completely forgotten her urge to reunite with her classmates for the moment, at least. Maybe she should just stay the rest of the day and finish helping this sweet old woman.

The afternoon passed quickly, and Mrs. Periwinkle was kind enough to bring out another tray stacked with refreshments in the late afternoon, shortly before Katharine finished up the weeding in yet another area of the garden.

After Katharine's stomach was again full, Mrs. Periwinkle asked her, "So, you'll be back in the morning then?"

"Well, umm, I don't rightly know, umm..." At a loss for what to say to the strange old woman, Katharine finally just stopped and stood there, fishing for words.

"Well, the church had said that whoever they sent was to help me around here each day for several weeks! Is this job going to be too much for you to handle? Not only do I need help with all of the gardening, but I needed someone to help with all the painting that needs to be done around here too!" Hands on her hips now, Mrs. Periwinkle was back to her irritable mood of their introduction from earlier this morning.

Katharine looked from Mrs. Periwinkle to the house, and all around the yard full of gorgeous blossoms, to everything that needed painting, and then back again at Mrs. Periwinkle.

Although the work that needed to be done to this place was overwhelming, she just did not have the heart to tell the old woman that she knew nothing about what some church had promised her, or about painting.

"I...uh, well, uh...umm, yes...I'll be back in the morning then." she finally managed, realizing suddenly that she actually was glad, and meant what she had just promised. "Well, good evening then, ma'am."

And with that, Katharine skipped off down the driveway. The ancient woman watched her disappear from sight with her hands still on her hips, and a slightly astonished look on her wrinkled old face. Katharine headed back towards the little abandoned shed where all of her belongings remained.

What now? she wondered silently to herself. She made her way down the winding road, admiring the nature that had been impossible to observe in the dark the night before. *I suppose I wouldn't have to try to connect with all of my classmates just yet. Should I remain here a couple more days? It is so very peaceful here, and I feel almost as if I have finally made it home. And even though the old woman seems to get quite testy at times, she still is quite nice. Why do I feel this way? And why do I not care if I ever make it back to my school? What's wrong with me?* she wondered.

Finally, giving up on all of her confusion, she reached the old shed, and all of her belongings.

Arriving there, she realized that Larry the cat had followed her to it. "Oh, you silly boy!" she exclaimed to the furry orange ball of purr, and she squatted and rubbed his fur all over. "Mrs. Periwinkle must be right, you do like me! Well, I like you too! Yes, I do, you fuzzy boy!" She stood and opened the creaky shed door, and Larry just followed her right into it like he owned the place!

"So now you think you own *this* place too, huh, silly boy? Well, that's fine I guess, you can keep me company for awhile while I try to decide what I should do." With that, she flopped onto the mound of straw, and Larry climbed up onto it with her and cuddled in the crook of her arm, purring loudly and rolling all around affectionately. Katharine had not realized just how tired she was!

Sometime in the middle of the night, she awoke to the night sounds of the woods all around her, and the warm, orange ball of fur still next to her in the straw. Rising only to pull the door shut and latch it from the inside, she then lay back down and cuddled with the cat for only an instant or so before she was again sound asleep.

The Garden Arbor

She vaguely remembered the dreams she had dreamt during the night. Something about butterflies and rainbows and soft, whispering voices that kept saying, "Welcome home, Katharine. Welcome home!"

Shortly after daybreak, the crowing of a rooster again awakened Katharine. Only this time, she realized that it probably was the same one she had seen at Mrs. Periwinkle's place just yesterday. Today when she rose, instead of just brushing off the same clothes she had worn the day before, she decided that it was time to change.

What she really wished for, however, was a chance to wash up first before putting something clean on. She remembered the small stream running through Mrs. Periwinkle's property and down the mountainside yesterday, and wondered just how far away from her little shed it was.

Katharine decided that it was time to explore a little. So, as she opened the creaking shed door and Larry ran out and took off, presumably toward home, she remained behind for awhile longer to have a little look around.

She had brought some soap and toothpaste and shampoo along, as well as a towel and washcloth. Perhaps she would get lucky and be able to put them to some use. After wrapping all of her toiletries in the towel along with a fresh change of clothes, she stepped outside and stopped to enjoy the fresh smell of the mountain air mixed with the new morning dew and sunlight for a moment. She breathed the sweet perfume in.

Certainly this place was the best-smelling one that she had ever encountered! She even thought she could detect the fragrance of some of Mrs. Periwinkle's numerous blossoms from there.

Basking in the brightness of the sunlight, and just enjoying the new morning and stretching, she suddenly noticed something she had not seen before. There was a narrow, well-worn rut from the shed leading off toward somewhere. *Probably an old wheelbarrow path leading to some forgotten garden, maybe even one of Mrs. Periwinkle's,* she thought. Perhaps this shed was on part of her property!

Following the path of the old rut, she soon encountered a creek, perhaps the same one she had seen yesterday. Bubbling and bursting with crystal clear, frigid mountain water, it was quite a bit wider than the one running through Mrs. Periwinkle's yard. It looked immensely refreshing to Katharine, who was used to bathing and washing her long blond hair every day. She looked around to make sure there was no possibility of anyone observing her, and then decided that this area was too secluded to have to worry much about that.

And so, with a high-pitched squeal at the chilliness of the water, she rushed through everything as quickly as possible, not only because of the water's temperature, but also that thought that someone could maybe inadvertently invade her privacy.

In minutes, she was quickly scrubbed clean from top to bottom, and then toweled dry and dressed in fresh things. Her only regret was that she had not brought more ordinary clothes to wear. The dresses that she had packed had been some of her nicer things, and would probably be ruined within a few days if she decided to stay.

What was all of this that she was thinking anyway? Of course she should try to get back to the city. She couldn't stay! By now her classmates and teachers were surely worrying about her! *Oh, she wondered vainly, what should I do?*

Mulling over all of this on her way back to the shed, and not being able to come to a decision, she realized again that her stomach was growling. She dropped off all of her belongings at the shed, latched the door, and took off for the road again, in search of those same juicy raspberries that she had found the morning before.

Once her hunger was satisfied, at least temporarily, she again traversed the short distance to Mrs. Periwinkle's house. Once more, this morning, coming up the long, winding drive, she was awestruck by the beauty of the entire place, even in its need of much repair and a brand new paint job.

Boy, just to imagine what it would look like if it were all fixed up! She gazed at the house for a moment, and could almost picture it, shutters mended and all freshly painted up, with maybe several different colors on all of the gingerbread. *The place would surely take your breath away!*

"Mrs. Periwinkle!" Katharine called out. "Mrs. Periwinkle!?" Just then the old woman tottered out onto the front porch.

"Well, you're up and about early! What do you know? Maybe you'll work out okay here after all! However, we do need to do something about your choice of work clothes, dearie! I noticed yesterday when you left that your dress was torn! I have some old work clothes in the house that my dear, departed Herbert left behind, God rest his soul! You don't want to ruin that pretty little dress. You'll need to change before we get to work today!"

Grateful for the opportunity to put on something more practical, Katharine let Mrs. Periwinkle usher her inside the house, to the large pantry just off the kitchen, and hand her some men's work clothes.

The inside of the house looked also as if it had once been beautiful. Even though it was slightly run down with age and in need of a little tidying up, it still seemed a luxury to her in comparison to her tiny shed!

In minutes she was changed, with her locket tucked safely inside the old button-up shirt. Though she felt that she probably looked a little foolish, the clothes didn't fit her too badly at all! She was rather tall for a girl, and apparently, dear departed Herbert had been rather short and slight for a man. All she needed to do was to fold the pant legs up slightly, and she was ready to roll.

Changed now and all set to work, she appeared on the front porch, and flung her arms up, saying, "Ta, da!"

Mrs. Periwinkle looked up from filling her watering can at the pump, and had to smile slightly. *The girl is quite adorable, and even more so in dear Herbert's old clothes!*

"Well, all right then, dearie, why don't you go on over to where you left off yesterday and get that weedy mess all taken care of first thing? After that, maybe I'll have you tackle the mess all around the arbor. I've been trying to get that cleaned up for years, but the weeds and vines in there always grow back way too fast for me! Probably because I'm so old and slow!" The venerable woman chuckled a little at that.

Katharine smiled, and went on over to where Mrs. Periwinkle had directed her and got to work.

Morning passed quickly, and Katharine's enjoyment of the place just kept growing. This morning she became amused by the antics of a couple bluebirds near the giant Victorian birdhouse. They appeared to be male and female, and busily taking care of some babies inside somewhere. In and out their little door they went, chirping often.

Soon it was lunchtime again, and she joined Mrs. Periwinkle up on the porch in the shade once more as she had done the day before.

"So, Katharine, how do you like your job here so far? You are doing quite well, and I do so appreciate all that you have taken care of for me already. Work always goes faster when you have someone to do it with!"

Katharine agreed, and told Mrs. Periwinkle that she liked it here, that the place was absolutely beautiful, and that she would try to make it even more so.

Mrs. Periwinkle smiled at her, with a twinkle in her kind, bright blue eyes. "Please," she said to Katharine, "just call me Penelope. It's slightly shorter to say, anyway!"

Katharine agreed that she would try to do just that. Sitting there, rocking in the shade for a few more cooling moments before resuming her weeding, Penelope suddenly leaned in and scrutinized Katharine closer.

"My dear, I am not sure why, but I feel that I know you! Do I? I remember you saying that your last name is Abernathy. I haven't been down into the town for quite some time, and don't go often, so I really don't know of everyone down there! I have heard from my grandson that there are quite a few new families living there now too!"

Katharine didn't quite know just what she should give away to the old woman yet, and finally said, "No, ma'am, I don't believe that we know each other. I do live in the town below, but I was adopted when I was quite small. However, something does seem familiar about you to me, too. Maybe it's just this beautiful place you have here, I don't know. I think the beauty of it kind of sucks you in, and makes you not want to leave."

"Oh?" asked Penelope. "How old are you anyway, Katharine? Shouldn't you be in school?"

"Well, yes ma'am, I'm fourteen." was Katharine's reply. "I'm taking a few days off."

"Oh, on vacation then, are you?" Penelope asked her.

"Yes, I guess you could kind of say that." Katharine answered evasively. Then, afraid of divulging too much yet to her newly-made ancient friend, she said reluctantly, "Well, I should probably get back to work!"

With that, Katharine got up and headed back toward the garden that she had been working on before lunch. She was not ready to go into too much detail with Penelope just yet. The old woman would probably see to it that she was returned to school, and soon! Besides, the longer Katharine stayed and helped her, the longer she wanted to. There wasn't really any reason for her to return, except to let her teachers and classmates know that she was safe. Maybe in a few days she would be ready, and then she could tell Penelope what was going on. For so many years she had done what everyone else had told her to do, and now she was enjoying her little bit of freedom!

About two hours later, a teenage boy came up the drive. At first Mrs. Periwinkle and Katharine did not notice him, until he finally yelled a loud, "Hello!"

"Oh, excuse me for a minute, Katharine," Penelope, who was working nearby, told her. "Let me see what this young man wants!"

Mrs. Periwinkle doddered on up to the house, and Katharine stood up from her work to see what all the fuss was about.

"Yes, young man, how can I help you?" she asked the boy rather sternly.

"Well, uh," slightly flabbergasted, the boy replied, "the church told me that you were needing some help around the place. I'm here to help you now."

"Young man, that was supposed to have been three days ago! Besides, this young lady has been doing an excellent job helping out!" Mrs. Periwinkle exclaimed, motioning toward Katharine.

"Well, uh, yes ma'am, but my mother took ill at the beginning of the week, and I had to stay and help her out till she was doin' better. I got me several other brothers and sisters, some of them young 'uns, and she couldn't handle them all when she wasn't feelin' good. Then, I had to get permission from school," the boy offered nervously.

"Well, stay then if you like, but I hope you're hard working and reliable!" Mrs. Periwinkle finally said, as if to admonish him for his tardiness.

"Yes, ma'am, I'm a real hard worker, you just wait and see! Anyway, my name is Alex, ma'am. Alex Brock. My older brother, Aaron, should be along later in the week to help with some of the harder stuff, like the real high up paintin' and such, and maybe my dad will come for a while too. They said they might not be able to help until Saturday, though, seeins' how they both have to work."

"Well, all right then." Mrs. Periwinkle replied, looking a little surprised. However, she finally shrugged her shoulders and directed Alex to some paint cans and brushes, all the while contemplating to herself that she could use all the volunteers she could get here!

She put Alex to work painting a couple of sad looking trellises, and headed back toward the garden and her weeding. The rest of the afternoon passed relatively quietly, but there was never a dull moment at Mrs. Periwinkle's place, Katharine soon discovered.

Penelope's three cats: Moe, Larry and Curly, were indeed hilarious. Larry was usually the instigator, and although he was probably the most loveable of the three, he was also the most playful and rambunctious. He constantly annoyed the other two cats, trying to get them to chase him around the yard and wrestle.

Moe, true to form, was the more surly of the three, kind of a weird combination of loveable and grumpy. He never appreciated or tolerated any guff from the other two cats.

Curly was a good natured, gentle giant of a cat, large-boned and rather tall with a very long tail. Unfortunately for him, he was quite often the target of Moe's wrath, particularly when they were both near their food dish.

In between watching the threesome's antics, and enjoying the absolutely beautiful weather, and nature in all of its glory, Katharine began to feel as if she never wanted to leave! With the hundreds of butterflies, bees, maidenflies, dragonflies, and numerous other insects, and all the birds and their lovely birdsong, Katharine felt entirely at home here. There were awesomely gorgeous flowers everywhere. She reveled in nature's glory!

After a while, Katharine finished her present task of weeding the small flower garden, and she stood up and brushed herself off a bit. She took the basketful of weeds to the compost heap and dumped them. She remembered that Mrs. Periwinkle had wanted her to start by the arbor next, so she took her basket and tools over to it, to begin weeding there.

Katharine was temporarily sidetracked by the sight of a beautiful, iridescent green hummingbird with a ruby-red throat, flitting quickly between the deep orange blossoms on the trumpet vine that covered the picket fencing. After watching the small creature with entrancement for several minutes, it finally whizzed away, out of her sight, and she knelt at the base of the arbor to resume her weeding.

Here, she discovered, much to her annoyance, that there was a weedy mess indeed! Brambles and cockle-burrs and all sorts of nasty stuff resided in there and around the thing, along with morning glories and some of the trumpet vines. She put on her gardening gloves and started using a pruning shears to cut it all back.

The morning glories that still managed to find their way through all of the thickety mayhem were lovely, but this arbor would definitely need a lot of work, and could use a couple coats of paint as well! It was quite rusty in spots, and she didn't know if it would even be worth saving, once she successfully had the mess cleared out of there.

After trying to get the brambles out of it with no success without damaging the morning glories, she finally got frustrated with all of the scratches that were beginning to cover her forearms. Now, she just took the pruning shears and started whacking away at everything!

Penelope eventually came by, and agreed with Katharine that although she had loved her morning glories, it was probably the only thing that Katharine could do. Katharine worked at the weedy chaos for a couple more hours, filling her basket and dumping it several more times.

Finally, Mrs. Periwinkle decided that Katharine had worked sufficiently for the day, and invited the girl to stay for dinner. She also invited Alex, who politely declined, saying he had to go home and help his mom with their dinner. He took off down the drive at a run, turning around and yelling, "Be back tomorrow!"

While Penelope prepared dinner, Katharine sat up on the porch and took turns petting all of the cats, getting cat hair all over her face and giggling at the antics of each one. They sure were cute!

Dinner was delicious, and afterwards, Mrs. Periwinkle finally suggested, "Well, shouldn't you be heading home, dear? It's quite a walk into town, and I'm sure you would want to make it back before it starts getting dark!"

"Yes, ma'am, you're right, I guess I should be heading back. I'll go change out of these things and then be on my way!" Katharine agreed.

After promising to return bright and early the next morning, Katharine cheerfully headed away down the drive, and toward her old shed, which she was now laughingly and secretly referring to as her home. Again, Larry the cat followed her there, and spent the night cuddled next to her, each other's warmth keeping both of them snug and cozy.

Penelope Periwinkle

his was beginning to become an everyday ritual, Katharine mused to herself, waking again to the telltale rooster crow, and the fuzzy orange Larry-cat. Vague images and sounds of butterflies, rainbows and welcomes disappeared as she awoke and rubbed her sleepy eyes. She had to smile slightly to herself. Even though the roof over her head wasn't much, it was better than nothing at all, and she had plenty to busy herself with during the day.

She rose, opened the door of the shed wide, stretched in the glory of the early morning sun, and bade Larry farewell as he ran off toward what she suspected was his food dish up at Mrs. Periwinkle's house.

Spying again the worn broom in the corner of the shed, she dusted the cobwebs out of the windows with it, and then swept the straw that was now her bed into a nice round pile for the next night. She then swept the remainder of the floor clean and out toward the shed door.

Placing the broom back next to the wheelbarrow, she repeated her ritual of the morning before, venturing to the creek again to wash up, and found that she was also beginning to enjoy that as well. Although the water was shockingly cold, it was very refreshing, and helped wake her up and wash the sleep away from her mind and eyes as well.

This morning, however, after she was all cleaned and dressed, she decided to try out the narrow wheelbarrow path that had led her way to the stream to see just where it did lead to. Sure enough, after she had made her way up the steep hill for several minutes, she began to see Penelope's place off in the distance.

Closer to the house now, she was able to see why the stream was so wide further down the mountain. Another, wider branch of it joined the narrow one coming from Penelope's yard.

As she kept climbing, it became obvious that this was just an extension of the same property. *Well, then, the shed where I have been sleeping is most likely hers,* Katharine confirmed to herself! She ventured a little further, over the top of the hill past tall grass and small, scrubby trees. The arbor where she had scratched both her arms all up yesterday afternoon began to come into view.

In total surprise, she stopped dead in her tracks. The morning glories that she had finally resorted to cutting all the way back to the ground just yesterday afternoon were covering the arbor fully, and in wondrous, resplendent bloom! *How could this be?* she wondered.

Certainly nothing could recover and grow back that fast! She stood there a few moments more, still astonished at the beauty of the morning glories on the arbor, and then finally decided that it was time to take her armload of clothing and toiletries back to the shed and close it up before trekking up to Mrs. Periwinkle's again.

Grabbing more raspberries yet again before she reached the old place, she marveled to herself at the fact that she was not even missing the field trip that she should have taken, or her friends and teachers either. *I suppose I should do something about all of that,* she reasoned. *But, I'm just not ready yet,* she reflected to herself. *Maybe I never will be. Ha!* The thought of just staying here forever and living in the little shed made her chuckle to herself.

Soon she was approaching the marvelous old property again. She was beginning to love this place. *A person could live here their whole life, and never want to leave!*

Mrs. Periwinkle was sitting on one of the rockers on the front porch this morning, working on what looked like some kind of fancy needlework. Katharine went up the stairs and looked at it, fascinated with its intricacy. "What are you working on?" she asked Penelope after several minutes.

"Oh, I'm just tatting a doily. Helps keep the old, arthritic fingers nimble!" Penelope remarked, standing up rather slowly and painfully while setting the doily-in-progress aside. "Too bad it doesn't help the other old, creaky bones!" she added, with a slight smirk in her grin. "Getting old is no fun, I'll tell you! Be grateful for your youth, it'll be gone before you know it!" she admonished, holding a gnarled index finger up.

Katharine smiled back. Penelope was beginning to seem like an old friend to her.

After Katharine had again changed into a clean pair of dear, departed old Herbert's clothes, and tucked her locket on its long chain safely inside Herbert's work shirt, they headed off to do their chores in the garden again. Then, Katharine remembered the morning glories on the arbor. Approaching it, she stood there, newly amazed all over again for a moment or two, and then went to get Penelope so that she could show her.

"Well, my goodness, dearie! I can't say I've ever seen anything like this before!" the old woman exclaimed to Katharine. "Well, you must have done a good pruning job indeed! The flowers are beautiful! Keep up the good work!" she directed Katharine, as she doddered away to work on something a little ways away.

Much to Katharine's dismay, however, when she picked up her pruning shears again, she noticed that most of the weeds that she had cut back just last evening had also returned. Vaguely, she remembered Mrs. Periwinkle saying something about never being able to keep up with the weeds around there, but she had thought that perhaps it was just because the old woman was rather slow.

Painstakingly, she removed briars and thistles and cockleburs again. After awhile Alex showed up again too, picking up his paintbrush and can from the day before and giving the old trellises a second coat of paint.

On into the day Katharine worked, and even though she was slightly dismayed with the return of all the weeds around her, she gloried in watching all of nature at its best while she worked.

Nearby, a hummingbird visited the trumpet vines along the fence-line again, flitting here and there with wings that were almost invisible on a body of pure, iridescent emerald green with a ruby colored throat.

Enchanted, she watched silently for several minutes, until finally, its hunger satisfied, it zoomed away off into the distance where she could no longer observe it.

During their lunch, which she again enjoyed with Penelope and Alex, Alex reminded Mrs. Periwinkle that tomorrow his father and older brother would be joining him to help her around the place.

Never one to look a gift-horse in the mouth, and knowing that her old place certainly could use a lot more sprucing up than both Katharine and Alex combined would be capable of, she pleasantly agreed and told him that she was looking forward to their help tomorrow.

While they enjoyed all the different selections on the large tray that Mrs. Periwinkle had prepared, Katharine decided to ask her a question.

"Penelope, you said that you had a grandson in the area. How many children did you and Herbert have?"

"Only one, my dear. A daughter. We named her Helen. She lived a little further up the mountain path. Unfortunately, she and her husband, Thomas Meriweather, have both already joined my dear old Herbert."

Penelope reflected sadly for a few moments, and then continued. "However, Herbert and I were still very blessed. We were together for forty-three wonderful years, and Helen and her husband had four children of their own, giving us four grandchildren."

"Oh?" Katharine asked. "Where do they all live now? Are they up here on the mountain also?"

"No, dear, I'm afraid not. Their youngest son, my grandson Patrick, does live in the town below. He comes up here to visit often. I rely on him for quite a lot, I'm afraid. He does all of my shopping and banking and such for me. He is a real blessing! I just am not able to get around like I used to be. He and his wife, Berta, attend the little white church down there, and they're the ones that are responsible for you and Alex coming up here every day to help me out."

Katharine didn't reply, not ready to divulge the true reason that she was here just yet.

"Anyway," Mrs. Periwinkle continued, "my other grandchildren do not live around here anymore. They are all busy, with lives of their own, and who could blame them?"

"My oldest grandson, Norman, served in the war," she continued, "and after he left the service he married a nice girl and they live in South Carolina with their three children. My oldest granddaughter, Imogene, is also married and lives with her husband in Pennsylvania. They had two children. And then, there was my youngest granddaughter, Cassandra, whom I haven't seen since she was seventeen."

"Poor Cassie had lots of problems growing up. She was never satisfied with the simple life up here on the mountainside. She always had big ideas, wanted to be a famous actress, and felt that she was too limited living up here. Perhaps she was right." Penelope stopped to take a breath.

"For whatever reason, she was quite promiscuous with the boys, and rumor had it when she disappeared that she might have been pregnant. No one has seen or heard from her since." Penelope paused and reflected with a sorrowful expression.

"Shortly before she disappeared, she stopped by to visit with me for a few hours. It seemed like there was something that she wanted to say to me. It was as if she had the weight of the world on her shoulders, but whatever it was, she never did tell me. That was the last time I saw her…I do miss her so, and now I wish that somehow I could have found a way to help the poor girl." Penelope ended with a rather wistful look on her face.

She gazed at Katharine then, and imploringly said, "So many times life does not give us a second chance, dear, and if ever there is any advice that you remember that came from me, please remember *that* most of all." Penelope finished pensively, not saying anything more for several minutes afterwards.

Finally, Katharine, feeling so bad for Penelope's loss, said to her, "Well, Mrs. Periwinkle, if it makes you feel any better at all, you seem like a very nice lady to me. I'm sure that you said and did everything with your granddaughter that you thought was appropriate at the time."

Penelope gave Katharine a rueful smile, and then told her, "Well, thank you, dear. I do appreciate that. You know, in some ways you actually remind me of dear Cassandra. She had the same mannerisms as you. I have noticed that on more than one occasion."

Katharine smiled, glad that she had been able to make Penelope feel a little better. "Well, I'd probably better go get back to work. That ornery arbor has got me quite frustrated, and if I'm going to get the mess around there cleared away today, I'd best get going."

Penelope nodded, as Alex had already returned to his painting some time before.

Later, as Katharine was finally able to make some headway with the weedy tangle in the arbor, Larry, Moe, and Curly again amused her by getting testy with each other, and running about, all over the place. They scurried in and out amongst all of the flowers, making her laugh out loud. What silly cats! Oh, how she enjoyed watching all of their antics, and how she loved them!

Remembering Penelope's words of earlier, she thought about how Penelope had warned her that sometimes life did not dole out second chances.

Katharine mused that in her own life, she had been left abandoned, and that there had been times when people such as Constance or Ingrid had treated her badly. Neither of them had wanted a second chance with her. They had *always* treated her horribly, and never tried to make amends. If only they could have been kinder to her. A large butterfly hovered overhead of Katharine, shading her temporarily, and making her feel oddly chilled, but for only an instant. It then glided off.

It had never been her will to see anyone fall. She had never held any ill will toward them, and had only wished for them to know that. She was happy now, and only grateful that their torment of her had not lasted forever.

Time was wearing on at the arbor. It was *hot* this afternoon! Since she didn't seem to be getting much of anywhere anyway, Katharine, feeling as if she needed a break from her arduous task, decided to wander a bit. She wiped beads of perspiration from her forehead with the back of her hand.

Off to the left of her, the coolness and stillness of the woods called to her. She stood, dusted herself off a bit, and walked over into the shade by the cooling refreshment of the tiny, enchanting, gurgling stream.

Penelope was nowhere to be seen for the moment. Off in the distance, beneath the shade of the trees at the edge of the forest, she could still see the large butterfly that had shadowed her briefly only moments before. It was quite some ways away now, lilting and fluttering about gracefully in the stillness below their drooping branches. *It appears to be a soft shade of white. No, now it looks pale green!* thought Katharine.

"Katharine!" she almost thought she heard it summon her. "Katharine!"

Intrigued, she hopped over the cheerful, sparkling stream, and tried to follow it, in order to see it better.

Just when she would begin to gain on the butterfly, it would flutter deeper and deeper into the woods.

Soon, she was surrounded by the coolness of the forest. Sunlight streamed in here and there throughout the woods, illuminating it enough that she did not realize just how deep into the forest she had wandered. Birds chirped and fluttered about, their calling echoing between the large trees.

There is the huge butterfly again! she thought. Still, she followed, now gaining on it. Soon, she observed it landing near a grouping of bright blue wildflowers.

As she approached, she realized that it was not a butterfly at all, but rather, a large, Luna moth. Intrigued with its almost iridescent pale green color, she moved even closer still.

As if sensing her presence, the moth lifted from its greenery perch, and again lilted away further into the forest.

Since she had gotten a good look at it already, Katharine debated whether she should return to Mrs. Periwinkle's place, or continue to follow it for a short distance longer in the hope of seeing it one last time.

In all of her life, she had heard about the beautiful creatures, and glimpsed them briefly now and then, but they were always elusive, and gone before she had ever gotten a good chance to see them. Of course, she had seen pictures before, but until now, had never actually observed one up close for herself. They really were quite graceful creatures!

Climbing through the ever-thickening greenery of the forest, Katharine saw it again! Now, the moth had alighted on a smooth brown rock, next to a small, algae-covered pool of water. Several unusual-looking water lilies floated on top of the algae, with dark blue, nearly purple blooms that almost hurt her eyes to gaze upon them. Large, circular leaves floated amongst the flowers. Slowly, she approached the moth, not wishing to frighten it away again. Nearby, was a cluster of several large rocks, sitting at the base of an ancient, gnarled oak tree.

Carefully, she moved toward them, thinking how nice it would be to sit there for a bit and observe the beautiful moth. The moth stayed put, moving its wings up and down slowly, but otherwise staying still.

Climbing on top of the biggest rock slowly, Katharine appreciated its coolness, and felt slightly refreshed from the heat of the day.

Carefully brushing wisps of hair away from her face so as not to frighten the moth again, Katharine sat and guilelessly observed it.

Suddenly, the moth rose, almost instantly transforming from the beautiful, pale shade of green to a wicked black color. The shape of its wings changed from slightly and gently rounded, to horrible and jagged looking! While doing so, it unexpectedly, swiftly and purposefully flew straight towards her face. As it neared, for an instant Katharine was aware of a diminutive, frightful, evil face with glowing red eyes directly in front of hers. The horrid form hissed, grinned and then laughed obscenely. Then, as swiftly as it had come, it zipped past her and disappeared directly into the darkness of the woods.

Startled at what she wasn't even sure that she had just witnessed, she was left with only the sense of something purely evil hovering nearby. Katharine shook her head, which was now beginning to feel thick and foggy. Knowing with certainty that it would be wise to head back to Mrs. Periwinkle's place as quickly as possible, she began to rise. Then, all of a sudden, the murky water in the pool beneath her began to bubble and boil.

By now, she was quite frightened, but her mind became increasingly thick with mist. She felt unable to move, as if a spell had been placed upon her! As she stood watching with huge eyes, mesmerized with the bubbling water, a slimy form began to emerge from within its depths. Huge round, bloodshot eyeballs appeared first, followed by a slime-covered, rotund body.

Finally, the water began to still, as a large, sickly green, wart-covered toad-like creature with huge, bulging eyes slithered and climbed onto one of the large water-lily leaves.

Turning toward her, it opened its awful mouth, and wisps of what appeared to be a green vapor began to come forth out of it. Then, in a raspy, beckoning voice, it called to her. "Welcome, dear Katharine!" it intoned. "Welcome to the Murky Pool of Evil, Sorrowful Intentions and Unwise, Heartbreaking Choices!"

Still unable to move as if she were rooted to the spot; and not knowing why, Katharine began to shake uncontrollably. "I don't understand!" she was finally able to manage; her body and mouth trembling terribly.

The afternoon light began to wane, and gray clouds began to roll in across the sky. In the cover of the thick growth, Katharine could no longer see the sky, yet the forest darkened perceptibly. The wind picked up slightly at first; then the forest blackened even more, and became enveloped in a chilly, murky fog. The horrible green vapor that had escaped the creature's mouth had begun to pervade everything with a horrendous, poisonous stench, making Katharine gag.

The toad's eyes bulged even larger than before, the whites of them turning an even more sickly bloodshot red, and then it finally spoke again. "You, my dear, are the result of unwise, heartbreaking choices, and have been the victim of evil, sorrowful intentions more than once in your lifetime. *Is this not true?*" it demanded of her.

The horrible, slimy creature sat on its awful lily-pad perch, surveying her with distasteful, hate-filled eyes. "Look into my eyes and deny it!" the creature abruptly demanded. As horrid as it was, Katharine could barely force herself to gaze upon the ugly creature, but finally she complied.

Suddenly, its face was replaced with first the hatred-filled visage of Constance Abernathy, gazing on at Katharine with evil intent as she almost drowned when she was four. Then, Ingrid's fat, stupid one appeared as she tried to strangle Katharine the rainy day that they had watched the movie in school. Both horrid countenances had appeared as if in example.

Ingrid's face faded from Katharine's view, to be replaced now by the face of a teenage girl that she did not know, but thought she recognized. Sorrow and regret filled the young woman's blue eyes, while she watched over and bade farewell to a tiny baby. This unknown face was again replaced by the horrible toad's.

Green, slimy snot flowed sinuously from its wide, nasty nostrils, reminding her again of the abhorrent Ingrid. Its long, skinny tongue lashed out, capturing the nasty green mucous, and whipping it into the creature's warty mouth.

Faces of evil demons swam round and round in the murky water, as if they were trying to escape. Then, they mocked and beckoned her at the same time. Slimy hands reached up and out of the putrid slime as if trying to grasp something in order to climb out. Then, they seemed to change their minds, and began to motion to Katharine to come join them. Red-eyed serpents slithered amongst the demon-faces.

Katharine's stomach and mind were both by now doing loop-di-loops. She felt violently nauseous, not only from the horrible stench, but also the dreadful scene that was playing out before her. She placed her hand over her mouth, not sure if she would be able to hold in the contents of her riotously roiling stomach much longer.

Grasping the ancient oak tree next to her for stability, as her head was swimming now too, she felt powerless to turn away from the horrible creature in front of her. It still had her under its dreadful spell.

Finally, she was able to manage, in a voice almost as croaky as the toad's, "What do you want?"

The creature began to spin before her in a horrible, putrid green spiral, rotating faster and faster, and causing her stomach to lurch uncontrollably.

"Why you of course…you, *dear Katharine!*" it suddenly and horribly screamed at her. "You have not forgiven your enemies for all of your past hurts in this lifetime. And for that, you will pay with your *soul!*"

Katharine's poor legs began to tremble violently now also,

and, with sweat running profusely down her forehead, she felt her stomach began to lurch rebelliously again.

"But I have forgiven them!" she protested adamantly. "I have! I've never wished anything bad on anyone in my life!" Her trembling legs could no longer handle her weight, and she fell to her knees, using her forearms and hands to keep herself from falling flat on the ground.

Breathing heavily, she was sure that she was about to die. Her heart was pounding so wildly that it felt about to burst. Her locket on its fine, golden chain fell out of the collar of Herbert's old work shirt.

With her head hanging, ultimately, she lost all remaining power she had over her roiling, boiling stomach. She gave up all of its unfortunate contents, surrendering to wave after wave of painful vomiting.

When she was certain that she would die if it happened again, it did, and still she continued to feel horribly ill.

Lifting her hand to push her hair away from her regurgitating mouth, she brushed her butterfly locket, still dangling from her neck.

Swiftly, glowing, iridescent lights began to appear. Then, even quicker still, the form of a beautiful, fairy-like butterfly-winged maiden materialized in front of her eyes. "Katharine!" it whispered to her. "Dear Katharine! Safety has found you!"

Then, the winged maiden turned toward the horrible creature, as again it licked away the slimy green mucous flowing without restraint from its dreadful, wart-covered nostrils. It then captured Katharine's vomit in the same hideous manner!

"Be gone with you, horrible, evil creature of the swamp!" the diminutive, flying maiden commanded. "Katharine *has* forgiven all of her enemies, and we know this because we have always watched over her, to protect her from those of your type! Be gone! You have no power over her any longer!" the butterfly-maiden shouted.

That said, the specter pointed a long, slender, graceful finger at the evil blob, and a lengthy, glowing, radiating iridescent light protruded from it, its beam touching the evil abnormality's fore-head. Before Katharine's eyes, the monstrosity began to blow up like a balloon. Larger and larger it grew, along with the fear that it might burst evident in its bloodshot, bulging eyes.

The winged maiden turned to Katharine, kindness radiating from within her very soul. "Dear girl, your soul will now be free, I command it!"

A dreadful weight instantly began to lift off Katharine's very being.

Again, the fairy-like specter turned back to the toady blob. Shaking her fist twice at him, then pointing her graceful finger at him once more, she caused him to let out a thundering, rumbling belch that shook everything in the forest to its core. With the reverberating belch, the toad-like creature began to quickly shrink. Putrid green gases and demon-like tormented images escaped from the horrid abyss of its mouth, only to be vaporized by the fairy's magic, as she pointed once more.

As the horrible, nasty belch occurred, Katharine's soul was freed from the vomit he had consumed. The terrible burden of the weight of the world lifted completely from Katharine's shoulders. She immediately began to feel a wonderful sense of release and freedom. The illness that had pervaded her entire body only moments before disappeared as quickly as it had grasped a hold of her being in the first place.

Tiny, rainbow-colored lights surrounded her and the butter-fly-maiden. The specter hovered near her a few moments longer, while the nasty toad continued to shrink. Finally, with a tiny, vain sound of protest, it disappeared into the glugging, thick, and putrid water completely. The swamp surrounding him shrunk along with him, until first the indigo water lilies, and then the tiny cesspool itself disappeared completely, from her view.

Now, the intriguing butterfly-maiden turned toward her again. With much kindness in her glowing face, and a look of contemplation about her, she said one last thing to Katharine. "Evil lurks everywhere, my dear girl. It is within everything and shadows one, looking for opportunity! Always take care not to let it consume your heart. Protect your soul! There is kindness and forgiveness within you, I can feel it, and have witnessed it!"

"Don't dwell on bad thoughts, or memories of the past. They can only hurt and diminish you. And, unlike the people that inflict bad memories upon you, they will not fade away, but instead infect you to the core of your very soul! Always protect your heart! Go now, with love, and only look forward to your future!"

With that, the benevolent specter smiled at Katharine one last time, put her hands together as if in prayer, nodded at Katharine with a radiant smile, and gently faded from view.

Katharine now found herself alone again in the forest. The fog had dissipated, and the birds chirped happily once more, flitting from tree to tree. The day still appeared to be somewhat overcast, however, and Katharine knew that she should be getting back along to Penelope's place.

Not quite remembering which direction from whence she had come, however, it took her quite some time to finally track the lovely old place down. More than one time, she had believed she was lost for good, and each time, a pair of lovely, brilliant swallowtail butterflies would appear and lead her onward.

She noticed her antique locket dangling outside her work shirt absently as she searched, and tucked it safely back inside, straightening her collar a bit.

Finally, she was back at Mrs. Periwinkle's place, much to her relief! Apparently, the old woman had not even noticed her absence. Katharine could see the old woman doddering around up by the large old house, putzing away.

She jumped over the little merry stream, glad to encounter something cheerful and normal again, and headed back toward the arbor. Naturally, all of the work she had accomplished again this day had been in vain! The weeds and brambles were back once more, thick as ever, and Katharine set her hands upon her hips and sighed with anger and frustration.

Not much later, after she had hauled several more basket loads of garden waste to the good old compost heap, Mrs. Periwinkle called to Katharine to finish up what she was doing, since it looked as if a storm was brewing. *It is getting near to the time when we should be finishing up anyway*, Katharine thought to herself. She tugged on some more vines and clipped away, finally dropping the entire heap into her basket to make one last trip to the compost heap.

Memories of the awful adventure of the afternoon repeatedly seeped into her mind as she worked, and then finally dumped the clippings, and she put it from her mind as well as she could. *It is amazing how quickly the sickness left me after the butterfly-maiden helped me! I feel absolutely fine now!* she marveled to herself.

Tomorrow, she vowed, she would tackle the mess toward the back of the arbor, and hopefully be able to go onto something else.

She had rather hoped that Mrs. Periwinkle would agree to let her paint some of the finishing touches on the ornate front gate out by the road as she had suggested, decorating the flowers periwinkle blue and the leaves and vines green, all individually.

After she had dumped her basket of weeds, it was becoming quite windy, and beginning to sprinkle. Penelope emerged from the kitchen in the shelter of the front porch with a tray containing their dinner, and called out to her, "Better hurry dear, it looks as if the sky is going to let loose any second now!"

Katharine ran up towards the porch carrying her basket and tools, as Alex came tearing down the drive with his paint can and brush in hand. Just as they both made it onto the covered porch, the sky did indeed open up in a downpour.

Since it was quite windy, Penelope decided that it would be best if they all ate their dinner tonight in the kitchen, with the weather so nasty at the moment. This time, Alex decided to join them too, as he did not want to traverse the mountain path toward home in this weather.

As they sat at the table in Penelope's large kitchen, Katharine finally got her first good look around at the inside of the old house. It was quite beautiful, though rather unkempt, and she thought perhaps one day she could suggest to Penelope that she help her straighten it up. However, for the first time all day, she realized while they ate that she had not thought once about her school field trip, or her teachers or classmates, and she began to feel slightly guilty about that.

After they had eaten, Alex took off for home anyway, disregarding the rain that still came down at a steady rate but had let up somewhat. Not long afterward, Katharine noticed the beautiful grand piano sitting in the parlor just off the kitchen, and complimented Penelope on the beauty of it.

"Ahh, yes dear," Penelope remarked. "I used to play it myself, but it's become so out of tune that I just can't bear the sound of it anymore. I guess I really should speak to my grandson, Patrick, about sending someone up here to give it a good tuning up."

As Katharine walked and Mrs. Periwinkle hobbled in to observe it more closely, Katharine noticed the large, ornate Victorian fireplace at the other side of the room. The whole room was filled with lovely old antique furniture.

Moving closer, she noticed all of the old family photographs sitting on the beautiful mantel. Mrs. Periwinkle followed her over there, and pointed out who each and every person in all of the photographs were. Every photo was quite old-looking, and very charming. One stood out in particular.

Penelope had pointed to it, telling Katharine that this one was her granddaughter, Cassie, that she had spoken of, earlier. Katharine admired the photo, telling Penelope that Cassie had been a very pretty girl indeed. Penelope had agreed, again with that wistful, faraway look on her face. Even to Katharine, something had seemed vaguely familiar about the photograph. *The girl reminds me of Mrs. Periwinkle*, she decided.

Finally, the storm was beginning to let up, reduced now to just a light sprinkle. So, Katharine told Penelope that she should begin to head home herself, before it became too dark outside.

After changing, she bade Mrs. Periwinkle goodbye for the evening, promising to come back bright and early in the morning. She returned to her little shed, which she now regarded as her own little home of her own, with Larry following close behind once again in the lightly sprinkling rain.

As she plopped again onto her pile of musty straw, cuddling soft, purring Larry close, she remembered once again her classmates far away in the city. Surely by now, they had become quite worried about her. Hopefully, her absence had not ruined their trip, she thought ruefully to herself.

Tomorrow, she decided, as the warm Larry-cat nestled once again in the crook of her arm. Tomorrow she would have to tell Penelope the truth. Tomorrow…tomorrow…and before she knew it, she was out like a light, dreaming.

Images once again filled her nighttime visions as she ran, carefree through lush green, flower-covered hills and valleys. Yet, her dreams remained continually haunted by the faraway likenesses of parents whose faces she could still not make out.

Then, the butterflies would invade her sleep-filled thoughts, and keep her safe and fill her heart with joy. She loved these images the most, the beautiful butterflies that had ceaselessly seemed to be with her, wherever her life had led her.

Soaring with the Butterflies

"Cock-a-doodle-doo!" Katharine stirred again in the brightness of a new day, as the perennial rooster crow woke her from her dreams. "Welcome home, Katharine, welcome home!" was the last thing that she had remembered from her butterfly-filled dreams, as they began to fade away.

Rubbing her eyes and sitting up, she remembered from the evening before that she had resolved on this day to tell Penelope the real reason that she was here, that she was lost, and needed someone to help her find her way back to her schoolmates. Larry trilled his good morning to her, stood, hunched and then extended his furry back in a great stretch. Katharine watched him, and then laughed.

"Merow!" he greeted her, and she patted him on the head and rubbed his furry back, running her hand up his tail.

She stood and stretched too, not unlike her feline friend, and then, opening the shed door, watched him once again disappear into the tall weeds and wildflowers as he headed up to Penelope's for his breakfast.

"Bye, Larry!" she called as the orange, fuzzy tail vanished into the lush undergrowth.

Looking around at the beautiful morning that presented itself to her, and stretching again, she sighed with contentment. After the rain of the night before, everything absolutely glistened with wetness. Small, rainbow-colored spherical droplets covered everything, lending a magical hue to the entire landscape.

Why anyone would ever want to leave this place was beyond her, she mused. She thought again of the story that Mrs. Periwinkle had told her the night before, about her granddaughter Cassie, and how the poor girl had never been satisfied living up here on the gorgeous mountainside. Katharine couldn't understand the girl's discontent—she loved it here herself, and personally was having trouble with her own prospect of having to leave the place. She had come to regard it as her home.

Bathing in the chilly stream in the cold, early-morning mountain air, a lone doe observed her from a distance. It munched on tall grass, as she continued to worry about what she knew she had to take care of. Certainly, her teachers were quite distraught at her disappearance!

Heading up the mountain path, Katharine again had to marvel at the beauty of everything up here. The remaining raindrops from last evening glistened like diamonds, as if the entire area was covered in precious treasure. Gorgeous butterflies fluttered everywhere. It was like an enchanted world! What a glorious morning!

She reached Mrs. Periwinkle's place, and viewed its beauty in its entirety rather wistfully, knowing what she would have to do this day. Mrs. Periwinkle came out onto the porch with a, "Good morning, dear."

Katharine changed again into Herbert's old work clothes, butterfly locket tucked safely inside.

She and Penelope exchanged some small talk about the beautiful, sparkling morning, and then it was time again for them both to get to work.

She tackled the mess once more in the arbor, which of course, much to her dismay, had all re-grown overnight into a brand-new, tangled mess.

Not long afterward, several horses and wagons containing tall ladders and other equipment came down the long drive in front of Mrs. Periwinkle's dilapidated old home, loaded with people. Alex and his father and older brother were amongst them.

Why, there must be at least thirty of them, Katharine thought silently to herself. She set down her tools and approached everyone, along with Penelope, who seemed quite astounded.

"Why, my goodness, what do we have here?" Penelope asked the crowd of people, who were all smiling. A kind looking, middle-aged gentleman, who introduced himself as Pastor Farley, informed Mrs. Periwinkle that they were all there to help her spruce up the place.

Mrs. Periwinkle's pruny old face reflected the joy that she felt at hearing that. With bright blue, sparkling eyes, she welcomed the entire crowd, saying, "Oh, thank you all so much. You have no idea how much this is appreciated. Thank all of you, again!"

People began climbing down off the wagons, with good humor in their eyes. They began looking around, pointing this way and that and discussing amongst themselves, as to which tasks each of them should begin to tackle. Many of them introduced themselves to Mrs. Periwinkle and Katharine.

Katharine met a nice girl her age named Megan, and her younger sister, Rosalind, too.

There were several older women in the group, and they all gathered around Penelope like a cluster of hens, chatting amicably and laughing. The women unloaded some rather large packages of food, and then the group headed inside to the kitchen, to prepare the noon-time meal.

The hustle and bustle in the yard began to grow. There were workers everywhere, holding tools and paint cans, talking and joking and moving ladders around the house. Hammers resounded as popped out nails were pounded back in, as well. Shutters were removed, gutters repaired, shingles nailed back down, and so on.

The old Victorian appeared, from Katharine's perspective down at the arbor, to be covered with an army of worker ants. She smiled silently to herself. Perhaps now, Penelope's house would be restored to its former glory, and with all of these people here to help, soon.

There was an aura of excitement surrounding the entire place, as people worked together jovially to renew the old mansion's luster. Even Mrs. Periwinkle's cats seemed to have caught the contagious exhilaration. They began scampering in and out of all the flowers constantly, swatting at each other playfully, flipping over one another acrobatically and getting into an occasional catfight. Katharine just had to laugh to herself. How she loved those cats!

She snipped away at the mess in the arbor, for the third exhausting day. She wondered silently to herself if she would ever finish up her chore here, as two bluebirds sang happily nearby at the lovely old Victorian birdhouse. A sparrow flew past them into a nearby nook in the same dwelling.

Another hummingbird hovered nearby on the trumpet vine and morning glories, while Katharine kept very still. She watched the iridescent green being flit to and fro, and then finally disappear high up into the green leaves of the tall trees.

Nearby, in the zinnia patch, several beautiful swallowtails sipped nectar from them as they enjoyed their mid-morning brunch. Katharine watched them admiringly also, while they secretly observed her back, as always.

Lunchtime came, as Mrs. Periwinkle and the other womenfolk began carrying trays of food out onto the huge, covered porch. Next, they began setting up extra chairs out there to accommodate the crowd, and brought out plates and eating utensils, and a large punch-bowl and cups.

Everyone was in good cheer, enjoying each other's company,

and the good feeling that comes with helping those in need. They all took a nice long break to relish the delicious food and camaraderie.

While eating, Katharine got to know Megan and her sister better, making friends with both in her easy way. She also got a better look at Alex's older brother Aaron, who, she realized with a bit of a blush; was quite handsome.

Aaron was quite a lot taller than his brother, and looked to be around seventeen years old. Katharine secretly wished to herself that she could get to know him better.

However, she knew that she would need to speak with Mrs. Periwinkle that afternoon. She felt it best to probably wait until after everyone else had left for the day. Now, she was feeling rather anxious and distracted, and wishing she didn't need to do what was necessary.

After the meal, all of the workers, including Katharine, headed back to resume their chores. Katharine watched, as the afternoon progressed and the true beauty of the old homestead was slowly revealed. It was a glorious sight to see. The old Victorian mansion was becoming even more beautiful than she had imagined it in her mind's eye to be!

Larry came by to demand another tummy rub later in the afternoon. Katharine was a bit tired and feeling in need of a small break, so she plopped herself down on the cool, green grass, and began rubbing his tummy.

Another hummingbird came by while she rested, to visit the nearby trumpet vine. She sat watching, next observing the swallowtails that were still clustered on the brilliant zinnias.

Laughter and clattering and hustle and bustle still abounded up by the house. Katharine felt slightly left out, sitting way out here by herself. Feeling pensive, she knew that in a couple of hours now, she would need to speak with Penelope. And, in a couple of hours, everyone would be heading home.

Katharine looked up at the arbor from her comfortable spot

with Larry on the grass. In spite of the tangled mess within, there was a bit of light shining through from the other side. She looked slightly closer.

The light appeared to have an ethereal quality to it, almost rainbow-hued. She gazed out at the rest of the sky. There, it appeared to be perfectly normal, just clear robin's egg blue, with a few puffy clouds here and there.

Forgetting all of the commotion that was going on up near the house, she gave Larry one last pat on his fuzzy head. Then, she got up onto her knees and again picked up her pruning shears. *I just have to get through this mess today*, she thought to herself with a vengeance.

What is this strange light coming through the morning glories? Since it was the afternoon, they had ceased their blooming for the day. Trumpet vines still wove their way through also, and she struggled to cut the remainder of them back.

A few big hacks and rips later, the ethereal light now seemed stronger. Mesmerized by it, she continued struggling with and hacking at the mess, which suddenly now seemed to be clearing away more rapidly than before.

The light was beginning to shine through it, and onto her face. It was almost blinding, now that she was nearly through! She could see her work finally progressing, and was energized by that. Closer she was getting, snip, snip; snip! She stood and cut away the remaining vines that wove their way through the sides and top of the arbor. Snip, snip, and snip some more!

Pulling away the last of the vines with a huge sigh, a small, rainbow-filled light suddenly penetrated the scrollwork of the arbor. It shone brightly on her face and locket, which must have fallen out of her work shirt in her eagerness and effort to clear the brush away from the arbor. Then, it increased in size, becoming full and pervading the entire arbor, and coming somewhere from the heavens above.

The nearly rust-covered arbor all at once began to brighten, as if the rainbow light was healing its rust patches. Katharine stared at it in amazement, while it seemingly was being made brand new right in front of her eyes!

Katharine watched in astonishment as the light aura brimmed over with butterfly-like creatures.

They were just like the ones that she had sometimes seen in the past when people had been horrible to her, and fairy-type beings had come to her rescue.

These were the butterflies that had filled her dreams. She had told herself before that they were probably only her very active imagination. However, there *had been* that scary incident just the day before in the woods. Perhaps she was just imagining it then, and she must be now. She had to be!

"Welcome home, Katharine!" many whispering, detached, childlike voices began calling to her, accompanied by ethereal, magnificent musical intonations, and childlike giggles. "Welcome home!"

The archway of the arbor still blocked her view of this firmament, and she slowly stepped through, completely awestruck at the spectral rainbow-colored "landscape" before her. Her very heart became enveloped with an emotion that one could only describe as love. What *was* this wondrous place that she was entering?

Now, fully through the arbor, the rainbow that had enveloped Katharine suddenly vanished. A technicolor dream of flowers covered the hills and valleys before her, much like her dreams of the past.

Nearby, the crystal-clear mountain stream from Penelope's yard still flowed, but in much greater brilliance than ever possible on what she had known as earth, for *certainly this couldn't be earth anymore!* Was she in heaven, she wondered? Had she died somehow, cutting away the vines around the arbor?

Without any warning, a large specter appeared in the sky, moving closer and closer toward her. As it approached, she realized that it was one of those butterfly-like beings that she had seen before, just like yesterday, when life was not at its best.

Closer now still, Katharine observed the rainbow-like wings

and diamond and rainbow covered crown on the head of what appeared to be the most beautiful female face that she had ever beheld.

"Welcome home, Katharine!" the specter said to her. "You are home!"

Finally, Katharine could stand her own silence no longer. "Home?" she asked the ethereal being. "Are you a fairy, or an angel, perhaps? Have I died and gone to heaven?"

The specter smiled at her, the most wondrous and radiant smile that Katharine had ever seen in her lifetime.

"No, dear Katharine," it intoned kindly. "I am only the queen of the swallowtails. And this is our dear king, my partner." she motioned as he in his magnificence too, approached Katharine.

"You have entered our ulterior world," he spoke now, "something that no other human being on earth has ever done. Many other veiled worlds also exist within your own. It is just not possible for humans to see them."

"Then, why am *I* here?" asked the astounded Katharine.

"Because we vowed to you, long, long ago, that we would care for you all of your life. You were abandoned as a baby, do you remember?"

Katharine nodded slightly; she did still vaguely remember her dreams during her fateful train ride of only days before.

"My godparents, who took me in after my adopted father Edward died, spoke of that," she told them. "I was only told that I had been found abandoned as an infant, in a small mountain town; and that no one had come forward to claim me. I was wearing this locket, with the name Katharine engraved on the back, when I was found. No one knew any more than that. Do you know? Do you know who my parents are?" she implored now.

The queen of the swallowtails smiled compassionately, and then the queen told Katharine, "I am not at liberty to yet disclose such details. However, in good time, you will discover for yourself just where you have come from. Please know in your heart that the answers lie within yourself, and your magical locket. You will not always be in the darkness, observe all the beautiful light!"

With that, the ethereal specter motioned all around her with her slender, semi-transparent hand, and then extended it towards Katharine.

"Come, join us all in flight, it is the least that we can do for you, and maybe you will discover some answers to your many questions."

Katharine hesitantly reached forward, and then clasped her hand with the translucent one of the queen.

"I don't understand." was all that she could still manage to say. Benevolently, the queen smiled again, and told her, "Here, in our alternate world, you have *wings! You can fly, Katharine!*"

Katharine looked behind her, astonished to find that indeed, she now had beautiful wings not unlike those of the queen's. Slightly different in size, shape and color, they were the most amazing things that she had ever seen.

"Come!" the queen beckoned again.

With bewilderment, Katharine let go of the queen's hand, and discovered that, true to the queen's word, her wings were now beginning to move to and fro. Then, suddenly, she was lifted off the rainbow-hued ground, now hovering slightly over the queen and king, with an astonished look on her face.

The queen chuckled slightly, with almost a tinkling, bell-like resonance, and then lifted off the ground herself effortlessly to join Katharine. "How do you like your wings, Katharine?" she asked.

"This is amazing!" was all that Katharine could manage. Now, many other butterflies had surrounded her and the king and queen, to join them in this wondrous dance of flight.

"Follow us!" they all whispered joyously, immediately following their encouragement with childlike, tinkling giggles. "Let's go!"

Off, they all raced into the sky, swooping gracefully down into huge, lush, green valleys, and up steep, glorious hills. Katharine's heart was filled with indescribable joy, as they all descended, and then lifted, over and over again. She thought it might explode, she was so completely happy. *Surely, no one on earth has ever experienced this! Certainly, I have to be dreaming!*

She soon began to join the butterflies in their laughter. She could definitely see why they were all so immeasurably happy!

On and on they flew, soaring for what seemed like hours, reaching the tops of mountains, swirling around the peaks on their delicate wings, and then plunging down with great speed into lush, verdant valleys filled with flowers and rushing streams.

Soon, dragonflies, maidenflies and bees also joined them, their iridescent wings glowing in the radiant, rainbow-hued sunlight that shone everywhere. Katharine had never known such an ultimate happiness and peace as that which she was experiencing now. She never wanted this magical flight to end!

Now, they were all racing upward again, swirling once more around a beautiful mountaintop, nearly touching the sun, and then plunging earthward yet again.

Heart nearly exploding with joy, Katharine observed a lovely Victorian gazebo, at first from a distance. Then, as they all approached it on their fragile wings, in their wondrous, dancing flight, she recognized it from her dream on the train. This was where she had been found abandoned as an infant!

There was the magnificent waterfall, tumbling out of the mountainside nearby, into the beautiful stream lined with weeping willows. The radiant rainbow that shone from within the depths of the waterfall seemed to end right in the center of the gazebo.

Drawing near, and then flying into the gazebo itself, they circled around inside. Suddenly, below them all, she could again see herself as an infant, with her young mother sitting nearby, sobbing.

Her mother had been a pretty girl; that Katharine could see. With blue eyes and hair not unlike her own, and a slim, willowy build that mirrored hers, there was a sadness in her mother's eyes that was almost unbearable to observe. There was also a familiarity about the girl that Katharine could not quite place.

All of the joy that had filled Katharine's heart only moments before now began to swiftly fade away. She was unable to tear her rapt gaze away from the pathetic scene playing out now before her.

Tears streamed down the young woman's lovely, vaguely familiar face, and an intolerable sadness now pervaded everything, including Katharine's heart. She could actually perceive the emotions that her mother had experienced when she had left her newborn daughter behind. How terribly sad. How utterly hopeless they were. She could read her mother's thoughts.

She had only been seventeen, and did not know who the father of her sweet little girl was. She had carefully hidden her pregnancy from her parents, wearing loose-fitting dresses and not coming home often, especially toward the end, when she knew she was really starting to show. Even then, however, with her slim build, her condition was not obvious.

She had visited her grandmother some miles away lower on the mountainside from time to time, but did not know her overly well because of the distance between them, and the secluded life that her parents had chosen to lead.

Her grandmother had always been kind to her, however, and one day, toward the end of her pregnancy, she had stopped by to see the loveable old woman. They had visited for a while, and had lunch, but the conversation had been somewhat strained because of the heaviness in her own heart. While she was there that day, she had stolen from her grandmother's beautiful old jewelry box a lovely, tri-colored golden locket that had the form of a butterfly on the front, and the name Katharine inscribed on the back. It had belonged to her great-grandmother.

Perhaps she would leave it around the neck of her baby, if it was a girl. Somehow, she just knew that the life inside her was female. *I can't leave you anything but this,* she thought, as she caressed her burgeoning belly a few weeks later. *I will name you Katharine, after my great-grandmother. It's the only legacy I can leave you, I'm afraid.*

Her parents had ridiculed her numerous times before she had discovered that she was pregnant. Young girls should not be so wild, and should stay away from boys, they had reprimanded her. What would your grandmother say?

She had, of course, attended the school down in the tiny town, and had been with several boys, wandering down off the mountainside on her own when she became bored with the isolation of her mountain life. However, the boys had all seemed to regard her as a hick, or someone beneath them. They did not consider a hillbilly from the mountains to be marriage material, despite her beautiful face.

She had been the town joke amongst all of the boys, a pretty little thing to be passed back and forth. First, one would tell her that he loved her, and that he would help her to become a famous actress. Then, later he would say that he didn't love her anymore, and pass her on to his friend, and so on and on her life had played out.

Desperate to get out into the huge world and be on her own, away from her life of isolation, in her innocence she had believed the first couple of boys. Later, she had simply accepted their lack of esteem for her, and adopted it as her own.

Her parents had never told her the facts of life, thinking that her relative isolation from the rest of the world would keep her innocent. She had been forced to discover them for herself, and now it was too late to go back, what was done was done.

After she had realized that she was with child, and begun to show, she had stayed away from home as much as possible, living in the woods and taking shelter under a small mountain cliff in inclement weather.

Now, where am I to go? She knew her parents would never accept this poor child. They hadn't much money, and would feel disgraced and overwhelmed if she returned with a daughter. She had no money, and no home, and she did not want to return to her lonely existence there, and the ridicule that was certain to come if she did.

And so, with tears brimming in her eyes, she leaned forward, and placed the delicate butterfly locket around her newborn daughter's neck. Clasping it, and then adjusting it slightly while her precious Katharine stirred, she then gently touched the baby's tiny cheek. The shadowy form of a Luna moth hovered briefly above the pair; then drifted away silently.

With heaviness in the young woman's heart at what she knew she had to do, she sat up, staring out at the lovely scenery before her. The morning was brightening with the first light of the crisp, clear dawn that was signaling the start of a brand new August day. *If I don't leave here before long, someone might discover me,* she anxiously worried to herself.

With tears now filling her eyes, and escaping to run down her face, she leaned forward one last time, kissed her newborn daughter, and took a deep breath of the sweet, tiny baby scent that enveloped the infant.

Then, finally standing with much remorse, she straightened her dress, wiped her eyes, and trudged off, disappearing into the trees surrounding the mountain. Following her quite closely, the elusive Luna moth also vanished into the thick forest. Katharine's mother would never return to her mountainside home, nor see her child, ever again.

Near the suspended; and now crying Katharine, the queen fluttered, with tears in her eyes also, as they circled lightly above the scene below them. The queen compassionately and gently reached out and touched Katharine's shoulder.

A tiny blue and green maidenfly alighted on the baby Katharine's nose.

The queen spoke softly to Katharine now. "This was where we came in, dear Katharine. We do know that sometime after your mother disappeared, she died in a nearby town."

"She had continued with her wild life, in her despair over her sad existence, and knowing nothing else. She took up with the wrong man, who became jealous and beat her to death late one night. Your mother is gone, dear girl. You will never know her. We are so very sorry."

"So why have you shown me all of this! What purpose could it possibly serve now?" Katharine demanded angrily, tears streaming down her face. The joy that had filled her heart previously was now totally gone, and replaced by dark, lonely desolation.

"Because, dear Katharine," the queen said sympathetically, "all of your life, there was a void in your heart. We knew this. You could not envision your parents, and did not know if they had even wanted you at all. Well, now you know the truth behind it all, sweet girl, and that is that they were simply too young to be able to care for you properly."

"Your father never even knew you existed. Your mother never knew for sure who he was. But she did love you, dear Katharine, and we wanted you to see that! She loved you enough to leave you for someone who could love you even more than she did, and care for you properly. And you have had a good life, Katharine, much better than what you would have known had she kept you and raised you herself!"

"However, there are still secrets that we may not reveal, that you will discover on your own. Only remember that there is a treasure at the end of each rainbow, and that you are beginning to discover all of that now."

Katharine was not at all happy about what she had just witnessed, and her heart was still terribly burdened with the weight of what her mother had gone through.

However, she just had to ask one final question of the queen. "What was that awful Luna moth yesterday? I believe that I have seen her on and off throughout my lifetime. In fact, she was in the visions that you just showed to me. Remember? Was she one of you? It felt to me as though she too, had powers of her own, although I do not believe that they could ever be used for good."

The queen acknowledged what Katharine was trying to ask with a kind nod and smile, and allowed her to continue.

"What I have experienced with you today, although terribly painful, was obviously for the greater good," Katharine went on, "as now many of my heart's questions have been answered. But, my experience yesterday was terribly horrible and frightening!"

"Yes, dear Katharine, we know. That was the Dark Luna Moth of Lost Souls. We do not associate with her. She knows when hearts are heavy and uses that to her advantage. Her singletary mission is to seek out and snare as many souls as possible for the horrible Toad of Doom. He escorts tormented, unforgiving souls to the abyss, one place we all wish to stay away from!"

"Will I see her again?" Katharine asked, still persistent.

"Not, likely, my dear. She exists only where souls cannot forgive. She lies in wait, hoping to detect hate and resentment. You, my dear, have always had a kind, forgiving heart. She simply misread your true feelings and motives yesterday afternoon when she happened by."

The lovely butterfly queen continued, telling Katharine, "We will help protect you from her always, as long as you maintain a kind, loving, and forgiving heart. It's that easy!"

Her heart and mind eased somewhat, Katharine's soul felt tremendously unburdened now, and greatly relieved.

The queen and king smiled benevolently at her one last time, and finally pronounced, "It is time to go back to the garden arbor now, dear Katharine. Time to go back, beyond the garden arbor. Time to go back... and once again, welcome home!"

The vision before Katharine then began to turn, slowly at first, and then with increasing speed, until she ultimately became so dizzy that she began to pass out.

Ethereal beings flew around her in the brilliant but dizzying, rainbow-colored swirl, calling out farewells to her, telling her that all would be well; and repeatedly welcoming her home.

Eventually, the swirl began to fade, deepening at first in color, and then the colors dimmed to gray, and lastly, black.

The blackness enveloped Katharine, seeping into her raw,

enlightened soul and ultimately causing her to descend into a soundless, lightless, but mercifully peace-filled sleep. The harmony of it filled her heart, and enveloped her with love.

Great-Grandmother

Katharine awoke at the foot of the arbor, dazed, not know-ing who or where she was for a moment. Lying in the soft green grass, with her wavy blond hair fanned out behind her, her blue eyes gazed unseeingly at first up at an equally blue sky filled with soft, puffy clouds. *That one is shaped like a butterfly,* she mused to herself in her distracted state.

Her locket on its long gold chain still hung outside the collar of Herbert's work shirt, laying on her chest upright but slightly askew with the tri-color gold butterfly design in full view. She was unaware of it.

"Mrreow!" Larry the cat announced his presence, trilling as if telling her to awaken, and rubbing against her shoulder and on the side of her head. "Meow!"

Katharine turned her head sideways to gaze at the silly cat, and then saw Penelope rushing toward her as fast as her old, spindly legs would carry her.

"My God, Katharine; what happened? Did you pass out?" Penelope implored, worry etching the deep lines that already adorned her ancient face even further.

Katharine, still slightly dazed, continued to lie there as Penelope approached.

"My dear, can you hear me? Are you all right?" Penelope repeated.

Katharine continued to lay there, mind still murky. Finally, struggling to push herself up, she rubbed her bewildered eyes and said hesitantly to Penelope, "Yes Penelope, I believe I am okay. I'm not quite sure what happened. I think maybe I just fell asleep or something. I had the most fantastic, colorful dream just now!"

Katharine pushed herself up into a sitting position; then stood fully, stretching slightly and rubbing her eyes again. By now, a few other helpers that had been working near the house had joined Mrs. Periwinkle, looking quizzical and slightly concerned, themselves.

Penelope peered at her through her coke-bottle lenses with wizened eyes, examining Katharine's face to ascertain that the girl was indeed all right. Assured now that Katharine was just fine, a look of relief passed over her wrinkled old face. However, it quickly changed to a look of pure disapproval. The ancient mouth puckered into wrinkled censure, along with the corrugated eyes.

"Where did you get that?" she pointed at the butterfly locket that graced Katharine's neck, with obvious displeasure written all over her face.

Katharine, still in a bit of a stupor from the "dream" that she had just awakened from, didn't understand at first. She then looked down to the source of Penelope's disparagement, and then up again at the old woman's puckered, angry face.

"Why, this is my locket! I've had it all my life. When I was abandoned as an infant, it was found on my neck. My adopted father told me all about it. This is how I got my name. Why?" she asked Penelope.

Penelope did not seem to be comforted in the least. "That was my mother's! It was hers when she was a baby!" she exclaimed sternly to the bewildered girl. "It's been missing for quite a number of years, but I always thought that I'd probably misplaced it somewhere around the house, and that some day I'd come across it again! Where did you find it, and why did you steal it from me?"

"B- but Mrs. Periwinkle, I'm telling you the truth! It's always been mine. Are you sure you didn't just own a similar one?" Katharine asked with increasing consternation, as more and more helpers from the church began approaching to see what the sudden commotion was all about.

Katharine was beginning to feel more than a little embarrassed at all of this, and wondered how she must appear to all of her new-found friends. She subconsciously hoped that they would not think she was guilty of anything, like Penelope obviously did at the moment.

"As I said, young lady, that was my mother's, and I can prove it! The name "Katharine" is inscribed on the back!" Mrs. Periwinkle retorted, still quite angry. "Take that locket off and let me look at it!" she demanded.

Katharine complied, still flustered at this new turn of events, unhooking the clasp in the back and plopping the necklace into Mrs. Periwinkle's creased, gnarled, and outstretched hand.

Penelope turned it over, examined the back side, and proclaimed, "I knew it!" while holding the locket aloft for everyone in her presence to see. "This was my mother's!" she again affirmed.

More and more helpers had by now approached, Pastor Farley being one of them. He was quiet at first; just observing their conversation, and then he became curious. He stepped forward, toward the testy Mrs. Periwinkle, and asked to see the necklace himself. She handed her long-lost treasure to him rather reluctantly, but none the same.

Holding it in his hand, and then turning it over, his

expression changed from one of curiosity to one of complete bewilderment!

Astonished, he looked at Katharine and finally said, "My God, I never thought that I would see you again! Dear Lord, how you've grown up, and into such a beautiful young lady!"

Pastor Farley looked back at Mrs. Periwinkle, and, still amazed, said to her, "Ma'am, I believe there might be a little bit of a misunderstanding here! This young lady is the same Katharine that we found abandoned down by the town in the gazebo, what—" he paused to consider for a moment; then looked back at the overwhelmed Katharine, "some fourteen or fifteen years ago?" he asked her. "This is the locket that she was wearing when we found her, and this locket is the reason she was named 'Katharine'."

Mrs. Periwinkle, still not entirely convinced, struggled to take all of this new information in. She held her lips firmly pruned together, remaining doubtful.

Finally, she un-puckered them. "Well, Pastor Farley, that is all well and good, but how does that explain how this locket that belonged to my mother suddenly ended up in a baby's possession?"

Now, Katharine, who was finally beginning to understand just what all of this was about, finally spoke. The new dawn of realization had finally begun to unfold.

"Mrs. Periwinkle… you said you had a granddaughter named Cassandra that had disappeared years ago, remember? You showed me her photograph and said that there had been rumors that she had been pregnant when she had disappeared! Remember? You told me that it had been very upsetting for you to never know what had happened to her! *Do you remember?*"

The beginning of understanding also began to spread across the wizened old face. Penelope said nothing for a few moments, taking it all in, and adding everything up in her mind to see if it made sense. She looked from Katharine to Pastor Farley and then back to Katharine again.

Finally, she spoke, the beginning words coming out in a bit

of a croak, "My dear…this means that you are my great-grand-daughter!" Wrinkly old hands cupped the ancient, puckered face. *"You are my great-granddaughter!"*

Suddenly, Penelope's distressed expression turned into one of pure, unadulterated joy. "Dearie, you are my great-granddaughter!" she exclaimed again. "You know, there were so many times that you reminded me of someone these past few days, but I never could quite figure out why! Why, now that I know the truth, I can't believe that I couldn't see it all along! Look at your eyes! They are almost exact copies of my own, only with many, many years less wear and tear, and still unwrinkled! *You are my great-granddaughter!"* Penelope laughed out loud, she was so surprised. She handed the antique locket back to Katharine in joy.

By now, everyone in the small crowd was looking on curiously and discussing the marvelous turn of events between themselves, also. There were a couple of people there that actually remembered that fateful day, along with Pastor Farley, who still could not believe what had just happened.

Finally, the reverend proclaimed to all that would listen, "Everyone, I think we have all done enough here for the day! This grand old place is beginning to recapture its former splendor. I think we should call it a day, and let Mrs. Periwinkle and her newly-found great-granddaughter have the rest of this lovely day to themselves!"

Everyone agreed, while he strode toward first the fully astonished Mrs. Periwinkle, and then the amazed Katharine, and gave them both great big hugs; and firm congratulations on their new discovery.

The men began stacking ladders and other equipment into neat piles until the next day, when they would all return after the Sunday church service and resume their refurbishing of the Periwinkle place.

Finally, the crowd of people began to depart.

Pastor Farley remained behind for a few moments after most of the other workers, and the first team of horses with their wagon, had ventured on down the long, winding drive. He approached Katharine and Penelope, wished them well again, and said that he would be on his way now also.

"You know," he said wistfully in final departing words to Katharine, "if I had been married at the time that you were discovered, I would have taken you in myself. As it so happened, however, I was just out of seminary school and had only been here a few months when you were born."

"Several years later, I met and married a lovely woman, my wife, Emily. We now have two young children of our own, a son that's seven, and a daughter that's five. I'm so happy to be able to see what a beautiful young woman you've grown up to be. I never forgot about you, not even after all of these years! You two enjoy getting to really know each other now! We'll see you both tomorrow!"

And, with that, Pastor Farley climbed up onto the remaining wagon, and soon the huge wagon wheels began to roll. The teenage girl and her great-grandmother watched the remainder of the group leave. They waved goodbye, with their free arms extended around each other, watching as the wagon disappeared around the bend of the long drive that led toward the mountain path.

Then, the pair gazed anew at each other with the anticipation of what their lives would now hold for them in the future, and smiled joyously.

Getting Acquainted

Penelope and Katharine went inside, and once again examined the old photographs on the mantle in the parlor together. Comparing similarities and differences, too, the young girl and the older woman both had to admit that there were striking similarities between not only Katharine and Cassandra, but many other family members as well.

Later, sitting in Mrs. Periwinkle's kitchen, enjoying their dinner, both Katharine and Penelope gloried in the new developments of the day. Not only was Penelope absolutely thrilled at all of the help that everyone had given her all day, but now, she had a newly discovered great-granddaughter besides to add to the several other great-grandchildren that she already had!

Finally, as they were winding up their meal, Katharine told Penelope the truth about herself. It had all fallen into place for her.

"There's something I think you should know." she told Penelope. "The only reason that I'm here is that I got lost on a school field trip into the city. My teachers and classmates are probably worried sick about me, not knowing my whereabouts or anything. I really should try to contact them."

Penelope listened with a concerned expression, as Katharine went over the events that had led up to her coming to stay there.

"Well, child, we can try to contact your school, then. That would probably be the best place for us to start. And, if we don't have any luck with that, we will have to contact the police department in the city. We must wait until tomorrow, though, as I have no telephone service up here on the mountainside. Perhaps, some kind soul that comes to help tomorrow would be good enough to give us a wagon ride into town so we can make a call from the mercantile."

Katharine agreed that doing so would be fine, and then Penelope asked her, "Where have you been staying then, dear? Certainly you don't know anyone down in the town!"

Katharine blushed slightly, and then told Penelope that she had been living in the old shed for the past four days.

"What?" Penelope said, rather shocked. "Why, that shed hasn't been used for years! It must be filthy and filled with all sorts of little crawling creatures!"

"Well, yes ma'am, it *was* slightly dirty," Katharine agreed, "but there was an old battered broom in there that served just fine for sweeping it out, and it cleaned all the cobwebs out pretty good too."

Penelope still couldn't get over this, asking Katharine, "Well dear, why didn't you say something sooner?"

"I was going to," was Katharine's reply, "but I became filled with such a sense of peace when I was at your place here, a sense of homecoming really, and now I know why! Frankly, I didn't really *want* to leave. I guess I should have let my teachers and classmates know a little sooner, though. They are probably all quite upset and worried by now!"

Penelope agreed with her, again affirming that in the morning they would take care of that problem together. "So dear, what do you plan to do now?" she asked.

"Well," Katharine told her, "the school year is almost over, and I do miss my classmates somewhat. Also, I was getting straight A's, and I don't want to ruin my perfect grades."

"Ahh, you're a bright one, then?" asked Penelope. "You know, my grandson Patrick was always extremely smart too. In fact, he is vice-president of the bank down in our town! Some people think that just because we were born and raised up here in the mountains, that we are not very bright, but they've got that all wrong, I'll tell you!" Katharine chuckled slightly at this.

"So dear, where have you been all of these years? Has life treated you kindly in the interim?" Penelope inquired of her.

Katharine proceeded to tell Penelope the story of her life from the beginning, leaving out very little. Her dreams from her ride on the train and everything that the butterflies had shown to her had completely refreshed her memory, and filled in some blanks.

Mrs. Periwinkle winced slightly at Katharine's tales of the abhorrent Constance, and Edward's subsequent death, and also at the stories of Ingrid's horrid behavior toward her during most of her school years.

Katharine wasn't sure if she should tell Penelope about the elusive magical butterflies or not, thinking that perhaps her great-grandmother would think that she was fabricating. Finally, however, she went ahead and told her about them anyway.

Penelope sat still in her chair, and listened to Katharine with interest. Katharine told her of how butterflies had always been there to help her in any time of need, and that she felt that they were responsible for sending her into a deep sleep and guiding her to this tiny town on the train.

Penelope then finally interrupted her. To Katharine's surprise, she said, "Well, you know dear, although I have never experienced anything magical about them, for much of my life I have felt a definite closeness to them, too. In fact, now that I really think about it, much of it seemed to start about the time my dear granddaughter, or your mother, Cassie, disappeared. I would see them in my garden, and they would give me such a sense of peace. Do you realize that your last name is really Meriweather?"

"Anyway, I remember that when I slept, I dreamt quite often about this house, the yard, and all its butterflies, and someone that always eluded me; that I could never quite see," Penelope added.

Continuing, she also said, "In those dreams, I would wander about on this lovely old place and could detect someone in the distance. But no matter how far I walked, or for how long, on my tired old legs, I could never quite make them out! I thought perhaps it was Cassie!"

Katharine sat, looking in astonishment at Penelope. So, the butterflies had also tried to contact Penelope in an attempt to convey their message to her about Katharine's existence!

"I don't believe this! Yes," she replied, hesitantly at first, "many nights I would have almost the identical dream! I would be running through butterfly and flower-filled fields, and always, there were two people in the distance, presumably my parents, but I could never reach *them* either. Maybe those two people were my mother and you! You know," Katharine sighed, "I always felt so different from all of the other kids. They all had at least one parent and knew who their parents were, and where they had come from."

"Well, child," Penelope returned kindly, "now you know who your mother was, and you have found me! Perhaps we should just be joyful and grateful for that."

"Yes." Katharine agreed, and then she surprised her great-grandmother by going on further. "I do know from my dreams that even my mother did not know who my father was, and that she died a couple of years after giving birth to me, at the hands of an abusive man whom she was living with at the time."

Penelope seemed surprised to hear this, asking Katharine how she could know so many details for sure.

"Because, Penelope, right before you found me lying in front of the garden arbor, the butterflies, they brought me beyond it, into their own world. I don't know if I dreamed it, or if it actually happened, but I went with them on a wondrous flight, up and down and throughout the mountains. It seemed to last for hours."

"It was the most spectacular, beautiful thing that has happened to me in my entire lifetime. Then, they took me to the gazebo that your Pastor Farley spoke about. There, they showed me everything that happened in the early morning hours of the day that I was born, before I was discovered."

"The flight with the butterflies was so joyous and wondrously uplifting. Yet, when they showed me how it had been there in the gazebo with my mother, my heart became so saddened and depressed, that I felt that I would die. They actually took me into a window of her heart, if you will, and I was able to feel everything that *she* had felt at that particular moment in her life. It was horrible, knowing fully the depth of her sadness and despair about her life. I also know that she is the one that took your locket. She left it with me, so that I would at least have a name."

"Oh, dear, dear, the poor misguided child! Such a waste of what had been such a promising life! She wanted to be a famous actress, you know." Penelope reflected, with a wistful look in her eyes.

"Yes, I know." was Katharine's solemn reply. Penelope seemed to some extent bewildered to find that Katharine already knew that, as well, but said nothing.

Now, Katharine reached behind her neck, unclasped her beloved piece of jewelry that had been with her for her entire life, and handed it to her great-grandmother. "I do believe this belongs to you."

"Oh, Katharine," Penelope protested, "you really should keep this. It has been with you all of your life, it is a part of you now!"

"No, great-grandma, it was your mother's, and my great-great grandmother's, and I wish to return it to you."

Penelope didn't know for sure what to say to Katharine. She didn't feel right about keeping the locket now, after all that the dear girl had been through, but decided it was best perhaps just to let things be for the moment. Things had come full circle for both of them, in their own way.

Penelope glanced at the small, teapot-shaped clock hanging on the soffet over the homey kitchen sink. "Well, dear, I just realized that it is after midnight! Perhaps we should consider getting some sleep. After all, all of our wonderful helpers are due to arrive bright and early again in the morning!"

Katharine glanced up at the clock then, too. The time was nearly twelve-twenty. She agreed with her great-grandmother, saying that she should be on her way.

"What do you mean, young lady?!" Penelope challenged in a feisty voice that reminded Katharine of the morning that they had met just days earlier, "You'll do no such thing! You are my family, and you will stay here, from now on, at least until you return to school, and whenever you come to visit me in the future! Tomorrow morning, if you wish, you can go gather your things from the shed and bring them up here! I'm certain that by now, you have dirty laundry that needs taking care of and such!"

"Well, yes ma'am; that I do. I'll help you take care of it in the morning. Oh, it'll be so nice to spend the night in a "real" bed!" Katharine agreed. Penelope then smiled warmly at her, shook her head, and led her upstairs to a wonderful large bedroom with sunny, yellow wallpaper embellished with tiny pink, green and white roses, and a large white canopy bed in the middle. Though the room was showing its age in a dated sort of way, it was still quite lovely.

"Oh, this room is beautiful!" Katharine exclaimed.

"Well dear, for as long as you need to stay here, it is yours!" her great-grandmother told her. "You know, this was our daughter's room—your grandmother's, by the way. It belonged to our darling daughter Helen!"

Penelope handed her an old, worn-looking nightgown from a dresser drawer, and then began turning down the beautiful yellow and white quilt that covered the luscious down-filled mattress and pillows. Katharine eagerly climbed in as soon as she was changed.

"Oh, this is the most *wonderful* bed I've ever been in my life, it is so very soft!" she exclaimed. "Thank you, Great-grandma!"

Penelope smiled at her benevolently. "Please dear, none of that, the thanks are all mine! After all that you have done for me these last few days, it's the very least that I can do for you!"

Katharine beamed at Penelope tiredly, eyes already growing heavy. "Well then, I will see you in the morning, Great-grandmother!"

Penelope smiled back, and then with one last "Goodnight, child." she went out the door of the bedroom and closed it gently.

Katharine's last thought seconds later as she drifted off to sleep was gratefulness at knowing, finally, after all these years where she had come from, and who she now belonged to.

And, beyond the garden arbor, the butterflies smiled in their dwelling of resplendent glory, joyous in the knowledge that all of Katharine's questions had at last been completely answered for her.

Former Glory Restored

Morning came, clear and bright and with a cock-a-doodle-doo as always, but closer and more loudly than before. Her new bedroom and late grandmother's bedroom was not far from the chicken coop. But that didn't matter to Katharine, as she lay snuggled in her soft, comfy bed in the bright yellow bedroom in the cool of the morning, listening to the rooster crow again and again.

Her good old alarm clock; was he, she thought as she smiled to herself again, stretching and yawning finally. What a wonderful day this was going to be, she reflected! What a wonderful life this would be from now on! She had found her great-grandmother! However, she was beginning to feel more than slight trepidation about the prospect of having to return to her old life once again.

After enjoying the delicious breakfast of eggs, bacon, and pancakes that Penelope had prepared for the both of them, they both headed outside onto the wonderful, old huge porch, to wait for their helpers to show up for the day. Since it was Sunday morning, they were all to arrive slightly later today, to allow for a short church service beforehand.

"Well, child, thanks to all of the helpers that my son has helped organize to get this old place in order, it should be in tip-top shape in no time flat! I am so very grateful, not only to him, but to all of those dear church people that gave so generously of their time. I will have to find some way to thank them all!" Penelope contemplated, plucking slightly at the long whiskers on her gnarled old chin.

Katharine smiled. She too was looking forward, as Penelope was, to seeing the finished result of everyone's hard work, knowing that the place would be breathtaking when it was finished! She could already picture all of it in her mind.

It wasn't long before the horses and wagons made their way up the winding drive, loaded with even more folks than the day before. Seems word had gotten around that the tiny infant that had been discovered at the gazebo more than fourteen years before, was back in the area. Many of the older men and women, remembering that exciting, slightly chaotic day from all those years before, had wanted to see it all for themselves.

Katharine was introduced to many new friendly folks from the village, and felt happy that so many had remembered the first few days of her life.

Even Penelope's son Patrick, and his wife Berta, had come along. Since it was Sunday, Patrick had no duties to worry about at the bank. They both felt that it would be the Lord's work to join in the sprucing up of his dear old grandmother's home anyway.

Both he and his wife were astonished at Katharine's resemblance to Patrick's younger sister, and were surprised that his grandmother had not noticed the similarity sooner.

Penelope spoke to them briefly about the urgency of letting Katharine's school know where she was, and Patrick agreed to take both of them down into the town and help Katharine notify the people in charge of the Catholic Academy.

Berta remained behind in the hustle and bustle of fixing up Penelope Periwinkle's place. Ladders were already being set up, and hammers were loudly and busily banging away when the small group headed away on the wagon down toward the town.

Slow and steadily, the horses traveled downward, with Katharine again recalling the details of the night that she had arrived here. Past the little shed they rolled, while Katharine began to worry with some trepidation about what would happen to her next.

Through the mountainside forest the wagon slowly wove its way, while birds chirped in the daylight and butterflies flitted past. Finally, the trees began to thin down, and the ground started to level out, and the horses were able to pick up their pace somewhat.

Approaching the little town, Katharine was entranced by the charming old houses and quaint town square, and old-fashioned-looking white church with steeple. There was the small schoolhouse at one end of the square. The town seemed to be such a quiet place, but, after all, many of the residents were up at Penelope's for the moment fixing up the old house. However, Katharine was sure that this appeared to be a wonderful, quaint place to live.

Patrick took Katharine and Penelope to his lovely home. He had telephone service there, as did most of the other small town dwellers. It had been quite some time since Penelope had visited her grandson's home, and she was happy to let him help her creaky old bones down off the wagon so that she could stretch her wobbly legs for a while and look around.

Patrick began his assistance by asking Katharine what the name of her school was, and in what town, and then phoned the operator and asked her to please help him locate the Catholic school.

After several minutes, he was speaking with the headmistress, who was absolutely thrilled to hear from him, and know finally that Katharine was safe. He let the woman also know that Katharine had turned out to be a long-lost family member.

She told him that she would contact the two teachers that had remained behind at their field trip destination after the rest of the group had returned. She also said that she would be more than happy to contact the police department that had been notified, when it had been discovered that Katharine was missing.

Once that business had been taken care of, the headmistress asked to speak with Katharine for a moment.

"Hello?" Katharine spoke hesitantly into the phone after Uncle Patrick handed it to her.

"Yes, dear," the kind woman said. "We are so *very* relieved here to finally know of your whereabouts! I just wanted you to know that after your absence was discovered, that the students and teachers stayed in the city for the full, scheduled length of the field trip, hoping that you would find your way back to them. They were afraid that if they left, you would not know where your group was. And, the police department was looking for you too! We also informed your legal guardians that you were missing."

Katharine was starting to become worried now. She should have told someone sooner that she was lost! George and Madelyn were most likely heartsick by now! She was sure that everyone had been very anxious in her absence. "I'm sorry, ma'am," she replied now. "I fell asleep on the train, and by the time I discovered that I was lost, it was already becoming dark. Then, there were no telephones where I finally ended up at. I was just so relieved to find a place to stay where I felt safe for the moment," Katharine told the woman.

"Well, yes, dear, and we understand now that you have found your long lost family! We are all very happy for you here, and just relieved to finally know that you have been found safe and sound!"

"However, you do know that the school term is nearly completed, don't you?" the headmistress added. "You really should come back here for the last few weeks, and finish up with your studies, so that you can take your end-of-the-year finals."

"Yes, ma'am, I'll see what these kind people here can do to see that I return. I'll make sure that I'm back at school within a couple of days, then." After saying their goodbyes, Katharine hung up the phone, and looked up sadly at Mrs. Periwinkle.

"Don't worry, dear. As soon as your schooling is finished up you can come directly back here! I'm sure Patrick here will help you see to all the details." Penelope reassured her.

Patrick agreed, saying that tomorrow he would make arrangements for her to ride the train back to the town where her school was, and have someone from the school there to meet her at the train station when she arrived.

Katharine also called George and Madelyn's home to let them know that she was safe. They were *so* glad to hear from her. They had just been at their wit's end, and had felt powerless on their end to do anything to help find her!

Katharine apologized to them too, and explained the entire situation to them also.

On the arduous ride back up the mountainside, Katharine worried that she was going to lose everything that she had just discovered. She was very quiet, and Penelope noticed, and put an old, arthritic arm around the girl to comfort her.

Arriving at the old, decrepit shed, Patrick stopped the wagon momentarily so that Katharine could retrieve all of her things. Penelope just smiled and shook her head in incredulity at her grandson. How that girl could spend several nights in that old moth-eaten place was beyond her!

Katharine returned soon, large suitcase and small bags in hand, looking quite sad. Another sad goodbye, at least for now. As the wagon moved away, she felt a tiny twinge of sadness, for certainly she would never sleep in "her" little shed again!

Approaching the Periwinkle place, Katharine's heart lightened a little as she noticed with some delight that a couple of boys were helping Alex put the finishing touches on the ancient, wrought-iron gate. Sure enough, the finished result was just what she had pictured in her mind, with periwinkle blue flowers connected by dark green vines covering the entire thing, and the name "Periwinkle" in the center of the top painted that appropriate blue also.

Penelope was just thrilled to see the new beauty of the gate. Before this day, she hadn't been to the end of her drive for quite some time, but remembered well the former dilapidated condition that it had been in.

All three of them admired the house from a distance as they approached it. The elegant old painted-lady was beginning to look as if it had returned to its former glory. Fresh paint and new colors replaced the old, tired finish, and shutters were being returned to their locations after new, vivid coats of paint also.

The heaviness in Katharine's heart faded even more now, at the jovial excitement that was present everywhere here. It was reflected on the faces of all of the helpers, and even the wildlife and animals that resided in this beautiful place seemed to find the atmosphere contagious, as well.

The three cats were chasing each other around the yard, in enthusiasm. Birds flew here and there, singing away in the glory of the morning.

Katharine again became enveloped by the joyousness of it too. As she was helped down off the wagon, she glanced up again at the lovely old homestead. What a glorious place this was turning out to be!

And, the beautiful gardens that she and Penelope had worked fastidiously on all week long were even more gorgeous, now that flowers and plants had been thinned out, all of the weeds had been removed, and room had been made for new flowers to thrive.

Women came out onto the porch, welcoming their return, some holding dishtowels and plates while they chatted away.

They informed Penelope with some delight that they had been busy scrubbing the inside of the old house down from top to bottom. Penelope had to smile; and just shook her head, thanking them for all of their kindness.

Eventually, lunch was served after the cluster of women had hauled large trays piled high with food out onto the porch for everyone's enjoyment. Katharine sat with Megan and her sister, Rosalind, while they enjoyed the beautiful day and the delicious food.

Megan finally asked Katharine about the events of the day before, when Mrs. Periwinkle had found her lying in front of the garden arbor passed out. "So, what happened, Katharine? Did the heat bother you?"

"No," Katharine told her, "I only was resting for a bit."

Megan looked at her doubtfully. "Well, Mrs. Periwinkle seemed awfully concerned, and then she sounded mad after a bit, asking you about the locket you wore."

"Yes, well it seemed we had a bit of a misunderstanding about that, but I have returned it to her now," Katharine replied. An idea began to form in Katharine's head. Perhaps if she took Megan and Rosalind down to the arbor, she would be able to let them glimpse for themselves the magical paradise beyond.

When they had finished eating, she and the two girls made their way down to the arbor. To Katharine's dismay, she discovered that yet again, there was a tangle of weeds and vines to contend with. She did notice, however, that the arbor itself still appeared as if it had just received a fresh coat of paint!

She asked the girls to help her once more clear away the mess, promising that when they finished, that she would show them what lay beyond.

Into the afternoon the girls worked, chatting about girl stuff and laughing while they snipped and pulled away at the weedy, tangled mess. While fighting with the interwoven confusion, the older two girls delved into their newfound interests in the opposite sex. Having other people to help with her struggle with the disorganized jumble for once made it go much faster, and their conversation was lively and enjoyable.

Katharine pointed out Aaron to Megan, saying that she found him to be quite good-looking. After Megan observed him from afar, high up on his ladder replacing a shutter, she had to agree with Katharine that he *was* becoming very handsome, and strong and muscular too. She had never really paid any attention to him before, even though they had grown up together. "Maybe you can get him to notice *you*, Katharine," she encouraged slightly.

Katharine only smiled shyly at that, she had caught his glance several times the past two days. When that had happened, she had experienced a thrill in her pounding heart. She was quite sure that he *had* already noticed her.

Finally, the mass of weeds and vines had been cleared away again, however, not once had Katharine seen the ethereal light shining through while they worked. Feeling vaguely worried, she took their hands, and they ventured on through.

The landscape was gorgeous, of course, with wildflowers and long grasses and beautiful trees dotting it here and there. And there was the frigid, bubbling mountain creek that ran through the Periwinkle place, joining with another wider creek from somewhere else further up the mountain. The creek was much larger where it joined than in Mrs. Periwinkle's yard, and the water was sparkling and dancing joyously in the afternoon light. Katharine's two friends seemed impressed with the delightful scene anyway, and for the time being she kept her thoughts to herself. The other girls ran happily toward the creek. Once there, they sat down on boulders near the water's edge in the cool shade of a crooked willow tree, slipping off their shoes so that they could dip their toes in the merrily churning, bubbling water.

Katharine lagged behind slightly, wondering if the secret world that she had shared with the butterflies was now closed away to her forever. Perhaps it was. After all, no mysteries about her life remained to be discovered now.

She underwent a slight feeling of abandonment, wondering if she would ever experience the miraculous, elusive world that lay beyond the garden arbor again.

She joined the girls at the creek for a time, and took part in their happy chatter about schoolmates that Katharine had yet to meet, and again about boys, always boys. They watched frogs jumping about from rock to rock, and dragonflies and maiden-flies skitter about also.

Finally, feeling refreshed, they headed back to resume their various jobs up by the house. The two girls thanked Katharine for showing them the cheerful, cool creek.

The work at the beautiful old house was winding up for the weekend, and as they approached it they all oohed and aahed about how different it looked in comparison to how it had just been the very day before.

Katharine was thrilled to see for herself just how lovely the old place was again, returned to its full, resplendent glory of former years. It was almost as if the old homestead had a new life of its own to look forward to, just as she did! Everything was brand new, and on the brink of a fresh, new start.

That didn't do much to ease Katharine's sadness about returning to her former life, however. She was happy with what she had found here, and did not want to leave.

She waved goodbye after dinner while the wagons disappeared around the bend, loaded with all the kind folks from the town below. With heaviness again returning to her heart, she knew that the next weekend when they all returned to finish up, that she would not be there.

Sorrow filled her heart at knowing this. She had *so* wanted to be here to help complete the job that she had begun.

Penelope noted the wistfulness in the girl's eyes, and doddered up to her and pulled her close. "It will only be for a few weeks, dear Katharine, you'll be surprised how quickly the time will pass!" she reassured her kindly.

Katharine nodded gloomily, and went inside with Penelope. In the morning, her uncle would be arranging for her safe transport back to school. She only had perhaps a day or so before she would have to return. Oh, how badly she just wanted to stay here!

All Over Too Soon

Kind old Mrs. Periwinkle had arranged for Megan and Rosalind to return the following morning so that Katharine would have girls her own age to do things with. Katharine was surprised, but grateful when they showed up.

Katharine led them all around the place, showing them all the secret places in the yard that she had discovered during her brief stay there. She pointed them out to her friends now. There was the bluebird's nest, here was where the cats loved to hide, and over here was a chrysalis of what would soon become a butterfly.

The girls all watched with silence and utter delight, as a diminutive hummingbird sipped nectar delicately from bright orange, bell-shaped flowers on the trumpet vines, its wings fluttering with such speed that they were nearly invisible.

They wandered down to the old arbor, which, as always before, was covered anew in a thicket of weeds. Katharine, by now more than slightly frustrated at having to clear all of that out of there each and every day, expressed her aggravation to the other two girls. They giggled and offered to help her clear it out of there again. They reminded her that, after all, when they were finished they could go dip their toes in the crystal-clear water of the gurgling creek.

The girls were enchanted when the iridescent hummingbird came by again to partake of the nectar of the trumpet vine. They all stood very still so as not to alarm it, wanting to watch it for as long as it remained.

After cutting through the remainder of the weeds for what seemed like the umpteenth time to poor Katharine, they joyously all ran through the arbor, and toward the glistening water of the creek.

Sitting and chatting with the other girls, Katharine wistfully remembered to herself the quick, chilly baths she had taken in there just down the hill a short ways for several days only last week.

If only she could return to last week, then she wouldn't have to be leaving for school just yet. Megan noticed that Katharine was rather quiet, and asked her if she didn't want to go back to school.

Katharine told her then that she didn't want to leave yet. It seemed as if she had just gotten there, and she was happy here now, with them, her friends, and her brand-new great-grandmother, and aunt and uncle. She finally had family that she could truly call her own now.

The entire time they sat conversing, no ethereal lights appeared, and only ordinary butterflies fluttered past them occasionally. Katharine could not understand why she could not see the magical butterfly kingdom again. She remembered, however, that the queen swallowtail had told her on that glorious trip that no other human had ever been allowed entry into their glorious sanctuary before.

Perhaps then, she would never again visit that elusive place, she mused silently in her mind.

The two sisters left for their home in the late afternoon, and the Periwinkle place seemed unusually quiet after all of the commotion and kind, helpful people of the last few days.

Uncle Patrick showed up shortly afterward to announce that he had taken care of all the arrangements for Katharine's return trip to her school, and that her train ticket was for early tomorrow morning. Katharine was saddened to hear that, but tried not to let on to Penelope or her uncle how she felt.

Shortly before her and Penelope's supper, Katharine wandered down to the arbor one last time before she would have to return to finish her year of schooling. There were some new tangled vines within it, but she quickly cut them away, wanting to venture through just one last time on her own. Perhaps the arbor had not revealed its magic because of the other two girls, and would open the elusive doors to it for her again if she were on her own.

However, it was not to be.

The scene on the mountainside as the sun began its evening descent was breathtaking, with everything tinted a golden glow from the setting sun. Katharine wandered down to the fork in the creek where it widened up, and stood enjoying the pleasant gurgling sounds that emanated from it. She sat on a large rock next to the water, watching the amber hue from the setting sun reflect off of it as well.

Still, she felt tremendous despair, as if the entire world were suddenly deserting her. Not only would she leave there in the morning and not be back for several weeks, but now, the ethereal butterflies were withholding themselves from her presence also.

A short time later, Katharine and Penelope enjoyed their last evening meal together, as the sun began to fall slowly over the mountainside. When they had finished eating the delicious meal that Penelope had prepared, she handed Katharine a small, wrapped package.

"I want you to have this, dear." she told Katharine. Katharine opened it and discovered that it was her beloved butterfly locket.

"My mother passed away many years ago, and it suits you better than it does me now anyway." Penelope told her kindly. "*Your* name is also Katharine, after all. I believe that she also would have wanted you to have it. At least I will always know that it will be in your safe hands. Please, take it with you back to your school, always wear it, and promise me that you will return as soon as you can to visit with me. I will miss you, dear child."

Katharine gratefully accepted the returned locket. At least she would have this one reminder of her true home with her at all times now. "Thank you so much, Penelope, for this, and for everything else that you have done for me!" Katharine said to her appreciatively, giving the loveable old woman a hug.

"Oh, nonsense, child!" Penelope returned, hugging her back. "And, it's me that should be thanking you! This lovely old home of mine looks spectacular again! And, it should for many years to come, thanks to not only you, but everyone else that gave so generously of their time to see to it that this place will long outlive me! You know how much I like caring for the gardens, and I am still able to get around fairly well for that. However, there was no way at my age that I would have been able to do all of the wonderful things that everyone has done for me, you included. I will be eternally grateful for all of that!"

After cleaning up the dishes from their meal together, both Penelope and Katharine said their goodnights to each other, hugged again, and went to their own separate bedrooms.

As Katharine changed into her nightie in the soft glow of the old-fashioned, hurricane-style lamp on her dresser, she wistfully reminisced about all of the wonder of the past week. She fervently hoped that the next several weeks would fly by, so that she would be able to return to her home, here, with her great-grandmother, in the sunshine on the beautiful mountainside in the Blue Ridge Mountains.

Cynthia Mueller

206

Peacefully she slept, the glowing butterflies accompanying her dreams, and reassuring her with their soothing voices that everything would be all right.

Morning came, and with it a dark, rumbling thunderstorm complete with streaks of bright blue lightning. Katharine awoke in the dreariness to Penelope's gentle shaking of her shoulder. It was time for her to rise, pack her freshly laundered things, and eat a good breakfast before her uncle arrived to transport her down to the train depot. *No crowing roosters this morning*, she noticed to herself. Apparently, the morning was too dark and dreary for even the chickens.

Penelope had prepared another delicious breakfast again this morning, with biscuits and gravy and several bowls of different fresh fruits for sampling.

"No doubt about it, Great-grandmother, you are an excellent cook!" Katharine told her as she finished up the last of her breakfast, wiping the corners of her mouth with a napkin. "Promise to teach me how to do all of this when I get back?" she asked her, hoping that if they planned something together that it would happen soon.

"Of course, dear. I have many old, secret recipes that I have never shared with anyone, and I really should pass them on before this tired old brain of mine gets too ancient to remember them all! We will begin cooking lessons as soon as you return." Penelope promised with a smile.

They cleared away the remainder of the breakfast. Then, too quickly for the apprehensive Katharine, Patrick came up the long winding drive with a horse and small, covered buggy this time.

Penelope had decided to come along for the trip to see Katharine onto her train, and luckily, by now, the rainstorm had dissipated to only a light sprinkle.

Riding slowly away, the grayness of the morning suited Katharine's mood. Reaching for her butterfly locket, she held onto it and fingered its delicate design lightly as they moved away from the beautiful old homestead, and on toward the train depot where the train would carry her away to resume her former life.

Soon, she would be back with her schoolmates, at the Catholic girl's school that Edward had wished for her to attend.

A pair of beautiful swallowtails glided past in the light mist, their watchful eyes always with her.

The horse navigated the hilly mountainside slowly, taking care not to slip on the rather steep, treacherous, and muddy mountain trail. Finally, the small group reached their destination.

There was the same depot where Katharine had gotten off another train just days earlier, looking slightly bereft in the damp grayness of the morning.

Exchanging hugs in the lightly sprinkling rain, Katharine couldn't help but think just how suitable this nasty weather was for her mood. It seemed to be crying along with her. She dabbed carefully at the corners of her eyes.

"Not to fret now, child." Penelope chided her. "I will be right here waiting for you when you return in just a few short weeks, Patrick will help me see to that! You call him now when you arrive at school and let him know that you arrived safely, all right dear?" Penelope asked her, pressing a paper with her uncle's phone number into Katharine's palm.

They all exchanged hugs, and both Katharine and Penelope wiped away tears as the approaching train whistle could be heard in the distance. Soon, the train arrived, and Uncle Patrick helped her unload her suitcase and bags from the buggy.

The train came to a noisy, screeching halt at the depot, and Patrick handed her up to the conductor, who took her ticket and nodded to them.

Katharine turned around and waved and looked at them one last time, memorizing their beloved features. She smiled sadly as all three of them called out their goodbyes to each

other, while the train began slowly rolling away. It would be a
long several weeks for all of them.

Back to the Old Life

The next few weeks of schooling seemed to drag by for poor Katharine, although she was happy to be back with all of her friends from there again. Now, however, she was able to tell everyone that she *did* have a family, and that she now knew who her mother had been!

At night, she told her roommates about everything that had happened to her since she had slept through her departure on the train bound for their field trip. They all seemed fascinated by her tales of magical butterflies and what the beautiful creatures had shown her at the gazebo, albeit a bit doubtful.

And, they were amazed when she told them how she had found her great-grandmother, and that Penelope had recognized Katharine's locket as the one that had belonged to Katharine's great-great grandmother. Katharine told the girls that she felt the butterflies had led her to Penelope's house, and that she now knew that her real last name was Meriweather.

By now, all memories the other girls had of images of butterflies helping Katharine when she was younger had faded from their minds. Even though they listened with interest to the tall tales that they felt their friend was telling them, they did not truly believe her when she told them that they were real. So, sensing this, finally, after awhile, Katharine just stopped talking about it.

The time for finals approached, and the girls all spent much time studying the last couple of weeks beforehand. Katharine's wondrous tales of magical butterflies were forgotten as she and her friends spent late nights getting ready for the yearly testing, and became too exhausted to think about much else anyway.

Ultimately, their finals came and went, and with them, a sense of relief and closure at yet another school year completed. Next year, they would all be in the ninth grade.

They were fast approaching adult-hood, and everyone was pleased to have school come to a close for the year. All the students were eagerly looking forward to the summer and the relaxation it would bring them all with their families. Katharine was especially thrilled with the prospect of being reunited with her great-grandmother.

First, however, she was to have a brief visit with George and Madelyn, who hadn't seen her since Easter. After her bags were packed and she had said her goodbyes to all of her schoolmates, for the summer at least, her aunt and uncle picked her up and took her home to be with them for two weeks.

Katharine's visit with them was very nice. These people had always been so kind to her. They had helped her a great deal over her formative years, and she felt a fondness for them that she knew she always would.

It was wonderful, also, to see her brother Michael again. He had grown at least an inch, and matured so much since she had last seen him. Together, the entire family attended his graduation ceremony, and she was so proud of the wonderful young man that her brother had become.

It's strange, she realized to herself. *I have never really thought about it before, but maybe in some ways I'm more blessed than other people. In my lifetime, I have belonged to three wonderful families that have all meant a great deal to me in their own way, families where I've known love, and kindness, and peace.*

Even though Constance had been a horrible mother, Edward had loved and doted on her, and she had fond memories of him to this day, even though she had been so small when he had died. Michael would always be her brother. She would not have had a brother at all had Edward and Constance not also adopted him!

George and Madelyn, though parents at a distance most of the years that she was growing up, through no fault of their own, were very good people. In many ways, Uncle George reminded Katharine so very much of Edward. And, since Edward had stipulated that she go to private school, she was not able to be with them much. However, she still loved them, and would always want to spend time with them. Also, because of Edward, and his brother George, she had yet another set of grandparents too, although they were quite old now, and could not travel due to the frequent medical care that they both required.

And, last but not least, she had discovered who her birth mother was, had been led to where she had been born, and now had acquired another aunt and uncle and a great-grandmother besides!

So, maybe after all, she had always had a family of her own, just different, perhaps, from those of her friends. And that gave her a great sense of peace. No longer did she dream of elusive parents that were always out of reach, although she still dreamt of the joyous hills and valleys filled with the butterfly-like apparitions, and her running alongside them, and now, sometimes even flying with them too.

While Katharine visited with her brother and George and Madelyn, they reminded her that it had been Edward's wish that she attend private school; and then go on to college after she had graduated.

With the passage of time, and her greater perspective of what her life could become in the future, she was able to understand that perhaps, for now at least, she should adhere to Edward's wishes for her life. She realized it would be best for her to remain at her school, which was an excellent one.

Maybe once she graduated, she decided at George and Madelyn's suggestion, she could attend a college closer to where she had been born, but that could all be determined at a later date.

After all, Michael had chosen to go to college in a different state, where he could be with his two best friends from his own private school, and she could probably do something similar herself.

When the time approached for her to be reunited with her great-grandmother, she became excited. The promise of the summer that they would share still loomed long, and full of anticipated excitement before her.

Finally, the long-awaited day arrived, and she and her brother, uncle and aunt arrived at the train station. They all exchanged hugs and warm goodbyes and promises that she would visit again before she resumed school in the fall.

Katharine boarded the train, and waved goodbye to the much-loved group as she sat in her seat next to the window.

Summertime life in the tiny quaint town with the gazebo

awaited her, along with her great-grandmother and uncle, and cooking lessons and friends that she had not yet met.

She was happy, and excited, and content in the knowledge that all was well in her life. Now, there was so much more to yet look forward to, and, she knew she belonged somewhere as well!

Cynthia Mueller

Return to the Garden Arbor

Penelope and Uncle Patrick were waiting for her at the train depot when she arrived on a bright, sunshine-filled summer day full of promise. The train then rolled away, fading into the mountains quickly, along with the lonesome sound of its whistle as it rounded the curve of the mountain and disappeared.

Katharine's great-grandmother and uncle welcomed her home. Everyone hugged each other warmly. After picking up a few things at the general store, they headed on up to Penelope's place in Patrick's buggy.

By now, summer was in its fullness, and many different flowers bloomed in abundance along the mountainside as the horse and buggy traversed the winding, difficult mountain path. Butterflies were everywhere, enjoying the height of their season. Here and there, between the thick trees, bright beams of sunlight reached the dense undergrowth, lending cheerfulness to the forest.

As they approached the gate of her great-grandmother's place,

Katharine again admired it. She reminisced once more about her first trip up this long, arduous trail. Next, she remembered all the hustle and bustle of several days later, when everyone from the little white church down below came up to help her great-grandmother spruce her beautiful old place up.

With the buggy past the lovely, ornate gate, and now nearing the house, Katharine drew in a sharp intake of breath. She was completely astonished with the resplendent beauty of Penelope's place now fully restored, and the many new and different flowers now in bloom, with the change of the seasons.

Two goldfinches flitted past, chirping happily and heading toward a pair of feeders that had not been there when Katharine had left. Penelope watched Katharine's reaction with a kind smile that contained a hint of amusement.

"Aren't they cute?" she asked Katharine, referring to the goldfinches. "They have a little nest right over there in that tree." Penelope pointed toward it. "So, isn't the old place lovely, after all of our dear friends' work?"

"Oh, yes!" exclaimed Katharine. "And, I am so very glad to be back here."

"Well," Penelope added with a twinkle in her merry blue eyes, "I also have other surprises for you, as well. I have arranged for your friends Megan and Rosalind to come up here on a regular basis. You should be surrounded by people your own age, and not just stuck up here with little old me!"

"Also," she continued, "people from the church have been coming often to help maintain things around here. I do so appreciate it! And Patrick here has offered to take us down to church on Sundays, so that you can get to know everyone in the town and make new friends that way too! And, by the way, the church is holding a picnic down at the park by the gazebo this coming Sunday afternoon to welcome you home!"

"Oh, Great-grandmother! That sounds just wonderful!" Katharine exclaimed. "So, when do the cooking lessons begin?"

Penelope chuckled, "Please, dear, I still just want you to call me Penelope. It's so much easier! We'll begin the cooking les-

sons soon, my dear. You can help me prepare our lunch!" she told
Katharine as Patrick began unloading her bags. They all headed
into the house. Uncle Patrick carried her things up to Katharine's
bright yellow bedroom.

It felt so wonderful to be home!

Later, after helping her great-grandmother put together their
lunch, and eating it with her out on the lovely old front porch in
the shade, Katharine decided to explore a bit and see what was
new and different in the gardens.

Baby bluebirds fluttered around the elaborate birdhouse,
along with their mother. Tiny maidenflies and dragonflies scurried about in the small stream running through the property,
flitting from rock to rock, sitting for a few moments, and then
moving again. Two brilliant goldfinches flew together into a pine
tree not too far off, and then came back again, with their charac-
teristic gleefully bouncing flight, chirping all the while.

Katharine just had to smile at it all. Penelope's place was
everything she had held dear all of these past weeks, and she
loved it still!

The silly threesome of cats followed her around the yard,
scurrying in and around all of the plantings, pouncing on each
other, and just making general fools of themselves. She loved
them all!

She observed with some dismay that the arbor was entirely
filled with weeds and brambles again. Perhaps that was the way
that it would always be. Maybe the butterflies that had protected
her all of her life protected their own existence in this manner.
She did not know, and perhaps she never would. The arbor itself
still maintained its sparkling newness, nonetheless.

The morning glories intertwined within it were radiant also,
the morning's blooms just now beginning to fade. Katharine
admired the arbor anyway, even with its flaws. An iridescent
hummingbird drank from the orange trumpet vine blossoms not
far away. Sparrows fluttered happily over to the coolness of the

birdbath. A wide variety of butterflies fluttered everywhere. All was well with the world!

Megan and Rosalind came by an hour or so later and visited until shortly before dinnertime. All three girls went up to Katharine's cheerful bedroom. They spent hours looking through Katharine's things that she had brought along for the summer; and some of the books on the large bookshelf in one corner of the room. Mainly, though, they spent their time gossiping about friends, and boys, and all of the things that young teen girls think about and dream of.

A couple of days later, two nice men from the church stopped by in the afternoon and took care of several things for Penelope that she could never have managed on her own. She thanked the pair profusely and served them lemonade and fresh cherry pie that she and Katharine had baked just that morning.

Rosalind and Megan came to visit Katharine again the next day, and then spent the night with her.

Katharine was beginning to enjoy the freedom of being through with school, spending her time now just relaxing and enjoying the beautiful summer. It was so nice to have a few weeks away from her studies, and spend some time getting to know her great-grandmother. She realized that Penelope was getting on in years, and would not always be with her. Katharine wanted to spend as much time as possible with her now, helping her in any way that she could.

Uncle Patrick and Aunt Berta came up to visit them on Saturday afternoon, and after socializing for quite a while, the two older women and Katharine all prepared their dinner together while

Uncle Patrick took care of several things for his grandmother outside.

Katharine was already becoming quite the cook, and loved to experiment with new and different things. Most of them were successes. Everyone enjoyed visiting and sharing their food together, and after all of the cleanup, they sat on the large, covered porch in the coolness of the evening after the long hot day. They all talked and drank lemonade for quite some time.

As the sunlight began to fade, and be replaced by the light of twinkling fireflies, they said their goodbyes. In the morning, Patrick and Berta would return to take Penelope and Katharine to church, and then later, they would all share in the joyous picnic that the town was holding to welcome Katharine home.

It had been a wonderful, relaxing day, and the summer had just begun. As Katharine and Penelope stood on the dirt path, waving farewell to Patrick and Berta, they glanced at each other, smiling warmly. Then, they headed into the lovely old large house, each enjoying an enveloping sense of peace and permanence within their overflowing hearts.

Magical Butterfly Box

Sunday morning dawned clear and bright and hot, like any typical late June day. Patrick and Berta came up the mountain extra early that Sunday, to help Katharine and Penelope load several dishes of prepared food and a picnic basket, blankets, and wooden folding chairs into the buggy.

After enjoying a large, delicious breakfast consisting of pancakes, bacon, fried eggs and orange juice together, they all headed on down toward the quaint town.

Katharine felt a mounting sense of excitement. Today, she was going to meet so many new people; many that had witnessed all of the happenings on the day that she had been discovered in the Victorian gazebo.

Pastor Farley mercifully kept the church service short and sweet, since it was so warm already. He then reminded everyone at the end of the service about the picnic that was to take place in the park at noon.

Everyone was in a cheerful mood, despite the heat. After the service, Uncle Patrick and Aunt Berta took Katharine and Penelope to their home for a while, to relax and sit in the coolness of the shade trees in their back yard until it was picnic time.

Beautiful swallowtail butterflies fluttered about in the gardens in the lovely backyard, sipping sweet nectar from first one brilliant bloom, and then meandering on to the next. Birds chirped and fluttered about, and even though it was hot, it was a perfect summer day.

Finally, it was time for the picnic, and they traversed the few short blocks in Patrick's car. It was difficult for Penelope to walk too far. Also, they had quite a bit of food and other items to take with them to the event.

Many folks were already there, blankets spread, claiming the shade under the numerous, large old trees. Set up underneath one of the trees were a cluster of several long tables. They already were beginning to fill up with casseroles, breads, cakes, and all sorts of other wonderful culinary delights. Women bustled about amongst them, uncovering and getting things ready.

A large container at the end of one table held enough lemonade for everyone to keep their thirsts quenched. Occasionally, a slight cool breeze would come through, helping to keep everyone comfortable.

There was also a large table set up nearby with bazaar and white elephant items, to help raise funds for the church's various missions. A couple of women sat behind it, fanning themselves and gossiping happily.

Not far off, the gazebo sat in solitary resplendence, with the waterfall slightly further back in the distance, sending a cool, misting spray into the air. The sunlight threaded through it, turning the spray into a brilliant, rainbow-colored aura over the bubbling brook beneath it. All of those things combined to create a radiant, majestic picture that was almost too beautiful to be real. Birds sang cheerfully, flying about between the graceful willows. Butterflies, dragonflies, and bees were everywhere in the flowers on both sides of the stream.

Soon, Megan and Rosalind showed up. After sitting in the cooling shade of a large oak with Katharine for a bit, watching folks arrive and catching up on girl talk, the girls decided to venture on over to the white elephant table. Picking through the numerous items, they chattered happily while the older women behind it fanned themselves and watched on in amusement.

Katharine dug through everything for long moments, not paying much attention to anything up until this point. However, suddenly, her attention was drawn to diminutive, rainbow colored lights sparkling over a small object residing in the middle of the crowded, long table.

Looking closer, she could see a small, ornately hand-carved ivory box. Inset into the top of the delicate pink-shaded receptacle, was a beautiful, intricately carved mother-of-pearl butterfly. As Katharine picked it up, minute, rainbow-colored ethereal lights danced briefly around it, and then vanished. She attempted to open it, but it seemed to be obstinately stuck shut.

She held it, gazing at it in entrancement as Megan and Rosalind continued their digging and chatter. Finally, they noticed how quiet she had become, and came back over to her side to exclaim over the beauty of the tiny treasure.

"How much is it, Katharine? Are you going to buy it?" asked Megan excitedly. Katharine glanced at the women behind the table, after turning it over and not seeing a price tag. The older of the two women stood and reached out her hand for it, and turned it over too.

"Goodness, dear!" she exclaimed rather enviously, albeit kindly finally to Katharine, after examining it fully. "I don't even recall having seen this when we were setting everything up just a short time ago! I don't know where it came from! It is indeed *lovely*, however! If I would have noticed it before you, I would have snapped it up and purchased it myself!" the woman chuckled a bit. She then assured Katharine, "The proceeds will go to charity, you know! How does ten cents sound to you?"

Katharine was not sure if she should buy it or not, ten cents was quite a lot of money, especially for someone her age. Still examining it, finally, she asked the woman, "Ma'am, would it be all right with you, if I carefully carried this over to my great-grandmother, and showed it to her first? I would like to ask her if she would be kind enough to loan me the money for it."

"Certainly, dear, we will be right here waiting, then! Take your time." the woman assured her agreeably.

Katharine and her friends ventured over to where Penelope, Patrick, and Berta were sitting on their wooden folding chairs along with several other townsfolk, all talking happily amongst themselves and enjoying the comfort of the shade.

She showed the lovely box to Penelope, who took it gently into gnarled old hands, inspecting it carefully. The venerable woman admired the ornate scrollwork intricately carved into it, and the mother-of-pearl butterfly inlaid into the top. "How exquisite!" she exclaimed softly, then ran a twisted old finger over the entire thing, testing its quality and smoothness.

"Dear, this is very beautiful *indeed!* I do believe it is an antique! Where did you find it?" she asked Katharine after a few moments.

"Over on the white elephant table, Penelope. Would you be willing to loan me a dime so that I can purchase it? The nice ladies over there told me that all of the proceeds would go to charity. Please, Great-grandmother?" Katharine implored, with barely-contained excitement.

"Well, certainly, dear girl!" Penelope replied, already reaching for her handbag before Katharine had even finished asking. Digging deeply into it, she finally pulled out a small change purse, opened it, and handed her a dime, and then also gave Katharine's two friends one each as well.

"Just keep the money. You girls go enjoy yourselves now!" she told them with amused, twinkling eyes, watching them dash excitedly back over to the little rummage sale while she chuckled merrily, charmed at their enthusiasm.

Katharine proudly paid the two women immediately upon returning, while her two friends picked through the pile of items with delight. After she had given them her money, one of the ladies wrapped her box with care, cushioning it in a piece of old newspaper, while the other held open a small brown paper bag for her friend to place it in once it had been wrapped. They then handed the small package to Katharine with a smile, and waited for the other girls to choose their treasures.

Finally, Rosalind decided on a beautiful, hand-embroidered handkerchief that had personally been crafted by one of the ladies from the church. Soon, Megan chose a lovely, lace edged hand-made scarf.

The two sisters declined bags for their purchases, happily handing over their money to the two kind women. Then, as she tied her lovely scarf around her neck and Rosalind stuffed her handkerchief into her pocket, Megan suggested that all three of them go visit the radiant waterfall.

Full of cheer, they raced to the waterfall. As they approached it, they could feel a drastic difference in temperature from the area over by the park. The frigid mountain water chilled the hot, sun-filled air as it evaporated, leaving a soothing hazy spray filled with rainbow lights from the sun directly over the small group.

The misty air was so refreshing that they decided to sit and stay awhile.

Rosalind pulled her embroidered hanky out of her pocket, and examined it carefully again. Then, she folded it neatly and returned it to the safety of her pocket, and the three girls made themselves comfortable on the large, smooth rocks of the stream bank.

Katharine carefully placed her tiny "treasure chest" in its bag next to the rock she sat on.

Then, all three girls began removing their shoes and socks, so they would be able to dip their toes into the soothing water.

It was an absolutely lovely afternoon, despite the heat, and everyone in the park was enjoying themselves immensely. Soon, Pastor Farley stepped up into the gazebo. He loudly announced to everyone that now that the entire town was present, that they should all make their way into line over at the food tables. He also proclaimed that since Katharine was the guest of honor; that she should go first.

All three girls reluctantly left the refreshment of the stream. They quickly replaced their shoes and socks, so as not to keep the other folks waiting. They were hungry, nonetheless, and soon became lost in endless chatter while they carefully chose items from the over-abundance of offered delights.

Sitting to eat their selections in the shade on a blanket, next to where Katharine's relatives had set up chairs, they watched as all the other townspeople one by one emerged from the long line, going to sit in their own spots.

Megan elbowed Katharine suddenly, pointing toward Aaron, Katharine's latest heart-throb from weeks before when he had helped at the Periwinkle place.

"Look, Katharine, there's your boyfriend!" she announced loudly, as poor Aaron, passing nearby to go join his own family, heard what she had said and acknowledged it with a bright red blush.

"Stop it, Megan!" Katharine protested, too late to do anything about the attention that Megan had drawn to her now. Two lovely swallowtails fluttered past the group of girls.

They finished eating, and waited patiently for everyone else from their group to do the same. Penelope and the other older folks eventually finished up also. Soon, Pastor Farley was back up in the gazebo again, along with Mayor Janssen.

"Dear people," he announced, "we hope you all have enjoyed the delicious food that everyone in attendance was so kind to bring. Thank you all for your kindness! We are here today to celebrate the reunion of Penelope Periwinkle and her great-granddaughter, Katharine."

"Many of you remember, from years ago," he continued, "that strange, fascinating morning when a tiny baby girl was discovered in this lovely old gazebo. It was a sweltering day, much like today. Unfortunately, at the time, none of us knew who she belonged to, and times were very difficult, so we were forced to surrender her to a Catholic Orphanage far away in the city."

"Not only was her discovery that morning a miracle," he continued, "but recently I witnessed another one involving this dear girl. Not long ago, she was reunited with her true family by pure accident, after being gone all of these long years!"

"It seems that Katharine fell asleep on a train bound for the city on a school field trip, and somehow miraculously ended up back here. God surely has had a hand in all of this!" The pastor held out his hands, looking skyward, as if to acknowledge the Lord's presence in this park as well. The mayor stood next to the pastor, smiling proudly and pompously, and began clapping.

Soon, everyone in the park had also risen from their chairs and blankets, clapping as well.

Katharine, feeling more than a little embarrassed, and Penelope, also rose, and both acknowledged the crowd with nods and thank-yous.

After a few more moments, people finished their clapping, and finally, Pastor Farley spoke again. "Well, I won't embarrass you dear ladies any further!" he said, looking pointedly their way. Chuckles could be heard throughout the crowd.

"Everyone, it is a beautiful day, let's all just enjoy the fine weather and good people, and the wonderful games for the children that some of our church helpers have planned. The Lord does indeed work in mysterious ways! A wonderful day, to all of you!" he exclaimed finally, looking rather pompous himself, and then the pastor and mayor came down the steps and began to mingle.

An elderly, distinguished-looking gentleman with a cane walked slowly past Penelope, attempting to catch her eye. Katharine watched as Penelope noticed. Even at her old, tired age, Penelope blushed slightly, inwardly feeling a slight thrill in her heart that she hadn't experienced in years—*why, since before dear Herbert passed away!*

Katharine and her friends mingled with the townspeople. Katharine was proud to be formally introduced to and shake hands with the mayor, and his wife, who now joined him. She was being introduced to so many new faces that it was impossible for her to remember all of the names that went with them.

The girls helped with some of the children's games for a while, until they began to tire and sweat. Then they decided to take a break and go back over by the waterfall to cool down for a bit.

Several other kids were already over there, enjoying the refreshing spray, and as they walked toward it, Katharine suddenly remembered her tiny, pink-tinted ivory box.

"Oh, my gosh!" she exclaimed to Megan and Rosalind. "I left my tiny package sitting over there by the stream. I hope that it's okay! I forgot all about it when the pastor announced that it was time for us to eat!"

Mildly worried by now, she rushed over toward where she thought she had left it earlier. Megan and Rosalind followed close behind, reassuring her that they would help her find it.

The rocks all along the stream bank, similar in size, shape and color, all looked the same to the girls, however. Soon, Katharine was despairing that she had lost her box forever, as the tiny thing was in a brown paper bag almost the same color as all of the rocks. The position of the sun had changed as the afternoon had progressed, and the shade on the rocks was different now than it had been earlier.

They all kept searching, however, and even asked some of the other children playing in the stream if they had seen her parcel, but none had.

The afternoon wore on, and some of the villagers were beginning to pack up their items and leave. The tables were coming down, and many of the dishes of food had been left empty, and cleared away.

Feeling quite frantic now, Katharine was certain that her tiny treasure was lost to her forever! The mother-of-pearl inlay on it had looked to be almost exactly the same as the design on her locket. Even the delicate carving around the butterfly had mimicked it to some extent. She hoped so desperately that she would be able to find it before it was time for them all to leave!

Beginning to cry slightly, Katharine whispered to Megan, who was searching nearby, that perhaps someone who had been playing here earlier had found her box, and taken it.

A group of teenaged boys was beginning to head toward the stream, and one of them was Aaron. A couple of them removed their shoes, socks, and shirts. They rolled up their pant legs and began to wade along the edge of the water.

Aaron, while removing his shoes and socks, looked the girls' way a few times. Then, he decided to leave his group of friends momentarily to try to overcome his shyness, wanting to be near the gorgeous Katharine, and find out what her little group was up to.

Penelope and her gathering of friends were still sitting in the shade of the large oak tree that they had claimed earlier. They were now joined by a new face, the one of the elderly gentleman from earlier, who was also contributing to their conversations as well. No one in their group seemed in a hurry to leave, Katharine observed from a distance. She was grateful, as she was still hopeful that she and her friends would find her tiny package soon.

Aaron approached the three girls, asking what they were doing, and when he found out about Katharine's missing parcel; he quickly volunteered to help them search for it.

The other boys, splashing nearby in the water, were already quite wet. One of them called over to the searching Aaron, yelling loudly, "Aaron, come on in!"

Aaron ignored him, and continued to help the girls search.

Megan's and Rosalind's parents called to them, and after telling Katharine goodbye, and that they hoped that she would find her tiny bundle soon, they ran towards the waiting couple.

Now Aaron was left with only Katharine nearby. After finally building up enough courage to speak to Katharine directly, he introduced himself to her.

"I'm Aaron. Your name's Katharine, right?" he asked her.

"Yes." she replied, simply and sadly, looking intensely at the ground and not him.

After pausing slightly, still searching for words to start up a conversation with her, he finally gave up, and just blurted out, "You're the prettiest girl here today! In fact, you're the prettiest girl in the entire town!"

Now he had Katharine's attention, and she looked directly at him, brightening slightly. "Well, thank you." she replied, smiling a little shyly. "I like you too!"

Aaron then smiled broadly at her with a crookedly handsome, boyish grin. Content to just be with her, they searched in silence for many minutes more.

Glancing again over at Penelope's group, Katharine noticed that they too, were now beginning to show signs of packing things up. She was quite worried by now, and beginning to accept that she might never see her tiny treasure again. A couple of the boys downstream hollered for Aaron to join them in their noisy rough-housing once more.

Finally, she spoke again to Aaron. "Thank you for helping me search for my little box. I'm pretty sure now that it's lost forever to me. Maybe you should just go join your friends." she suggested, glancing up at him now and feeling bad that she was wasting his time.

"Oh, no, that's fine, I'll help you a little longer at least!" he told her, eager to remain in her company for as long as she would allow him to. The warmth of the sun was beginning to cause him to sweat, and he removed his shirt, as his group of friends had done earlier. He wadded it up and wiped his forehead with it.

He is very muscular and tanned, Katharine observed appreciatively to herself. She blushed slightly when he caught her looking at him. *What a nice-looking guy! And he seemed nice too!*

Penelope's group was definitely starting to put their things away. The elderly distinguished gentleman remained, standing next to Penelope, and helping her with some of her items. Katharine began to despair.

Aaron looked at her again, now noticing her beautiful locket after its sparkle caught his eye. "What a nice necklace!" he offered. Then finally, "A pretty necklace for such a pretty girl!" he exclaimed, and then looked profoundly embarrassed, again. *That sounded stupid!* he reflected to himself with annoyance. He glanced shyly back down at the ground, in an attempt to hide his bright, red blush.

Katharine smiled, thought him to be quite sweet, and took hold of her tiny locket, fingering it gently. *It has seen me through so much*, she reminisced to herself.

Abruptly, a brilliant rainbow shot through the mist over the waterfall, encircling both her and the handsome boy, and ending right on the ground just a few feet ahead of them. Both of them stopped dead in their tracks. Tiny, iridescent lights filled the rainbow colored, widening space. Both of their jaws dropped, as the splendorous aura that now surrounded them filled wondrously with hundreds of butterfly-like shapes, swirling delicately round and round the pair.

The couple looked at each other fully for the very first time, and then at the scene surrounding them, filled with a sense of wonder, excitement and awe that neither had never known before! They were in love!

Simultaneously, both of them reached for the other's hands. The fairy-like creatures remained, joyously dancing about in the air, to what Katharine and Aaron could each have sworn was a wondrous music, lilting softly throughout the rainbow-hued space that still enveloped them both. They shared a first, sweet, innocent kiss. The butterflies sang!

Caught up in the wonder of each other, bright blue eyes gazing into brown ones, they remained, frozen in time.

Ultimately, the rainbow aura began to narrow, finally decreasing in size into just a very narrow, but extremely bright pinnacle of rainbow filled light, only a few feet away from them, and there it remained.

Tearing their eyes away from each other's brand new, overwhelmed, love consumed gaze, they glanced down at the rocks lying before them. There, sitting next to the largest one, directly in the beam of the rainbow, was Katharine's tiny missing bag!

"Oh, Aaron, look!" she exclaimed, moving swiftly away from him to retrieve her beloved treasure. In the instant before she lifted it off of the ground, the rainbow light disappeared swiftly into it, as if penetrating the tiny bag. "This is my missing package! Thank you so much for helping me to find it! Oh, thank you!"

He smiled broadly at her once more, with his handsome, crooked grin, and took her hand again, content in their mutual feelings for one another, and happy that her treasure had been found at last. Slowly, they began walking back toward the roughhousing group of boys.

"Hey, Aaron, come on in!" one of them yelled, noticing the pair approaching. "Quit wasting your time with silly girls and come in and cool off! We're having fun! Hurry up!"

Aaron glanced at Katharine, unsure of what to do now, and still holding her hand.

"Go on!" she told him happily, with a lilting laugh. "Thank you so much for helping me! Now go have a blast with all of your friends!"

"Um... thanks, uh, I'll see you later then?" he asked her. His brown eyes were shy and uncertain again now.

"Yes, Aaron, I promise! Penelope and my group are waiting for me anyway. I can see her over there looking this way. You go have fun now!"

Leaning toward her shyly again, he gave her another gentle kiss. Then, smiling crookedly at her one last time, he laughed out loud, shaking his head in astonishment. He turned and tore off for his group of buddies, screaming loudly as he approached them. He created a big splash as he hit the water, his arms flailing about joyously.

Katharine watched him, smiling broadly as he got himself soaked, while two large swallowtail butterflies fluttered closely past her face. They circled round and round each other, in a timeless, unchanging mating dance that was older than these mountains. She gazed at them in wonder, and could have sworn they both were smiling too! Then, off they flew, toward the rainbow that now only filled the mist coming from the waterfall, finally gracefully disappearing into it.

Katharine approached Penelope, who was standing and conversing with the elderly gentleman. Patrick and Berta still waited nearby.

Penelope spoke first, saying, "Oh, thank goodness dear! We are getting ready to leave now, and did not want to have to walk all the way over there in this heat!"

She then recognized the distinguished gentleman standing beside her, saying, "Katharine, I would like for you to meet Stanley Rutigier. He lives down here, in the town!"

Penelope smiled warmly up at the man, and then at Katharine. "He says he remembers the day you were discovered as a tiny infant here in the park, almost as if it happened yesterday!"

"Nice to meet you, sir," Katharine acknowledged the kind-faced gentleman, smiling. Then, looking at Penelope again, she said, "Thank you all for waiting for me. I left my little bag containing my tiny pink box over there, and for quite a while I was so worried that I had lost it! Aaron over there helped me find it, and Megan and Rosalind helped too!"

Penelope smiled, with a knowing look in her blue eyes, saying, "Yes, I saw you over there. It looks as if you've made a brand new friend!" Penelope scrutinized Katharine closely through her thick glasses lenses, with a benevolent smile. At that, Katharine blushed slightly.

Removing the tiny wrapped bundle from the paper bag, she unwrapped it from its newspaper to make sure that the tiny box had not been damaged. Thank goodness, it was still in perfect condition, and she was very grateful! She set the wrapping and bag on the ground, and attempted to open the delicate pink box again, while the rest of the group looked on, all of them curious to again see her little treasure.

The lid came off easily this time, as if it had never been stuck at all! As Katharine lifted it away from the bottom of the box, suddenly, a radiant rainbow light just like the one that had enveloped her and Aaron poured from it, enveloping them all!

Stunned into silence they all were, as the aura narrowed, now surrounding only Penelope and Stanley. Again, butterfly-like creatures filled the lighted, iridescent twinkling space, while the rest of them stayed, rooted to the ground, overwhelmed into watching on.

Penelope and Stanley gazed at each other, new-found wonderment filling their eyes. Slowly and arthritically, and losing their careful, age-induced control of themselves, each of them leaned toward the other, joining briefly in an innocent, first kiss.

Moving apart slightly afterward, they then stared into each other's time-worn eyes, both pairs of them filled with awe! They were in love, and much to their amazement, they both secretly marveled to themselves; each had believed that they would never know these emotions again! The pair of them, feeling at least twenty years younger than they had just a moment ago, slowly came to their senses, smiling joyously as the brilliant aura began to fade away.

There truly had been a treasure at the end of the rainbow, Katharine now realized, remembering what the queen swallowtail had told her when she and the king had taken Katharine beyond the garden arbor.

That treasure was love. She and Aaron had discovered it, and she could see it radiating from the eyes of the two elderly people standing in front of her, still entranced with each other. Also, she now observed it in the eyes of Uncle Patrick and Aunt Berta, who had both been temporarily encircled and touched by the rainbow themselves. The younger pair now also looked upon each other with a new-found appreciation in their middle-aged eyes, as well!

Pastor Farley awoke everyone from their momentarily trance-like states, striding up and informing them that all the clean-up and putting away in the beautiful park had been taken care of by church volunteers, and wishing them all well once more. "Thank you folks again for coming!" he said as he walked away merrily, and they too all thanked him for everything that he had organized on this fine day.

Heading back toward Uncle Patrick's car, Stanley bade Penelope farewell for the afternoon, imploring her to promise that she would attend church the next Sunday, and asking her to please sit with him.

The wrinkled old face smiled back happily at Stanley's equally aged and slightly unsure one. She promised him that she would be there, and that she would be very grateful to sit in attendance with him.

While the rest of the group watched on, Stanley extended his wrinkled hand toward Penelope's equally gnarled one, shaking it nervously now. He affirmed again that he would see her next Sunday, then. With an abrupt wave he headed toward his beautiful Victorian cottage only a block or so away.

It was time for the rest of them to be heading home now. Life

held only promise for everyone in the quaint little town bordering the Blue Ridge Mountains.

Full Circle

Summer passed quickly for Katharine and Penelope, and all of their friends from the tiny town at the base of the mountain. Much too quickly, in fact.

Although there had been numerous picnics over the summer, and joyous occasions for the townspeople to get together and enjoy each other's company, vacation time was drawing to a close.

School would be starting again soon. Katharine's birthday had come and gone. A small party had been held up at Penelope's place, with the all the food prepared by her and Penelope. Their many new friends were in attendance, in Penelope's lovely flower gardens. Katharine was fifteen now! She was growing up!

Hers and Aaron's affection for one another had only grown. They had seen each other often at the church, and at all of the other town gatherings. With time, who knew what their future might hold?

And, the same held true for Penelope and Stanley, whose regard for each other had also blossomed with each passing Sunday and town gathering. Since their first meeting, years had seemed to melt away from both of their elderly countenances. Penelope especially, seemed much more relaxed and enjoying of life's blessings lately to Katharine also. There was a spring to her step that Katharine had not noticed before, and she was moving more quickly and getting around better than she had for years.

The resplendent greens of summer were now beginning to turn into the brilliant colors of fall, with the weather becoming slightly cooler as fall approached.

Katharine actually was beginning to look forward to returning to school, as she *did* miss all of the friends that she had made and grown up with over the years. It had been decided that she would return to visit Penelope briefly over school break times, along with dear Uncle George and Aunt Madelyn, and her brother Michael. Visits with all concerned over school breaks now would have to be shorter in order to accommodate Katharine's burgeoning family.

Sitting alongside the cheerful stream in the shade of the crooked willow, beyond the garden arbor on a crisp, bright, early autumn day, she reflected on the joys of her life, and how it had all come full circle for her. No longer did she wish for family members that evaded her, or permanence in her young life. She had it now, and with it, a wonderful, heart-warming sense of fulfillment and love for everyone that she now belonged to.

Katharine had finally attained a success of sorts in clearing away the winding undergrowth from around the magical arbor. The weeds now only sporadically came in here and there, but without the ferocity that they once had. It had been as if they were there to keep the rest of the world locked out, until the time that she returned to her home.

The arbor itself still remained brand-new looking, though a paint brush had never touched it. Apparently, some of the magic from that special day still remained. Perhaps Katharine's butterflies had now realized that no one here was going to pose a threat to their eternal, joyous and ethereal existence.

Will I ever see them again? she pondered to herself as she watched the chilly stream sparkle and bubble, ever cheerful in its quest to reach the waterfall just above the base of the mountain. *Will the butterflies always be there for me, rescuing me in my times of need? Or, have I grown so, and become self-sufficient enough over these past few years, that I will no longer be in need of their benevolent assistance?* Pensively, she stood, as the chilly, early autumn breeze whipped her wavy blond hair around playfully.

Brushing it away from her beautiful face; she thought again of all the wonderful people that had filled her life. Each had contributed so many good things to her existence.

Edward had loved and treated her so kindly, and had left her with enough worldly means that she would never have to worry about money in her lifetime, providing that she managed it well. She was determined to do just that when she inherited it at the age of twenty-one. She only wished to honor his gift to her by always spending it wisely.

Edward had also seen to it that her education up to this point had been excellent, and would continue to be for as long as she wished it to.

Naturally, George and Madelyn had seen to it that she had known the love of a large family with them, and had always treated her and Michael just as well as their own children.

And Michael, dear Michael, had been such a wonderful brother to her for all of these long years. She couldn't remember a time when she hadn't known him, and it seemed to her as if he were of her own flesh and blood. What a wonderful young man he had become, with a bright future awaiting him once he finished college! She was determined to follow in his footsteps.

Many of her close friends from school were almost like sisters to her now. They all had grown up together, through the good times and the bad, and would stay best friends for the remainder of their lives, if she had anything to say about it!

Sweet old Penelope, her dear great-grandmother, and Uncle Patrick and Aunt Berta were always so wonderful to her, doting on her every chance they got, as she did with them.

And now, too, she had Aaron. They were both very young yet, and who knew what the future had in store? They both had so many years of their lives ahead, holding unknown promises for them. Maybe they would spend them together. Maybe they wouldn't. Whatever happened, however, Katharine basked in the glory of the moment, knowing fully that her once-empty heart ached with loneliness no more.

Never again would she wonder where she had come from, why she had been abandoned, or why she didn't have a normal family like everyone else that she had ever known.

Her heart was full of love and contentment, and excitement about what the promise of her future held for her.

Enemies of the past no longer threatened her in any way. George and Madelyn had told her quite recently, that Constance had passed away in the mental hospital, alone and forgotten to the rest of the world. *So very sad, and such a terrible waste of a life! How could one not know how to love?* Ingrid was never to return to her private school.

In the waning light of the early autumn sunset, a Luna moth materialized from beneath the darkening shadows of the trees, hovering briefly over the radiant girl as if waiting. It shadowed her for just an instant, and then glided off into the distant trees on the other side of the mountain, disappearing from view.

Katharine shuddered briefly as she watched it, remembering her horrible experience in those woods weeks before, and resolving anew to always forgive her antagonists if any new ones ever presented themselves. If and when they did, at least she would have the reassurance in her heart that her family members only held unconditional love for her. They would always be there, even years from now, after they were gone, as Edward still was, residing in her heart and soul and encouraging her still.

The setting sun began to disappear from view. A solitary swallowtail dipped and glided gracefully over the golden autumn grass and wildflowers, partaking of a quick sip of sweet nectar before retiring for the night. Soon, the frost would come, and the butterfly, along with all of the wonderful glories of nature that warm weather had brought to the mountainside, would disappear.

Snow and stark, icy winds would blow through the leafless trees, and the very thought of that made Katharine shiver slightly in the chilly, early autumn breeze.

The swallowtail took one last, lingering sip from a radiant, purple-coneflower, wings fluttering slightly and daintily as it worked.

Delicately then, it lifted from the spiny orange and brown center, light as a feather, fluttering toward the admiring and watching Katharine in the golden and purple hues of the magnificent sunset.

It drifted and encircled Katharine in its lilting flight... once... twice... then three times... softly brushing her cheek the final time with a fragile wing, causing her to giggle with delight as her hair waved in the crisp breeze.

As it began its flight away from her directly toward the lowering sun, it turned one last time, and Katharine could have sworn that it winked at her, just before disappearing totally from her view.

THE
END!

An Ode to the Butterfly
a poem, by Cynthia Jean Mueller

Rainbow colored like my garden
floating high and fancy free,
fluttering down to alight on a flower,
and taste of its tranquility.

I am enchanted by your simplicity
and yet, enthralled with your complexity.
Pollinating blooms is most likely your only purpose,
but your life contains astounding metamorphosis.

One of our Lord's truly amazing wonders:
you are the fairies of enchanted summers.
Iridescent prism hues of color
will soon break free of winter's slumber.

Then, fluttering to my flower fairyland, I will watch,
sitting on my garden bench, their lovely, fragile flight.
Oh, that I should live so utterly carefree.
Oh, that I could be a joyous, glorious butterfly!

www.ingramcontent.com/pod-product-compliance
Lightning Source LLC
Chambersburg PA
CBHW070525100726
47907CB00004B/985